Altaterra

Also by the author

The Awakening Earth trilogy

Innocent Earth
Divided Earth
Rebel Earth

Altaterra

Dale E. McClenning

Milton, Ontario

This is a work of fiction. All of the characters, events, and organizations portrayed in this novel are either products of the author's imagination or are used fictitiously.

Brain Lag Publishing
Milton, Ontario
http://www.brain-lag.com/

Copyright © 2023 Dale E. McClenning. All rights reserved. This material may not be reproduced, displayed, modified or distributed without the express prior written permission of the copyright holder. For permission, contact publishing@brain-lag.com.

ISBN 978-1-998795-03-1

Library and Archives Canada Cataloguing in Publication

Title: Altaterra / Dale E. McClenning.
Names: McClenning, Dale E., 1962- author.
Identifiers: Canadiana (print) 20230446019 | Canadiana (ebook) 20230446027 | ISBN 9781998795031
 (softcover) | ISBN 9781998795048 (EPUB)
Classification: LCC PS3613.C55 A78 2023 | DDC 813/.6—dc23

Part One
The Basin

Chapter One

Kaitja heard the two approaching through the brush long before he saw them. One sounded large, most likely a man he guessed, making no attempt to walk silently along the rarely-used trail through the underbrush. The second was smaller and quieter, taking advantage of the path the first person created, he assumed. There was no sound of the struggle associated with hauling a prisoner up the mountain, leading Kaitja to assume the other person was a wife or child. He had time to split two more logs, set the axe down on the stump, and walk across the yard to meet the pair before they emerged.

"Greetings Hon Marangoz," Kaitja said with a small bow as the man straightened before him from his uphill climb. "You honour my home with your presence."

"Well met, Arm Kaitja," Hon replied with a similar bow, "your greeting gladdens our hearts." Hon was easily over two meters tall with broad shoulders, thick arms and legs, and wide, strong hands. Being the village's carpenter kept him in such condition.

The young woman who stepped out from behind Hon shared his eyes and nose, but little else. A couple of hands' length below two meters, she was thin of body. Her legs and arms were long and her hair was cut well back from her eyes and short in the back, unusual for women in the village. She looked to be sixteen years of age, only a couple years from prime marriage age. The visit, though, would not appear to have anything to do with such matters since their ages were so different. That would be an act of desperation on Hon's part to suggest such a thing, too early for such a young girl.

"What matter brings you to my home, Hon Marangoz?" Kaitja asked in an even voice. "Not ill tidings, I hope."

"No, Arm Kaitja," Hon replied in an equally even voice. "I have business I would discuss with you."

"Business?" Kaitja could not help his tone from rising a little at the word.

"Yes. May I present my daughter, Xitano." Hon swept his arm to motion the girl forward. "She is an honourable daughter. I request that you take her as your apprentice."

Kaitja just looked at the man for a few seconds, his expression unchanged, before he found his voice. At least the request explained the bag the girl held behind her back.

"You wish her to be an Arm of the Law?" Kaitja inquired.

"I would not presume to know the qualities needed for an Arm," Hon said, lowering his head and eyes. "I thought she might be a tracker or even a hunter. If you find her suitable as an Arm, that is your decision."

Kaitja took a breath and steadied his stance and his voice before continuing the formalities. "And what brings you to think she will make a good apprentice?"

"Every chance she gets, she runs off into the woods, bringing back useful items. Once, she even had a bristle squirrel perched on her shoulder as if charmed."

Not succeeding in stifling a small laugh, Kaitja replied, "I guess one has to start somewhere. She didn't bring the creature with her?" he asked, looking the girl up and down.

"It made a tasty addition to my wife's stew," Hon said, raising his head, the memory causing his eyes to shine a little brighter.

Kaitja quickly looked at the girl's face. Anger showed in her eyes as she glanced at her father but was suppressed as she once again faced forward. It was the only emotion she had shown since arriving. Kaitja walked in front of the girl.

"And what do you think of this arrangement, Xitano?" Kaitja

asked. The girl's eyes quickly came up to his and widened briefly at the unexpected question. She set her jaw before answering.

"It's better than..." was quickly said and quickly stopped by the girl. Taking another breath, she forced herself to stand straighter before answering in a firm voice. "I am in agreement with the arrangement."

"And what payment do you offer?" Kaitja returned his gaze to Hon, who had been looking at his daughter. Hon's eyes quickly came back to the Arm's but were not as steady as before.

"I can have ten chickens delivered here tomorrow, alive or dressed as you wish. When the warmer weather returns I will deliver a new calf from a milk cow." Hon's lips quivered a little after the statement.

Kaitja let the man wait for a short while before answering. He held out his hand, flat with his palm down. "I agree to the arrangement. I prefer the chickens alive."

Hon slipped his hand, palm up, under Kaitja's and then gripped it firmly. Kaitja returned the firm grip before letting go.

"Would you care to enjoy the comforts of my home a while?" Kaitja asked, gesturing toward the structure.

"You are a generous man indeed. I am sorry to say that I must return at once to Ceno to attend family business." Hon made a small bow.

"As you wish, Hon Marangoz. Go in safety." Kaitja returned the bow.

"You have been an honourable host," Hon said before turning to the girl. "You will bring honour to the family," he said. Xitano only looked at him long enough to hear the statement. Once made, the man turned to the path by which he had come and walked away. Kaitja waited for Hon to be out of ear-shot before talking.

"Was he anxious to leave for some reason?" Kaitja asked without looking at the girl. She had not moved from where she stood.

"He hates to walk in the woods at dark," she replied, looking up in the failing light as if gauging when nightfall would arrive. "Carpenters are suspicious sorts."

"And what about you?" Kaitja asked, looking at the girl.

"I prefer to think on what is real instead of stories made up to frighten children." She looked up at the Arm, complete seriousness in her eyes.

"If you are going to spend the rest of your life in the wild, that is a good place to start. Lay your bag by the door and join me at the splitting stump." Kaitja let the girl move first and then made his way back to the wood pile. Picking up a section of log that was white on the outside and inside, he set it on end on the stump and then retrieved the axe. When the girl joined him, Kaitja handed the tool to her.

Xitano looked at the axe in her hand. It was a typical wood-splitting axe except that the handle near the head was bent back toward the holder at an angle. She looked at Kaitja, her brows pushed toward each other.

"Did my dad make this for you?" she asked.

"No, I made it myself from new hickory. Let's see what you can do," Kaitja said, waving at the wood standing ready.

Xitano gave a small huff as she laid the head of the axe on top of the wood. Lifting the axe, she swung it down into the pithy wood, driving the head three-fourths of the way through the log's length. Lifting the axe again with the wood still wedged at the head, she plunged the axe down on the stump, finishing the split.

"You can do better than that. It's only white bamboo," Kaitja said with a small amount of derision.

"I didn't know it was a test," Xitano replied carefully.

"Swing with your body and shoulders, not just your arms," Kaitja said, ignoring the comment as he picked up one of the split halves and set it on end on the stump. "Bend your knees and lower your body with the blow."

Xitano turned back to the stump and held the axe over the wood, one foot slightly in front of the other. Raising the axe, her arms, shoulders and body moved together as the girl drove the axe completely through the wood and into the stump.

"Much better," Kaitja said as he removed the new pieces and threw them onto a pile of similar wood.

"Why do you need so much white wood?" Xitano asked as she removed the axe from the stump. "Most people don't use more than one small stick to start a fire."

"When you are camping in the wild where all is drenched by rain around you, those sticks are vital to starting a fire to keep yourself warm." Kaitja picked up a log of brown wood and set it on the stump. "Now this one."

"You're testing my strength, aren't you?" Xitano asked as she lined up the axe.

"Yes," Kaitja said as he watched the girl drive the axe a little more than halfway through the wood. "And seeing how much wood splitting I will not be doing in the future. You've done this before, I believe."

"You know anyone in Ceno that hasn't, besides maybe that mayor's brat of a daughter?" Xitano raised the head of the axe out of the wood and made another swing, finishing the split.

"I would not know," Kaitja said with no emotion. Kicking the split wood aside, he placed a black log on the stump. The inside was the colour of charcoal with dark rings barely visible. Xitano stared at him, eyes wide.

"Ironwood? Are you serious?" she asked.

"Let's see what you can do."

"If you say so," Xitano replied, shaking her head. First sighting the axe on the wood, she drew it back until the head was well behind her. Swinging the axe in a wide arc, she drove the head onto the black wood. With a clunk that did not sound much like when the axe had hit the previous pieces, the edge rested only a finger width into the log. Her arms visibly shook with the impact. Placing her foot on the log, she worked the axe back and forth until it came loose.

"I hope you didn't expect much," Xitano said, holding the axe in both hands. Kaitja held out his hand and took it from the girl when offered. As she moved away, he moved into position to strike the wood.

"Ironwood is an enemy you have to know how to attack, just as the creatures in the mountains will be." Kaitja looked at the wood, shifting position slightly as he did so.

"Just how far do you expect me to be able to split an ironwood log?" Xitano asked as she watched.

Holding the axe in one hand, Kaitja placed his left foot in front of him and his right slightly behind. After studying the wood, he swung the axe in a circle behind him, still in one hand, and then with one motion from his hand to his ankle, swung it around and down onto the log, his feet leaving the ground when the axe was over his head and landing on the ground as it hit the log. The head impacted the log with a much different sound than before, hitting a weak vein, driven its full width into the wood.

"When you can drive it that far, we will divide the wood duty between us." Kaitja let go of the handle, leaving the axe hanging from the wood. "You can continue tomorrow. Supper should be about ready."

Kaitja walked toward his house made of hewn logs, as all the houses on the mountain were. A single storey dwelling, it was not large by anyone's standard. In contrast to some he had seen, it was well maintained. When he reached the door, Kaitja picked up the bag the girl had brought and held it out.

"There is a small room in the back currently being used for storage. It is the only room I have to offer. We will have to move things out for you to be comfortable, which we can do tomorrow. For tonight, you can sleep by the fire. Put your bag in the room, take the bucket that is there, and go to the stream and fill it. Since I was not expecting a guest, we will most likely need more water tonight. Go now."

Xitano took the bag and walked into the house without a comment. Kaitja followed. When she exited the small room, he gathered a few items from the room and took them to his sleeping area, separated from the rest of the house by a thick curtain whose edge hovered just above the floor. Once the items were stored, Kaitja made his way to the fire and stirred the contents of the pot hanging above it. Taking up a wooden hook, he raised the pot from the fire and placed it on the table. After replacing the hook, he walked to a table over which meat and cheese hung and took down a ham. He had just taken up a wide-bladed knife and was slicing pieces when Xitano returned.

"Place it over there," Kaitja said, gesturing with the knife. "There are plates, bowls, and such in the cabinet." He sliced some more pieces of ham, placed them on a wooden tray, replaced the ham on its hanger, then picked a length of cheese from which he also cut pieces. The finished product was a tray with six pieces of ham and six pieces of cheese. He placed the tray in the centre of the dinner table before sitting in the largest chair. Xitano already sat on the other side of the table, two complete dinner sets between them. Kaitja dished out stew to the two bowls.

"Since I did not know you were coming, you get a treat tonight. Don't expect it every night." Xitano sat, hands in her lap, not saying anything. The stew divided between the bowls, Kaitja placed the spoon in the bowl and sat back in the chair and waited. Xitano continued to wait, unmoving. After a few breaths, Kaitja spoke again.

"At least your parents taught you manners." Taking a piece of meat, he dipped it in the stew, letting it soak up broth before taking a bite. When he had put the meat in his mouth, Xitano took a piece of cheese from her side of the tray. Smelling it first with a long inhale, she took a generous bite, closing her eyes as she chewed.

"This is Margaro's cheese, isn't it?" Xitano said when the bite had been swallowed. "She makes the best cheese I have ever tasted. We can, I mean could, not afford it often."

"It is part of the town's tribute," Kaitja said without looking.

They ate in silence for a while until Kaitja spoke again.

"The next market day we will see if we can find you some hemp clothing. That cotton is already showing wear. If they do not have any in the village, we will have to go down to the plain."

Xitano looked at him when he mentioned the plain but continued to chew. She looked down, glanced up through the top of her eyes, and then back at her bowl. After swallowing, she spoke.

"Have you been to Prima?" she asked.

"Yes," Kaitja replied in a neutral voice, waiting for more questions.

"Do they still have machines that work?" Xitano was more animated but controlled.

"A few. Fewer as time passes." Kaitja ate without looking at the girl.

"Why don't they fix them?" Each question came faster than the last.

"Because those who know how to fix them are fewer with each generation and the sun-plates that power them wear out so less power is available."

"Why don't they make new ones?"

"Because the ore needed to make the parts is not found in concentrated areas like it was on Terra. We barely find enough iron to make the tools we have. If we had not discovered how to work tool-stone for axes, hammers, and such, we would not have enough tools to go around."

Xitano took a bite, chewed, and swallowed. "I would like to see a machine before they all stop working."

"I think there is plenty of time for that. First will be your training." They both ate a while before Xitano's next question.

"Do you believe the stories that someone destroyed the house that made power for the machines after the colony was set up? Why would someone do that?"

Kaitja took his time answering. "It has been almost three hundred years since then. Anyone who knew the answer is long dead. To me it makes no difference what happened, whether someone destroyed it or not, things are as they are. We live the life we are given to live. The colony only started villages in these mountains some fifty years ago. There is much of the planet left to explore and much we still don't know. Without all the machines that were originally brought to make settlement faster, we do what we can when we can."

"Wouldn't we be off better with more machines?"

"It is hard to tell. In the year after the colony lost the power house, half the colonists died from the cold or sickness. That tells me they were weak and too dependent on their machines. We are all stronger for their loss." Kaitja took a quick look at Xitano to see her reaction but she only continued to eat. He let her do so before asking the question he had been waiting to ask since their introduction.

"What were you going to say when I asked you if you wanted to be my apprentice?" That brought seriousness to Xitano's eyes. He could tell she was trying to gauge why he had asked the question—indecision showed in her face. To lessen her anxiety, he added, "If there is one thing we will need in the wild it is honesty, no matter if it brings pain."

Xitano swallowed and turned away her eyes. "I was going to say that being an apprentice would be better than being some man's servant as his wife."

Kaitja let the comment disappear into the walls before asking more. "So you do not desire to have a family, marry some boy you have set your eyes on?"

"They have never had much interest in me," the girl said while pushing what was left of her stew around her bowl with her spoon. "I am too skinny, they say. Even Matron Effero says that my hips are too thin to deliver babies and that I would probably die in the attempt. I never had much interest in domestic duties anyway." She picked up a piece of cheese and stuffed the whole thing in her mouth, Kaitja thought maybe for comfort.

"Is that why your father brought you here, because he did not think he would be able to marry you off?"

"He regards me as unruly," she said after swallowing. "Says I spend too much time away from home and not enough learning wifely duties. At least he won't have to provide a dowry for me."

"I think the boys are just afraid they won't be able to catch you," Kaitja said, peeking at the girl. He was rewarded by a laugh which she quickly covered with her hand. "You also did not look pleased when your father mentioned the bristle squirrel."

Xitano's expression changed to the opposite of laughter. She gripped her spoon tightly, pressing it against the bottom of the bowl.

"It was not his to kill. I befriended it, I brought it home. He had no right." She pounded the spoon onto the bottom of the bowl and then pushed the food away.

"Wild bristle squirrels only take a bit of food and a soft voice to tame. It may be their undoing." Kaitja chewed on his last piece of ham.

"We were not starving, there was no need to kill it."

"Did you eat the stew?" Kaitja asked. The girl paused before answering, her eyes focused far off.

"It wouldn't have brought the creature back if I hadn't. And it would have angered my father." Xitano played with a piece of ham in her hand. "They say bristle squirrels are so tame because the colonists brought them from Terra."

"No," Kaitja replied. "They are native. I was told that they are called squirrels because they look and act like squirrels on Terra. It is the same with many things here on Altaterra. It's a natural tendency for people to name things in such a way."

Xitano had been looking around the house. "You have no wife?"

"No," Kaitja said, finishing up the last of his stew. "But at least I have you now to clean my dishes and do whatever I say."

A few seconds went by before Xitano talked, staring at the man. "I will not warm your bed."

Kaitja stopped still and looked at the girl. Her face was the hardest it had been since she arrived. He took out the harshness from his voice his impulses would have directed at her before speaking. "I have no need for some girl to warm my bed. When I want it warmed, I can make it so. Women think it exciting to bed an Arm, though I have not met any that relish the idea of a husband who may not come back whenever he leaves their home."

Silence followed the statement, rich with tension. Xitano lowered her head and fussed with her fingers for a while before rising from the table and bowing. "I apologize, I meant no disrespect. I will clean up."

"I like my dishes very clean!" Kaitja called to Xitano's back in a lighter-toned voice.

Chapter Two

Xitano was bent low to the ground, following tracks that had led along and up the mountain through the blue-green brush and trees. Coming to a fork in the path often used by game, she had the choice of travelling farther up the hill or back down the slope. Examining the ground of both paths closely, she started on the path that travelled next to the rocky cliff and further up the mountain, still crouched low.

Kaitja waited on the cliff above, leaning back far enough so he could not be seen. He did not need to watch the girl to know where she was and could afford to take the time to look over the gently sloping mountain and into the basin. The basin was wide enough that he had never seen the mountain range on the side, though he knew that it ringed the land, ending in the ocean on both sides. While she was silent of step, he could still hear Xitano's breathing. They would also need to adjust her clothing since he could still hear a swish as she walked.

Waiting until she was below him, Kaitja leaned forward so that he looked down at the girl on the trail. He smiled at how good she had become in so little time. True, she had talent when she had arrived, but her ability had grown quickly. He was sure she would be ready when the need arose.

"If I were a mountain wolf I would be on your back now," he said over the cliff.

"And if you jumped on my back, you would be impaled on the end of my spear," Xitano said, making the end of the spear held under her armpit wave in the air above her without looking up.

"You don't think I could avoid your spear tip?"

"You, yes. A mountain wolf, no." Xitano looked up at Kaitja and smiled.

"I am glad," Kaitja said as he jumped down to the trail well clear of the spear, "that you hold me in such high regard."

Xitano straightened up. "Did I pass?"

"You can track anything in these woods," Kaitja replied, "except me when I don't wish it."

"Are you sure?" she asked with her head cocked to one side. "I found you, didn't I?"

"I wasn't trying my hardest, only close to my hardest." He smiled at the girl. All of her training had not made her any thicker in build but he knew her muscles were harder than twisted cords. She had grown a little taller since her arrival and was now one of the tallest females he had met. Her long arms and legs gave her leverage that she used with good advantage.

"So I passed?" Xitano asked.

"Yes, you passed. Lead the way home," Kaitja said with a wave.

Xitano walked lightly, almost skipping, down the path with a wide grin on her face. She looked back once using the corner of her eye to look at Kaitja, reminding him of the way children looked at adults when they think sly thoughts, but she didn't speak for several more paces down the path.

"Would you say that I have completed my apprenticeship in record time?" she finally asked.

"It depends on what you are apprenticing for," Kaitja responded in a normal tone of voice.

"And what would be left if I wanted to be an Arm?" Xitano's head swayed back and forth as she walked.

"You would need to track down a man and kill him," Kaitja said with the same tone.

Xitano stopped on the trail and slowly turned back to Kaitja, her eyes frozen in place. She swallowed before she spoke.

"An Infected?" Her voice quivered a little on the word.

"Possibly." Kaitja had stopped on the trail a pace behind her. "There are also times someone will run from the courts and we are called to hunt them. Few from the surrounding villages find themselves in such a situation but we can get ones from the plains who flee to the mountains."

"Is it true they have no Infected on the plains?" Her voice still quivered.

"Yes. We did not encounter them until villages were established in the mountains."

"Has no one studied them to find out what makes them Infected?" The girl's curiousness worked through her fear but did not dismiss it altogether.

"They are too dangerous. People have become Infected themselves by contact with both alive and dead Infected. That is why we use the forked spears and burn the bodies after they are killed."

"They sound like the most dangerous prey an Arm hunts."

"Actually not," Kaitja said as he started walking down the path, Xitano in tow, her head cocked to one side as she looked at him. "Infected are wild, unthinking creatures that act predictably under most circumstances. They would rather flee than fight and when they do fight, they charge with little thought to tactics. If you stay calm and quiet, you can get close enough to strike before they have a chance to react. Much more dangerous is a man who plans his actions, maybe even leaving traps in his trail to discourage others from following. I would much rather face an Infected than an intelligent foe who knows I am coming."

"Still," Xitano said, her voice still tense, "Infecteds frighten me more than any man."

"Fear, properly placed, is useful." Kaitja moved a branch out of his way and held it long enough for Xitano to catch it before he released. "Fear is your mind telling you something you have not taken notice of yet. Directed properly, it can save your life. Allowed to cause panic, it will kill you."

"Great," Xitano said with a forced huff of a laugh, "now I have to be afraid of myself."

"You will be your worst enemy," Kaitja said, his tone still serious. "If you become overconfident in your skill or worry too much your skill is inadequate, you will pay a price."

Kaitja looked back to see Xitano's eyes staring at him with absorption. She straightened her back, raising herself to her full height, and squared her shoulders.

"I will not forget your words," she announced.

"Good." Kaitja gave a small smile after the word was said, his eyes taking on a kinder tone. "Then a lesson as we walk."

Kaitja turned back to walking down the path. Xitano paused but quickly matched step just behind the Arm. "I thought I was trained."

"You will never stop learning, if you are wise. Now, answer this. How many days until the near-freeze?"

"About three weeks," Xitano said with a shrug.

"That is not what I asked. How many days?" Kaitja took several steps, feeling Xitano's eyes on him.

"How am I supposed to know? It doesn't come on the same day every year."

Kaitja reached up and broke off a leaf from a passing tree. It was a greenish-blue broadleaf about the size of his hand, trimmed with a thin yellow border. He handed the leaf to Xitano.

"The leaves of the blueleaf tree take twenty days to turn from blue-green to yellow. Each of those days the leaves turns one part more yellow. By looking at the leaf you can tell how many more days until near-frost."

"Interesting," Xitano said, not sounding entirely sincere.

"If the branch is bent," Kaitja continued, "the leaf turns twice as fast. If it is broken off and falls to the ground, it turns four times as fast." He waited for a response.

"So, if someone I am tracking bends a leaf, I should be able to compare the leaves and tell how long since they had passed." Xitano looked around at the trees they passed.

"Precisely. Now, how many days until near-frost?"

"Ah, seventeen?" Xitano said after examining the leaf.

"Eighteen, but close."

"Darn!"

"It takes some practice."

"How do the trees know?" Xitano asked, waving the leaf in the air.

"I have no idea. Maybe if we ever have use of the machines again, we will figure it out. There are other signs that you have not been taught yet."

"Are you sure you are not just looking for a way to keep me around to wash dishes?" Xitano's happy voice had returned.

"There is always that consideration," Kaitja replied, smiling but not looking at the girl. "The dishes have been very clean these last four months."

"Hmm," Xitano said to herself, "maybe I have been taking the wrong approach there."

"Only if you like doing them more than once."

"You just like torturing your apprentices, don't you?" Xitano said in a fake grumble.

"You are my first apprentice but I am quite enjoying it." Kaitja turned his smile toward her and received the tip of her tongue in the air in response. As he turned his head back he added, "Now it appears my apprentice is turning into a frog."

"Croak!" came from behind him.

Not long after they reached the house, a man crashed through the underbrush into the yard. His sweat in the cool day and his shortness of breath meant he had run all the way from the village. When the man drew enough breath to straighten, Kaitja saw that it was Charas, a farmer from the west edge of Ceno. He walked over to the man and held his shoulders in both hands.

"Friend Charas, breathe deep. What is the matter?" Kaitja talked in a calm, slow voice.

"An Infected!" Charas blurted out.

"Where?" Kaitja kept his voice calm and slow.

"On the west edge of Farmer Svan's land, headed north." The man took a couple of slow, deep breaths as if he felt he had the time now that his message had been delivered.

"Thank you, friend, for the prompt report, we will attend to this immediately. Do you feel you can make it back to the village safely?" Kaitja waved at Xitano to bring Charas some water.

"Yes, I will be fine. Just please kill that thing!"

"Stay here until you have recovered. Feel free to enjoy the hospitality of my home if you wish. Xitano," Kaitja said to the girl as he took the water cup from her, "take out two forked spears, two water skins, and a pack of white wood."

Xitano ran into the house. Kaitja handed the cup to Charas. "Was anyone hurt?" he asked.

"No, but his wife and daughter were frightened out of their wits."

"Have all the farms checked to make sure all are safe. Carefully."

"Yes, Arm, it will be done."

"Be safe, Friend Charas." Kaitja gave the man a light pat on the back and turned to the sound of Xitano coming out of the house. "We leave now. Follow my lead and listen to all I say as we go."

Slipping the waterskin strap over his head, Kaitja took a spear and started running west with quick, long strides. He could hear Xitano's even breaths behind him. Unworried that she would be able to keep up, Kaitja headed quickly across the mountain face on a game trail where it appeared.

"Infected are drawn to heat. We are lucky that the Infected was on the edge of town out of sight of any fires or someone might have been attacked."

"Where are we going?" Xitano's voice asked from behind.

"There are steam vents in the mountains. It is assumed that they are heated from underneath. It sounds as if the Infected is headed toward some vents that I know of near here.

"Listen. Remember what I said earlier today. Infected would rather flee. We will move up quietly, taking it from behind if possible. Aim for a kill thrust. If you are the one who makes the first thrust and miss, hold it down until I can kill it. Do not withdraw your spear until it is dead. Stay as far as possible from it at all times."

"It will let us get that close?" Xitano asked.

"If we do not try to corner it, yes it will. If cornered, it will charge straight at you. Extend your spear as far as possible and set your feet. Try not to get knocked over. That can be fatal."

Foliage and wildlife were ignored as they ran. The wildlife seemed to know there was no danger for they did not flee at the sight of the humans. Several miles later, the pair intersected the trail of the Infected. Compared to the one Kaitja had left for Xitano earlier, it was a scar on the land headed straight toward the mountain peaks. He turned up the trail to the mountains. The way the grass just started to bend back upright told him that the track was not more than minutes old.

"It won't be long now. Stay low with your spear pointed in front of you one man's height behind me," Kaitja instructed. Xitano's footfalls dropped back slightly.

They entered the upper forest of twisted pines, named so because their branches refused to grow straight. A stream flowed to their left close enough to feel an occasional spray when it hit large rocks. Without the tall grass, the trail was not as much a scar but was still plain to Kaitja. Habit made him check the tops of boulders and overhangs as they ran, though he knew that animals would flee the Infected. The footprints got close together. The Infected was slowing due to the slope of the mountain. Kaitja moved his hand at his side in a downward motion before slowing his pace to half speed. He gripped the spear with two hands.

Several turns later, a man came into sight. His hair was drenched in sweat, his clothes were torn, and he breathed in ragged fashion. He was still making his way up the slope but had encountered rough, steep terrain and kept looking around as if looking for an easier path.

"Careful," Kaitja whispered, "it may feel cornered. Stay back."

With long, careful steps Kaitja closed on the man. Red skin showed where the man's clothes had been torn, almost the colour of fire. Kaitja stopped once when he thought the man would turn around and then continued. As he pulled back the spear to strike, the Infected turned, its eyes wide and its face grimaced in pain. The Infected started to charge as Kaitja started his thrust. The Infected's movement made Kaitja's death-strike miss its target and sink into the right shoulder. Continuing to drive with his legs, Kaitja pushed the Infected backwards onto the slope, driving the end of his spear into the ground behind it. Still pressing the spear against the struggling man, Kaitja moved to the left.

"Xitano, now! Kill it!"

As he spoke the last word, Xitano's spear pierced the man in the heart and lung. The man's arms and legs flailed several times and then went limp, his body still. Kaitja pulled his spear out of the man and backed up.

"You did not hesitate, that is good. Set the spears aside. We will clean them in the fire with which we burn the body." Kaitja threw his spear aside. "Gather dry wood, as much as you can find."

Xitano looked at the dead man, turning her head from side to side. After removing the spear, she threw it next to Kaitja's but did not gather wood.

"Get away from that!" Kaitja yelled.

"Something is happening in the body, the midsection I think," Xitano replied. "It's … expanding."

Kaitja dropped the wood he had picked up and ran back toward the body. As he neared Xitano, the belly of the man expanded as if he had swallowed a large melon. Kaitja pushed Xitano to one side but as he did, a fine hole appeared in the man's belly and a geyser of steam struck him in the chest. The steam burned his skin through his thin shirt. As much as the steam hurt, there was something else. His chest felt as if a dozen or more spears the size of small seeds had struck it.

Kaitja screamed at the two kinds of hot pain. The seeds were hot, not as hot as coals but much hotter than something he would want next to his skin. He stepped back and tried to raise his arms but found they were becoming unresponsive, as were his legs. Stumbling, he fell to his knees. Xitano jumped to her feet but stood where she was.

"*Kill me!*" Kaitja commanded. "Kill me before I become one of them! I can feel their seeds burrowing into my skin! Kill me!"

Xitano passed where he could see as she ran to the spears. He could hear her take up a spear, hear her run back to him. Not able to turn, he looked at the Infected man in front of him. The pants of the man's legs were perforated with the same small holes that he knew were in his shirt. He breathed in and tried to prepare himself for death. He heard Xitano raise her spear.

The blow did not come. Kaitja yelled, "Strike me! What are you waiting for!"

The sound of the spear hitting the ground came to his ears. He felt hands under the backs of his arms.

"What are you doing?" Kaitja said in a soft voice, all he could force out of his lungs, as he was lifted backwards. The trees above started to pass by at increasing speed. He could feel the ground sloping downward below him. Unable to move and speak, he could only watch the scenery. The seeds in his chest continued to bore into his skin. He heard the splash of water ahead. The sky appeared briefly before he caught a glimpse of the stream as he was thrown face-first into it.

The water was almost as cold as the ice that appeared rarely in the lakes and streams. Kaitja held his breath as he was pushed under the water, held there by hands on his back. His breath did not last long in his weakened condition. Unable to hold it any longer, his diaphragm spasmed. The first gulp of water he forced down to his stomach but the demand for air caused his body to draw the next into his lungs. The cold water bit his skin inside and out as bubbles travelled from his mouth to the water's surface. He felt himself losing consciousness.

He did not notice being taken out of the stream but found himself lying face down on the ground coughing up water as Xitano's fist pressed under his ribs from behind. The water was not as cold as it had been but now his whole body was shaking. When he stopped coughing up fluid, Xitano rolled him onto his side.

"I will start a fire," Xitano said, her face near his. Kaitja lost consciousness as he watched her run off.

Kaitja woke up with a fire in front of him. He was lying under a blanket, his clothes drying to one side. His chest hurt, both inside his lungs and where the steam had hit his body. All his muscles were sore but he was not shaking anymore. Xitano sat on the far side of the fire watching him as one would a child with a cold, not as if she expected him to attack her.

"Why?" He tried to stare down the girl but didn't have the energy.

"You have been out for several hours," Xitano replied calmly. It wasn't until she did that Kaitja noticed that most of the light was gone. "I believe that if you were going to become an Infected, you would have done so by now."

Kaitja wanted to ask a long question but could only manage, "How?"

"The man wasn't from our village. This meant that he had been travelling. The steam from the body reminded me of the steam vents you talked about. Since the nights are getting near frost and the man had most likely slept outside, I reasoned that he found one of the vents you spoke of and bedded near it. I think that was when he became Infected. I reasoned that the infection needs heat to survive. When a body dies, it cools, so the infection would look for another host. It would have been me that was Infected if you had not saved me. I apologize, I was too curious for my own good. All this told me that the need for heat to survive was also the infection's weakness. The streams here are cold, very cold. Hoping that the cold from the stream would kill it, I brought you to the stream. Because I did not know if any of the infection had gone into your lungs, I had to drown you. I apologize for that too but I had to be sure."

"I appreciate your thoroughness," Kaitja responded after a pause. "Truly I do."

"I know I risked that we would both end up Infected but if there was a chance I could save you, I had to take it." Xitano paused and gave a forced smile. "How do you feel?"

"I think I can travel if you give me my clothes back, though I might be slower than normal."

"Don't worry; I will protect you on the way home." Xitano's smile became more generous and sly.

The next day his chest still hurt and he didn't want to move, but Kaitja was alive and not an Infected so everything else could be endured. Even with a healing salve he knew it would take more than a couple of days to recover. He did not rise as early as was his habit and it took longer than normal to reach the village from his house.

By the time they did, everyone had gathered in the centre. Xitano walked by his side as he headed into the centre of the crowd. He took a deep breath.

"The Infected is destroyed," Kaitja said in a loud voice so all could hear. A sigh passed through the crowd. People laughed in relief or said quiet prayers of thanks. He let it go on for a while before speaking again.

"Something very important was also learned, something we need to share with the other villages." All conversation stopped. "I will let the person who discovered this information tell you of it."

Turning, he said, "Arm Xitano, if you would, please."

Chapter Three

The train of horses could be seen for dozens of miles from the hillside. Watching them was slow entertainment and few did it for long except the very young who had never seen a horse before. Most checked the trail every hour or so. When the train turned onto the road that would lead them to the village, people became more excited. A twenty-horse train was a large one and no one had a clue as to why they would be headed for their small village.

The horses did not go unnoticed by Kaitja or Xitano, who made sure they were in the village before the troop arrived, standing in the middle of the small lawn. Heads down, the travellers looked saddle-weary, like those who did not spend a lot of time riding a horse on a regular basis. A few even accepted assistance from villagers or their fellow travellers to dismount, stretching as if from a long sleep. At the head of the troop was a gentlemen of some years crowned in white hair and sporting a short, white beard. His eyes, though, were bright and spoke of intelligence as he looked around the village, taking stock of each house and building. When no one from the village stepped forward, Kaitja approached the man and held out his hand.

"Arm Kaitja. How may I be of service?"

"Director of Science Phillipee Robterns. Most people just call me Robterns." Dismounting and shaking Kaitja's hand, Robterns continued to survey the village. "Quaint little place you have here."

"My assistant and I actually live up the mountain a ways. Is there something you needed from the village?"

"Just a place to stay the night." Robterns turned and gave him a grin. "I know it's early but most of us aren't used to riding for so long, so I think it best we stop here while there is still someplace to get real food and maybe a roof to sleep under."

"I'm sure the villagers will be happy to accommodate you. They are always anxious for news from the city." Villagers were already helping the troop, removing baggage as directed and handing out cups of water, asking questions as they did so. "May I ask to the nature of your visit?"

"Yes, of course." Robterns straightened himself into a business-like stance. "We are in need of a guide or guides, as can be provided. You and/or your assistant would be preferred."

"And exactly where will we be guiding you?"

"Over the mountain." The words were said with confidence.

"Over the mountain?" Kaitja's look became puzzled. "I don't know that anyone has been over the mountain, except maybe some over-eager boy."

"Precisely."

Contorting his face in concern, Kaitja glanced more at the growing pile of baggage. "So this is an exploratory expedition?"

"Yes. We will be looking for metal ores. About time, too. Given the shape of the mountain on this side, we believe there may be exposed veins of ore just on the other side. We intend to find them, if they exist, or probe the ground if they are not exposed." The pride on Robterns' face was clear.

"And why has such a trip been undertaken now?"

"It's your own fault." Robterns almost laughed with the words. "Now that we understand the cause and habits of the Infected, it was felt safe enough to mount an expedition over the mountain."

"It wasn't I who gained the necessary knowledge, it was Arm Xitano." Kaitja's arm swept toward Xitano.

"Whoever, it doesn't matter." Robterns rocked back and forth on his feet.

"Do you know you brought too much baggage for a trip over the mountain?"

Shock registered on Robterns' face. "But the horses don't seem to have trouble with it."

"You can't take horses over the mountain. In fact, you best leave them here because there isn't any place further up the mountain to leave them. Your people will have to carry their own baggage." The stare Kaitja gave the man expressed a firm position.

"Do you think we could hire some locals to help carry our things?" Robterns asked in a weakening voice.

"They're too busy making a living. Besides, if you believe you need all of... that... you're going to spend all your time caring for the baggage. You need to cut it down by at least half."

"Half?" Now Robterns looked worried.

"Yes." Kaitja took a deep breath and let it out. "Take only what you absolutely need, no more. Your things will be safe in the village, at least from all but the curious. And don't forget a couple changes of clothing and food. There's no game to speak of near the top of the mountains that wouldn't be hiding long before this crowd gets there. And everyone needs at least one water container. We can fill those as we go."

Wringing his hands, Robterns looked around at the travellers, unsettled. "This, this will take some time. We need to discuss what we will be leaving. I already made people cut back on what they brought. They wouldn't be happy to leave more behind."

"Well, if they have to carry it, then I'm pretty sure they'll come to terms. Oh, and by the way, before we head out tomorrow, I will be inspecting everyone to make sure they're not carrying too much. The air only gets thinner from here on up and we're not leaving stuff on the mountain if their packs are too heavy. Understood?"

"Yes." A heavy sigh followed. "This is going to be painful."

"Not as painful as it would be later, and I mean physically. I will leave you in the hands of the villagers. Be ready at first light tomorrow." Kaitja made a small bow.

"First light? It's going to be a long night." Turning toward the rest of the troop while shaking his head, Robterns clapped his hands for attention as he walked toward them.

"He didn't look happy." There was a sense of glee in Xitano's voice.

"I told him each person has to carry their own baggage."

The statement brought a huff of a laugh from Xitano. "Are there fifty more people around that I don't see?"

"I'm sure it will be hours before it all gets settled. Come on, I told them we would be back at first light." Kaitja turned uphill.

"You don't want to stay to listen to the arguments?" Xitano asked as she followed, a smirk on her face.

"No."

The next morning, Kaitja and Xitano found the science team not ready at sunrise, to neither of their surprise. Some still yawned as they came out of the buildings they had slept in. When they appeared ready, Kaitja inspected the backpacks. Most needed weight removed, which caused unhappy faces and sour comments under their breath. When Kaitja pointed up the mountain, most did not argue. One, a young man of stocky build with a square head of short hair, did argue.

"This is my job," the young man protested.

"You have to carry that all the way up the mountain," Kaitja said emphatically.

"I know that." The response had an element of dealing with someone stating the obvious.

"It looks heavy."

"I've had to carry worse, a lot worse." The young man's stance displayed his determination. "All this is essential, which is why I am carrying it."

Throwing up his hands, Kaitja turned away. "Have it your way. But I'm not carrying your stuff or dragging your weary ass back down the hill."

"Good. I'd rather you not touch my ass," came the reply to Kaitja's back.

Xitano's snickering did not go unnoticed by Kaitja, but he made no comment as he moved to the next person. It didn't go unnoticed by the boy, either, whose face turned red when he saw her reaction.

When Kaitja returned, she gave him a sly smile.

"This trip might prove interesting yet," she said as her eyes glistened.

"Don't start. It's going to be hard enough herding these cats in the mountain. If we don't lose a couple I will be overjoyed. And I'm not carrying any bodies back."

"Or asses?"

"I said don't start." He gave her a stern look. Glancing back at the young man, his eyes went questioning. "You taking his side?"

"He looks to be made of farm stock, the kind that can do hard work all day and barely break a sweat. If any of them can carry that pack up the mountain, it's him. Looks like a lot of equipment."

"Probably stuff Robterns told him was necessary. We'll see how long that lasts." Turning to the scientists, Kaitja talked in a loud voice. "Okay, people, let's get moving. It's going to take all day to get to the top, if we reach it. I'll lead, Xitano will take the rear. Don't go wandering off and don't go near any vents. And don't fall off a cliff because if you're dead, you can lie there as far as I'm concerned. Got it? Then let's go."

At the start, the trail was obvious. Kaitja slowed his normal pace to one he felt the scientists could match, knowing it would get slower as they went. Talk among the crowd was animated and eager. Most appeared awed by the sight of wild animals, the small ones and birds that dared investigate the intrusion into their domain. Xitano's bristle squirrel friend, her third in a year, named Brave Feet, hopped on her shoulder a short way out of the village but did not stay long. He didn't appear to like the attention he drew from the others even while she was petting him.

"I wish I could have held him," one woman said after the squirrel left.

"You can't blame them for being nervous. The villagers hunt them for food." Xitano tried hard to keep her voice neutral.

"Food? That little thing?"

"A little meat is more than some have."

"I didn't know people up here were so poor." Pity was heard in the woman's voice.

"Life can be hard and it's not like we have people bringing food into the village every day like in the city or even the money to buy it if they did. Which is probably why they don't."

"Why don't they have money?"

Trying hard not to react to the woman's ignorance, Xitano just smiled. "When your income is based on agriculture, pay comes a couple times a year, or maybe only once. If you don't manage it well, you run out quickly."

"Oh, right." The woman's head nodded.

"What do you do?"

"I'm a meteorologist."

"You study… meteors?"

The woman laughed. "No, the weather."

"So why aren't you a weatherologist?"

"It's just the word that's been used for centuries."

"So why do we need a weather person? We can tell you when it's going to rain." Xitano gestured toward the sky.

The woman laughed. "I also study the effect of weather on the topography, the landscape. Most of us are multi-disciplinarians." She paused a second. "We have more than one area of study. Not enough of us around to specialize in only one. Plus, I've also never been this close to the clouds. Might not get another chance."

"So if we're lucky, according to you, we'll get a fresh cloud over the mountain that fogs us in." Xitano made the statement in a tentative voice.

"That would be great, wouldn't it! The chance to be *in* a cloud. It would be awesome." The woman's whole body shook with excitement.

"Trust me." Xitano let out a breath as she talked. "It's mostly just wet."

"But it's water that has never touched the ground. At least since it evaporated off that is, so it's like brand new."

"It's still mostly just wet." Xitano's head bobbed back and forth as she spoke.

As the trek progressed, conversation lessened and breathing became heavier. Xitano expected the boy carrying the heavy load to start lagging, but he didn't. In fact, he seemed to be doing better than the others. As her curiosity grew, she asked the woman who had talked to her before, "Who's the guy carrying all the gear?"

"That's Tarn," the woman replied between huffs. "He's the director's assistant. Poor thing gets to be the pack animal all the time, but he never complains."

"So he's a scientist?"

"No. Engineer, in training that is. He's on loan to work the equipment. And repair it if necessary if he can out here."

"I didn't know they could repair machines." Xitano kept her speech slow so as not to wear the woman out trying to keep up.

"Simple repairs, like a loose wire or something. If one of the board components blows, no way unless you salvage another board from another piece of equipment. I don't know how people used to make those parts but it would be interesting to watch. They are so tiny!" The woman took a couple of extra deep breaths.

"He doesn't look like he's from the city."

The woman looked at Xitano for a second. "Good eye. He's not. Came in from the farms. I think his folks got tired of him trying to make new gadgets for the farm, though some weren't bad from what I hear. Plus I'm told they knew he was an engineer from the way he talked."

"What do you mean?"

The woman laughed. "Kept saying, 'There's got to be an easy way to do this.'"

While the woman continued to laugh, Xitano gave a half-hearted laugh in response, then silently wagged her head back and forth while her lips moved when the woman wasn't looking.

As they passed a stream, Kaitja called a break. After taking a drink, people refilled their water containers from the stream, commenting on how cold the water was. They got to sit for only ten minutes before Kaitja had them on their feet again, to many groans.

"Can't let your muscles stiffen, people," he replied.

After several hours, the trees were left behind. A much thinner trail led through the bushes, but even that soon disappeared and people had to watch where the person in front of them walked to know the path. Animals became few and they passed the first of the vents for the day. Xitano watched the suspicious looks that the scientists gave the vents as steam curled out of them. The woman in front of her turned her head to speak again.

"There is really... things... living in those vents?"

"It would seem so."

"It would be nice to get a sample but we didn't bring any equipment to collect it. Not the purpose of the trip and the committee couldn't be convinced to take the chance. Said it would take a special trip and equipment just for collecting samples from the vents."

"Why would you want one?" Brow furrowing, Xitano made sure the woman stayed on the path.

"To study them, of course."

"But they would be dead by the time you got them to the city."

"We could rig up a heated water chamber to keep them alive, I suspect. But even dead they would tell us a lot about themselves." The woman's breathing was heavier than before.

"So you know how to kill them?"

"Who knows what we would discover. We might find a medicine or new compounds that could be used for something else. Like, how do they keep their hosts from rejecting them? How do they control their urges? We could learn a lot." The woman's voice sounded animated for the first time in an hour.

"Or you could get yourself killed," Xitano added with a growl.

"It's the risk you take."

"No thanks." Xitano's tone was firm. "Not me. Rather they just die off."

The woman let up a little guff. "You're not a scientist."

"If that means I'm sane, no I'm not."

After another couple of hours, Kaitja stopped the group to eat. Most flopped onto the ground as if they couldn't reach it fast enough and sat for several minutes before digging out food. Xitano sat next to Kaitja, knowing he would want an update on the group.

"How they holding up?"

"Better than I expected."

"How's Mr. 'I can handle the heavy load'?"

"Better than the rest."

"Good. I don't want stuff scattered all over the mountainside." Grabbing his pack, Kaitja dug into it.

"Couldn't they just pick it up on the way back down?" Xitano pulled over her pack.

"What kind of shape do you think these people are going to be in by the time we come back down the mountain?" Taking a bite of cheese, Kaitja raised his eyebrows.

"Alive for one, I hope. Who knows, they might surprise you."

"We can hope. Don't get me wrong, I hope they surprise me, but I'm not counting on it. At least that Robterns guy seems to be in good shape. Been talking ever since we left the village. I'm beginning to wonder if the guy ever shuts up." Kaitja shook his head as he took another bite.

"You've just been spoiled since I don't talk much." Xitano took out her own food: a ham and cheese sandwich and some raw vegetables.

"Much?" Kaitja huffed. "I didn't know what a lot was before this guy. He puts you to shame and I thought you talked a lot."

"You just don't appreciate me enough," Xitano teased.

"Before apprenticing you, I could go weeks without someone talking to me." Pausing as he chewed, Kaitja added after a while, "And I liked it that way."

"Selfish," was Xitano's reply.

"Isn't everyone?"

After lunch, the scientists walked slower than before. Robterns didn't talk as much either. Kaitja adjusted his speed to accommodate but didn't act happy about it. The thinner air played a part and pushing through the brush didn't help either. The sun passed overhead and the shadows grew with increased speed as the afternoon wore on. Concern showed on the faces of the scientists, as much as their fatigue would allow. When people started to stumble, Kaitja called a halt in a small clearing even though they had not made the peak.

"I think we should camp here," he announced.

Altaterra   37

"Yes," Robterns agreed with enthusiasm. "It's getting much too dark to be walking around." Turning to the rest of the group, he said. "Let's make camp."

When Xitano made it to the small clearing, she looked confused. "Tents?" The scientists had pulled out hammers and stakes and were driving them into the ground.

"I guess so," Kaitja said in reply.

"That will be interesting. Kind of looks like they are having trouble driving the stakes. I haven't even seen those types of tents before. They seem to be made of a really thin material. Wonder what it is."

"Silk, maybe. I heard a rumour that they were growing the caterpillars in the mulberry grove but wouldn't let anyone near them, so it was hard to tell if the rumour was true." Setting down his pack, Kaitja looked around. "Doesn't look like anyone is starting a fire."

"Yes, over there." Xitano pointed.

"Isn't that the stubborn kid?"

"His name is Tarn."

Twisting his neck and furrowing his brow, Kaitja asked, "And how do you know?"

"I asked." An eye roll went with the answer.

"Well he seems to have more sense than the rest."

"Probably because he grew up on a farm."

Doing a slow head turn, Kaitja looked down at his assistant. "What did you do, interrogate him?"

"I asked one of the scientists."

Kaitja pointed with the hand that held food. "You think he'll get that fire started?"

"I was going to give him a couple of more minutes before I helped." Xitano started on her own food.

"Waiting for him to fail or just want to laugh at him?"

"Hey, you have to get your entertainment where you can out here." A small laugh shook her shoulders as she waved her arms over the scenery. "Naw, just want to give him time to do it himself. And there it is."

A tiny flicker of red and yellow appeared at the base of the stick pile. Fanning the pile with a large leaf, Tarn piled thicker wood on the growing fire. The others still worked in a frustrated manner on their tents.

"Shall we tell them that the soil is too shallow here for tent spikes?" Kaitja asked. "I don't want them getting too frustrated. Then I would have to hear them complain about things all night."

"I was leaving that to you. I took care of the guy making the fire." Xitano waved at Tarn while chewing her food.

"And that was such hard duty." Frowning, Kaitja stood up. "Fine."

"You're the leader," Xitano said without looking at him.

"I could make you leader."

"If you can make me leader, you are still the leader," she countered.

"Not sure it works that way," Kaitja said as he walked off.

"I am."

Chapter Four

The next morning the scientists demonstrated their inexperience at sleeping on the ground by bending in all directions as they rose, groaning, and acting much older than they were. Shaking his head, Kaitja turned away so as not to stare. "If they're like this after one day…"

"They'll get used to it." Xitano's voice came from his right. She, of course, was ready for the day's hike, her equipment already packed, if not on her shoulders. Yesterday's clothes were still on and would be until they were required to be changed by wear or offensive odour.

"And we have to put up with them until they do, which hopefully happens before the end of the trip." Giving a huff with his comment, Kaitja stirred the fire's embers, spreading them out inside the circle of rocks.

"No hot breakfast?" Robterns walked up to the circle with a warm smile on his face.

"It's going to take these people long enough to be ready to go. When we have a fixed camp, we can worry about hot breakfasts." Kaitja poured the last of the water in the leather water-pot onto the embers before folding it into a neat bundle.

"Shame, but I can't say you're wrong. Guess I better see to my pack." As the man walked away, he used hand gestures and words to encourage people who looked like they would rather still be sleeping.

"This going to be soooo fun." The words came out as a groan

from Kaitja's throat.

"At least there is one person functional." Pointing a finger, Xitano indicated Tarn, who had one full pack and was working on another, one that suspiciously looked like Robterns'.

"One out of twenty. If we get one functioning a day, it will still be a long trip." Putting the leather pot away, Kaitja's expression was not improved by the sight of Tarn's efficiency.

"Just don't let the scientists catch on to your mood. Things will be hard enough as it is. They're going to need all the encouragement we can give them." She gave him a stare.

Holding his hands up in mock surrender, Kaitja put on a big smile. "All smiles and cheer, that's me." He batted his eyes. In response, Xitano rolled her head and eyes, and sighed, turning away from the sight.

It took almost half an hour for everyone to be ready. Even then, Xitano checked all the backpack straps to make sure no one was going to lose one or themselves. Several thanked her but others looked annoyed. Those she scowled at.

The trip to the summit took well into the afternoon, given the pace of the scientists. Kaitja led them to a small pass between peaks with a small clearing—enough for everyone to sit down but not big enough for a camp. Breathing heavily, most plopped onto the ground and leaned back against the rocks, not even conversing. After a five-minute recovery, Robterns dragged himself over to Kaitja.

"I am anxious to look over the edge, but first things first."

"And that would be?"

Pointing toward a peak, Robterns continued in short phrases. "We need to put... a communication relay... at the top of a peak. When we go over the mountain... we will lose line-of-sight... with the city... and thus communication. We need to set up... one of our relays... that can see the city... and us in... whatever is over the cliff."

"Not a bad idea, though I don't know what anyone in the city is going to do for us if something happens."

"At least someone will know."

"Or not get a report and figure something has happened. If that is what you want, fine, but I'm not counting on it doing us any good in an emergency." Kaitja shook his head.

"Granted. Still, protocol." Robterns was recovering his breath faster than Kaitja would have expected.

"How many you need to make the climb?" Assessing the lack of a trail did not fill Kaitja with confidence.

"One. Tarn's our equipment manager. He has the relay." Some colour was returning to Robterns' cheeks.

"Xitano!" In answer to Kaitja's call, Xitano looked over with suspicion. "The scientists want to set up a relay on one of the peaks. Think you can get one of them up there without letting them fall over?"

"Sure." Her confidence started to disappear from her voice. "Ah, which one?"

"Me." Tarn stood behind her, relay strapped to his back, his breathing showing no sign of stress.

"You ready?" Her voice held a little shock.

"Anytime you are." Tarn gave her a smile.

"Fine. Follow me. Step where I step as much as possible." She gave him a stern look before turning away.

"You're the boss."

The tilt of her head indicated that Xitano was going to comment, but it never came. Picking her way though the brush, she took a path near the edge to avoid most of the vegetation that grew at the peak. It was small and wind-torn so it did not present much of an obstacle. It didn't take long, though, for a feeling to grow inside of her that was not related to Tarn's ever-deeper breaths. Placing the exact feeling, she spoke without looking over her shoulder.

"Are you staring at my butt?"

"Well," Tarn started with hesitation. "It is right in front of me."

"You should be looking at my feet."

"Those are nice too," Tarn said quickly.

Taking in a breath, Xitano stopped herself from replying, thought, and then grinned where Tarn could not see.

The peak was a hundred meters above the group's location. About halfway, Tarn's breathing started to sound laboured. Stopping, Xitano turned to look at him. "You okay?"

"I can make it," Tarn said between breaths.

Holding out her hand, Xitano said, "Here, I'll take it." When Tarn hesitated, she added, "You have to have enough energy to set this thing up, which you can't do if you are flat on your back trying to get enough air in your lungs to think straight."

With sagging shoulders, Tarn removed the pack and handed it to her. It weighed fifteen kilograms from what Xitano could tell.

"Not light," she commented as she swung it around her shoulder.

"Please be careful with it. It's irreplaceable. And old."

"So treat it like a grandpa. Got it." She buckled the straps together. "Let's go." After a few steps she added, "At least it will cover my butt."

"Darn," Tarn managed to say in mock disappointment. Or at least it was intended to sound that way.

When she reached the peak, Xitano turned and waited for Tarn to make up the steps he had lost. He didn't sound winded, though the thin air made him breathe hard. "Where do you want this?"

"Just hand it to me, please." Holding the device, still in its travel configuration, with two hands, Tarn pushed a latch. Three legs extended downward.

About the time the two younger people were halfway to their goal, Robterns started to make his way over to the edge of the cliff. Even though he was not asked, Kaitja joined him, hand ready to grab the man if he started to fall.

"Definite defined edge," Robterns said even before he reached the cliff.

"Yes, it's a rather steep drop-off," Kaitja said in a soft voice.

Robterns' breath gasped in awe as his vision cleared the edge to the sight beyond. The world beyond the cliff was not green. The cliff, while not sheer, was magnitudes steeper than the slope they had come up. From the bottom for a distance was a barren rut of dirt and boulders. On the other side of the rut was a small cliff with jagged peaks that looked like sharpened teeth. Beyond that could be seen a broad plain of brownish-green with a blue smear in the distance running north to south. How wide the plain was could not be seen. Fewer clouds roamed the skies above it, in fact almost none at all. Robterns was taking it all in when he heard Kaitja speak.

"Strange. This close area almost looks like a giant, dry river bed."

"It might have been at one time." Robterns' voice was weak. "Or it may have been a lava flow path. Hopefully we will find some evidence when we get down there." As he leaned forward and looked down the cliff, Robterns pointed, his hand shaking and his voice coming out in unintelligible spurts.

"What?" Leaning to look below, Kaitja scanned the cliff. "Spit it out, what is it?"

"There! There! I can see it from here! Right on the exposed cliff face."

"What am I looking for?"

"Ore! There, the coloured rock most of the way down and to the left." Robterns was almost jumping up and down by now.

"Oh," came Kaitja's much calmer voice. "What kind?"

"I don't know, don't want to say until we are sure. But it's there! Right there! Exposed on the cliff face, easily accessible. We couldn't have asked for better."

"Well, I guess we know where we will be going tomorrow then." The comment drew a look of confusion from Robterns.

"Tomorrow? But it's right there."

"And all your people are exhausted. Climbing down that cliff is not going to be easy, a lot harder than the one we came up. The ore's not going anywhere and your people need a good night's sleep."

"How about just me?" Robterns asked with a hopeful plea.

"No, we're not splitting up. You can wait until tomorrow." Turning back toward the camp, Kaitja started a determined walk. "You better pick your spot, there's not room enough for everyone to sleep apart up here. Not that I think anyone is going to even notice unless they have to get up in the night."

"Such a pity." Taking one last look, Robterns slowly withdrew from the cliff and walked back to the rest of the group. With a sigh, he added, "Don't know if I will get any sleep tonight."

"Trust me," Kaitja replied, "you will."

*　　　*　　　*

The next day, excitement raced through the group. Everyone wanted to gawk at the ore vein, but after a few quick looks, Kaitja made them back off so the descent could be planned.

"Looks doable," Xitano said, nodding her head.

"For us, sure. For them, pff." Kaitja's finger indicated points on the cliff. "We'll need to string a rope-line down the face so they have something to hold on to, anchoring it at regular intervals like there, there and there. Best to lower the packs from the top by themselves and letting the people go down unburdened."

"The packs will slide and maybe stick along the way," Xitano commented.

"Yeah. Wish we would have known, we could have brought some wooden skids. We might have to station people along the way at the landings to make things go smoother."

"Make sure you tie those people to the cliff so they don't fall." A suppressed laugh joined the comment.

"Of course." Kaitja shook his head. "This is going to take a while. We'll leave the rope-line once we are down."

Xitano gave him a grin. "So who's going first, you or me?"

"Me. I'll drive the anchors in as I go."

"Fine by me." The girl sounded happy.

"Just remember, if I start to fall you have to catch me."

"Or you could just not fall."

"That's the plan, but I like having a safety line on me."

"Don't fall," Xitano said in a flat voice. "I don't want to be left with these scientists all by myself."

"Such tempting options," Kaitja said in a sarcastic voice. "Come on, let's start rigging the ropes. Good thing we made sure everyone brought a coil."

Hovering like anxious chickens, the scientists did not help speed the process, though they did manage to stay out of the way. Their constant conversation proved to be something Xitano had to block out. Since it was repetitive, it was easy to do. She hadn't noticed the whole group for a while when, retrieving another rope, she found one being handed to her. On the other side of the coil was Tarn.

"Thanks. At least someone is helpful." She grinned as she took the rope.

"You probably don't want their help," he replied with a small chuckle.

"You're probably right." Xitano's comment was more serious. As she turned back to the cliff, she added, "You climb any?"

"Where?" came the surprised question.

"Good point, just thought I would ask." She tied the end of the new rope to the end of the previous one. "You know knots, though, right?"

"Sure. It's actually one of the skills they make sure engineers have since rope is used for many constructions."

Xitano noticed that Tarn hadn't moved closer to the cliff. "You afraid of heights?"

"Nope, just hitting the ground at the end of the fall." The comment brought a laugh from Xitano. "You know," he continued, "if you could fall without the impact at the end, it might be quite fun."

"How would you do that?" Xitano fed the new rope down the cliff.

"Land on something really soft and thick?"

"Like water?"

"No. You get too far up and water is as bad as hitting the ground unless you do it just right."

"Really?"

"Guess it can't move out of the way fast enough. No, it would have to be really soft like a pillow. The size of a house." Occupied with the rope, Xitano didn't see Tarn's gestures.

"The size of a house? I can't imagine anyone making a pillow like that, much less moving it where it's needed."

"Yeah, I know. I'm still trying to think of something else to use."

With the rope freely feeding, Xitano turned and laughed. "Why?"

"Who knows when it might be useful, like someone has to jump out of the window of a burning building?"

"Wouldn't the pillow catch on fire?"

"That's another problem."

Glancing back down the cliff, Xitano took quick note of Kaitja's process before talking again. "Do all the scientists come up with such wild ideas?"

"Some, but most are busy with their research and don't have time for much that has a practical application. That's for engineers to worry about." Tarn's eyes rolled to the side.

"So why don't we have more engineers along?" About half of the rope had been fed over the cliff.

"One, because this is an exploration and the scientists insist it's their job. They do happen to be the experts in mineral ores, at least identifying them. It also doesn't help that a lot of the engineers are assisting with the dig up north."

"What dig up north?"

The casualness of the question caused shock in Tarn. "You haven't heard?"

"We don't hear about much out here. You're the first visitors we've had in months. Hand me another rope, will you?"

"So you haven't heard about the mass grave they found?"

"Grave?" Xitano's face compacted as she took the rope. "Whose grave?"

"A whole group of people. I've heard numbers up to three hundred."

"And no one knew about it?"

"It's not in any of our records." Tarn made small shakes of his head.

"Wouldn't someone have noticed a lot of people missing? I mean, someone would have known, wouldn't they? They'd remember."

"It's not recent, it's old. Really old."

"How old?" Xitano had stopped feeding rope.

"From what I hear, several hundred years at least. Back to when the colony was established." Noticing that Xitano had stopped feeding rope, Tarn looked more concerned. "Hey, it happened a long time ago. Maybe it was a breakout of disease or something."

"Or maybe it wasn't."

The serious tone shocked Tarn. "You can't be serious."

"I'm an Arm. I'm trained to think that way."

The conversation stopped and, at an insistent tug, rope was again fed over the cliff. Tarn mostly stared, eyes wide and mouth slightly open. Somehow he managed to hand Xitano rope when she needed it. After the next coil, the rope went slack and Xitano secured her end to a large boulder, pulling it tight as she finished the knot.

"Tarn." She paused a couple of seconds before saying his name again. "Tarn! Get the backpacks."

"Ah, right." As if on automatic, Tarn turned back toward the camp.

Xitano clapped her hands. "Okay, people. We can start the descent. Make sure all your stuff is in your pack and give it to Tarn before you descend. We're going to start one person at a time, got it? One person at a time. That means before the next person starts, the first one is all the way to the bottom. We're going to do it this way until you demonstrate that you're not going to hurt yourself. Go slow. I know you are in a hurry but you won't do any good if you're dead." She looked at the group of eager eyes and people at the end of their restraint. "Who's first?"

To her shock, Robterns didn't volunteer to go first. "You're the one they can afford to lose?" she teased the woman who stepped forward.

"I'm the mineralogist," she replied with a sneer as she grasped the rope and started down the cliff.

"Hey, it was only a joke." She watched the woman descend and after a few moments said under her breath, "Wow, sensitive."

After six people had descended and none of them were Robterns, Xitano started to get a suspicion. When the current person was near the bottom, she walked over to the man and stared him in the face. "You scared of the descent, Robterns?"

"No, of course not." The way he threw away the comment looked suspicious. As Xitano continued to stare, Robterns grew nervous. After looking away and back several times, he said, "Fine, I'm scared of heights."

"Then we need to send you next while there is enough people up here to help. Get strapped in." She threw the man the end of a rope.

"But the others weren't strapped in," Robterns protested in a weak voice.

"They weren't scared. Have Tarn help you." Xitano coiled the rope around her body as she moved over to the cliff. "Come on, others are waiting."

The time it took to lower Robterns over the cliff would have been enough for two or three others to descend. Xitano wrapped the rope around her, had Tarn do the same, and then had another let it pass through their hands just in case. They gave her a strange look, but the noise from Robterns as he descended, not to mention the fact that they basically had to do all the work, removed any doubt as to her arrangement. Once he was down, she pulled the rope back up and turned her head to Tarn.

"Start getting the packs ready while I help the others."

"Sure." A sigh of relief came with the statement as he let go of the rope. Tarn made a hand-wave at another and the two moved toward the packs. The next scientist looked over the edge before starting.

"Is it safe?" the woman asked. "I mean, that was quite noisy."

"A lot safer than he made it sound. Just hold on to the rope as you go and make sure each step is steady before putting weight on it." Making small jerks with her head, Xitano encouraged the woman to start.

Finding a steeper descent close by, Tarn and the other man started lowering backpacks far enough away that no one had to worry about being hit by them while they descended. It also meant the process went faster than Xitano had anticipated. She shook her head as she watched the packs being transferred. "Handy guy to have around."

It wasn't long before shouts came up from those who were already at the bottom about the ore veins. Xitano didn't recognize any of the names used, and made a confused look at Tarn.

"A type of iron ore," he said, only taking his eyes off the pack he was lowering for a moment.

"That's good, right?"

"Depends on how pure it is. If the concentration of iron is too low, it won't be worth it."

"How do they tell?"

"Back at the lab," Tarn said, still looking at the pack.

"So we have to lug the rocks all the way back to the city." Xitano exhaled a breath. "Fun."

"We should probably haul some samples up while we're here. Not like they'd go anywhere."

"Good idea," Xitano said, turning before smiling. "You do that."

"Thanks." It almost came out of Tarn as a groan.

"Hey," she said back in a playful voice, "it was your idea."

"Someone else would have thought of it."

"Then don't say anything until they do and let them do it."

"I'll still get assigned."

"Just make sure whoever takes the samples has to carry them home." As Xitano snuck a peak, she saw Tarn smile in mild glee.

When the people and packs had been lowered to the canyon, Xitano and Tarn were left at the top. Ropes for the return trip secured, Xitano turned to find Tarn next to her with a pack strapped to his back. It had three poles with pointed ends and a separate box in a pocket. She gave him a questioning look.

"This is too sensitive to lower by ropes." When Xitano didn't respond right away, he added, "One bump on the rocks and it could be ruined. Don't worry, it's not heavy."

"You sure?"

"Heck, I've had clothes heavier than this." Tarn put his thumbs under the straps and shifted the pack as if to demonstrate how light it was.

"It's your..." Xitano's statement stopped at the sound of a low growl. As she turned her head in a slow motion, her eyes caught a glimpse of a small mountain cat edging from behind a rock. The rumble of its voice and its stalking steps belied its intent. "Shit. Don't move."

"Not a problem," Tarn's weak voice came in reply.

When Tarn spoke, Xitano felt some panic run through her at the realization that she had no idea where she had put her spear. A quick scan of her eyes revealed it was too far away to reach. "We have a problem."

"You mean your spear leaning over there on the rock next to the cat?" Tarn asked as the cat looked back and forth between them as if to decide which one to eat.

"That would be the problem."

"Can you slide your hand behind my back without that thing attacking?"

"I'll try." Leaning her right shoulder against Tarn, Xitano slipped her right hand behind his back, searching for the poles. It found Tarn's right hand doing the same. Giving his hand a quick squeeze, she grabbed one of the poles.

"Twist and pull down," Tarn said.

As she twisted the pole, something made a small click. The noise caused the cat to stop, lower its head, and create a deep-throated rumble. When the head stopped its downward motion, Xitano pulled the pole from behind. It wasn't an ideal hand location for throwing, but she only took time to point the pole at the cat before throwing it. Under normal circumstances it would have been an embarrassing throw, but the cat did jump out of the way and away from them. Without losing any time, she reached behind Tarn for another one. As she did, she watched Tarn throw a pole. Spinning around its centre like a spoke on a wheel, somehow the pole managed to hit the cat a glancing blow. The actions were enough to cause the cat to think twice about attacking and run back down the hill.

"What was that?" Xitano asked with almost a laugh.

"Better chance of hitting the thing," Tarn replied with a shrug.

"You have to hit it with the pointy end to kill it." Xitano handed him the third pole she had removed from his pack.

"We were trying to kill it?" Tarn gave her a questioning look before retrieving the other poles.

"I was trying to kill it. You obviously were not." As Tarn picked up the poles, she added, "If that had been a full-sized adult, we'd have only pissed it off."

As Tarn walked back, he was examining the poles. "Did we break them?" Xitano asked.

"Only a little bent, I can fix it," Tarn replied while examining the equipment.

"Better it than us. Come on, big hunter, let's get down with the others."

At the bottom of the cliff, Xitano was greeted by a stare from Kaitja. When he didn't say anything in a few seconds, she shrugged. "It was a little one."

"Did you kill it?" he asked.

"It ran away. I doubt it will climb down the cliff."

A harrumph was his reply before he turned back to the surrounding activity. Many of the packs had been broken into but no camp had been set up. Two groups of people had developed at the exposed vein and those examining the ores removed from it. As soon as Tarn hit the canyon floor, Robterns beckoned him over to set up the instrument he had carried down. Xitano looked at the canyon floor. It was relatively flat but hard like tool stone. No soil was seen and barely any pebbles, except near the cliffs. After examining her surroundings, she approached Kaitja.

"No one's started setting up camp yet, have they?"

"They're probably waiting for your friend to do it," he replied.

"Not that I can see any place that looks comfortable." Xitano's tone was one of disappointment.

"Place looks like a seasonal run-off channel in the mountains, only a lot bigger."

Huffing, Xitano said, "If this is a seasonal run-off, I'm not sure I want to camp down here."

"I said 'looks,' not 'is.' Ground feels like it hasn't seen water for decades." Grinding his foot on the ground for emphasis, Kaitja waved at the channel. "What bothers me is that there are no rocks in the channel-way or trees. Like the whole thing was swept clean."

"Maybe it was a *lot* of water."

"It would have to be as big as the river in the basin, or bigger. Not sure the mountains could hold enough snow for that amount of water."

As they talked, Robterns fast-walked up to them holding a smile on his face and a blackish rock in his hand. When he got close he said with joy, "Hematite!"

"Which is?" Kaitja asked.

"Iron! There may be some trace amounts of other elements but this is iron! We can make steel with this." Shaking the rock in his hand, Robterns stared at it. "And the amazing thing is, I think there is a different ore further down the canyon. We need to examine the other side."

"Why?" Kaitja said the word in a slow manner.

"To see what else is here. If there is more on the other side, it will confirm my suspicion that this canyon was formed by a lava flow." Robterns' head bobbed in small nods.

"Lava? Like a volcano?" Xitano's voice sounded a little worried.

"Yes." Robterns looked at her and then curled his mouth in dismissal. "Don't worry, any volcano has gone dormant long ago."

"How do you know?" Xitano challenged.

"Because we have never recorded any tremors or seismic activity. It was suspected at one time that the whole basin was the top of a volcano but that has been disproved years ago, though volcanic ash would explain why the soil is so rich. But I am sure there are other reasons, like sediment brought down by the river."

"But it flowed down through here at one time," Xitano asked.

"Yes, probably back when the planet was formed. The lava could have deposited the ore along the canyon as it flowed, which would explain why it doesn't appear to be very deep."

"Then why isn't there any in the middle of the canyon?" Kaitja's voice was less worried but more exacting.

"Faster flow, carried down-stream. You know what, if we could find where this canyon comes out, we might find a large deposit of multiple ores." Eyes going up, Robterns' expression showed a head full of thought.

"Not this trip," Kaitja said flatly.

"But at least we need to go to the other side of the canyon and investigate there." Robterns' voice was insistent.

"It will take a day to get there, after you're done here of course."

"Well worth it, well worth it." Hand flailing in the air, Robterns returned to his thought.

"You need to get some of your people setting up camp," Kaitja continued. "You don't want to wait until it is dark and it is going to get dark fast down here."

Sighing, Robterns replied, "I suppose we can spare a couple of people for that."

"Try five or six at least. You'll have plenty of time to look at rocks tomorrow."

"But this is so exciting." The glee on Robterns' face diminished as he looked at Kaitja. "Fine, we'll set up camp. Can we make a fire and have a hot meal at least?"

"Did you bring any wood?" A smile grew on Kaitja's face.

"Wood! I guessed there would just be some around." His head quickly swivelled back and forth, looking at the canyon.

"There might be some along the cliff but I won't count on much." Kaitja's tone was almost a tease at this point.

"Better send some people both directions to look," Robterns said while looking.

"Tell them not to go too far. I don't want anyone getting lost."

"Lost where?" Robterns said with a laugh.

"I don't know and I don't want to find out. Get them moving."

With a slight murmur, Robterns turned back toward the others, taking his rock with him. He didn't look happy.

"At least that will keep them from digging up too many rocks." Picking up her pack, Xitano moved toward level ground.

"Oh, I am sure we will be leaving a pile around here somewhere for later."

"The more you let them dig, the better they'll sleep," Xitano called back as she walked.

"Sleep, I miss a good night's sleep. Maybe once this is all over." Kaitja looked at the surrounding ground. "Might as well pick my spot before the scientists get all the good ones." He shook his head. "Good ones, ha."

Part Two
The Plains

Chapter One

The right foot and left hand moved up. With hook and spike embedded into the tree, the left foot and right hand moved up while pushing the body up. It was a crawl that Atami had done so many times that it was automatic, but at more than ten body lengths high a fall could be fatal, so he never let his mind forget to check each move. The hook in his left hand, once sunken into the tree, was given a small tug to make sure it was secure. The right foot was wiggled just a little to make sure it would stay. Only after being so assured did he raise himself up to the branch that was his goal. He wore full length leg leathers. Warm when on the ground, they protected him from not only the bark but also the wind higher up in the tree. After his first ascent, he always wore them despite their inconvenience while not in the tree.

The tree he ascended was large even by the tree standard. Easily over one hundred meters of thick trunk, that did not include the height from where the branches started to form. He didn't know why they grew so tall, competing only with the grass and some bushes on the ground. Maybe there was something in the upper air that the trees needed. If so, he had no idea what it might be. Maybe it was to keep people and animals away from the tree's nuts until they were ready to be thrown onto the ground. Not that the nuts were that delicious, but they were edible when other food could not be found.

The branch that was his goal was grey and missing about half of its bark, a clear indication that the tree had stopped caring about the branch and let it die. As the tree grew taller it let the lower branches die, transporting the nutrients to those above that caught better light. At least a full hand-breadth across, it was the right size for one of the younger men below to haul back to the village.

"On the right," Atami called down before turning the hand-axe around in his right hand and chopping at the base of the branch. Pairs of swings, one slanted, one straight down, progressed around the branch both top and bottom. Once circled, the swings concentrated on the top of the branch until its weight tore through what was left and the branch fell. At first it fell tip first, but the cluster of smaller branches at the end allowed the base to catch up and pass the tip. The branch hit base first with a thud, conveniently avoiding a spray of broken smaller branches showering the three young men below.

As Atami positioned himself closer to the place the branch had come from, he talked to the tree. "Thank you, father tree, for your gift and your protection of those below." Sliding his hand close to the blade, Atami carved on the knot until thick sap flowed from the whole area that had once held the branch, covering any wood that was not clothed in bark. "Be safe, my friend."

With that done, Atami reversed the axe and continued to climb. Three more branches awaited his axe and thankfully this tree could provide them all. He looked at the sky as he climbed, judging from the colour that they should be able to get back to the village before sundown. Not walking around on the plains at night was always a good idea.

Having to work his way around to the left, he came to a branch that was only half a hand-breadth wide. "On the left," he called. "This one's for Idula."

"Give the smallest branch to the smallest boy?" came Gorve's voice back.

"Of course," Atami replied as he started to chop the branch.

"How's he supposed to build up muscle if you give him the smaller branch?" Gorve called back.

"How are you supposed to keep yours if you only carry small branches?" The comment brought laughter from the other boys. The branch fell before the laughter had stopped, floating more than the last one. Atami paused a moment after bleeding the tree to listen to the sound of the boys trimming the smaller branches from the main branch. Satisfied at their progress, he continued his climb.

The next branch was in the front of the tree, or at least the direction they had come. After it hit the ground, Atami called out below, "Once you have stripped that one, Gorve and Idula, head back to the village."

"I'm not afraid of the dark," Idula called up.

"You're not a trained spear-man and if you get eaten, I will never hear the end of it from your longhouse." The other two boys laughed at Atami's comment. "And stay well away from the river."

"We know," two voices replied in unison.

Atami climbed to the last targeted branch. This one was the largest, definitely over a hand-breadth. The branch extended well out from the right of the tree. It was also the least grey of the four, taking more strokes to produce the same cuts. Before it broke, he called below again to make sure everyone was clear. With the branch down and the knot trimmed, Atami started the slower descent. He had never figured out why descending was more difficult. Maybe it was because you could not really see where you were going. It was also on the descent when the last wood trimmer had fallen. He had vowed after the funeral that he would never fall.

On the ground, Atami removed his foot spikes and stored them and the hand-hooks in his belt. Cerati, the only boy left at the base, was trimming limbs from the last branch, his branch ready to be hauled to the village.

"Just trim off the big ones and I will take care of the rest," Atami said, approaching the branch.

"Thanks!" Cerati started to swing his axe faster.

"But still be careful and do it right." Cerati's face turned slightly redder and his swing slowed a little but was still faster than it had been before.

Atami took a quick survey of the area. The boys had done a good job of piling the unused parts at the base of another tree. Even a casual look showed many smaller branches, a thumb width or less, that would be coveted wood back in his longhouse. Making a decision, Atami attacked the large limb with the hook at the back of his climbers axe, slicing the small branches from the limb in swift motions. By the time he was half-way down the branch, Cerati had lifted his branch onto his shoulder and was starting his journey home.

Practice made preparing the branch for travel short work. With all the smaller branches removed except at the tip, the shoulder notch cut, and his leather cloth wound around it, Atami started selecting smaller branches and cleaning them. A quick look at the sky told him he had plenty of time. "One can never have too many spears," he joked to himself. With many other uses for the wood, the twenty smaller branches that he cleaned, bundled with the hair rope he brought for just this reason, and then tied near the end of the large branch, would be appreciated by his family.

"Maybe Father will even let me keep a few this time," he said with a huff.

Bending his knees, Atami lifted the thick end of the branch and with one practised motion, turned and placed the notch onto his shoulder. Once happy with its placement, he started a slow walk which over many steps increased to an easy jog, one that kept the branch from bouncing up and down on his shoulder. The steps were more of a slide than a run. An easy look behind showed the array of branches left at the end making a broad, flat trail, one that did not look like a person dragging a piece of wood. Turning forward, he shook his head. "Amazing what the terror birds can learn."

The sun was just touching the horizon when Atami entered the village. Stopping at his longhouse and placing the smaller branches next to the building, Atami dragged the large branch in front of the chief's longhouse. Knaake was standing in front, examining all that had been brought for that day's assigned tasks. He was head and shoulders taller than Atami and broader of shoulder, but then he was older also, so that was not surprising. He wore the vest that announced him as chief, as if that was required by anyone in the village. Knaake had defended his place twice in combat and beaten his challengers without seriously injuring them, a true demonstration of his martial abilities. His hair held eight knots, one for each enemy he had killed. Four of them he had earned before he was chief. He had not been challenged again for over ten season cycles.

Placing the log next to the others the boys had brought in, Atami removed the leather and walked over toward the chief, awaiting his turn to be recognized. When Knaake turned to him, Atami lowered his chin to his right shoulder before speaking.

"As you instructed," Atami said as he bowed in the ritual manner, "four branches."

"One is smaller," Knaake said without emotion.

"One of the boys was smaller," Atami replied. The comment brought some snickers from Knaake's best men.

"You have completed your assigned tasks for the day," Knaake said loud enough for all to hear. Before Atami could turn, Knaake continued. "I have a task for you tomorrow."

"Yes, my chief." Atami turned his eyes back to Knaake.

"You are to bring twelve branches, each half a hand-breadth and at least two body lengths long, to the village."

"Will anyone go with me?"

"No." The word was firm.

"Then I will require an ox to transport the wood if I am to finish in one day." Atami kept his voice calm and even without any challenge. The statement seemed so obvious to him that there was no chance the request wouldn't be granted. No one could haul twelve such branches on their own with any hope of staying safe on the plains.

Knaake paused long enough to make Atami wonder if he was going to deny the request. Atami knew that he was not a favourite of Knaake's, more to do with his father than him. As worry started to settle in, Knaake spoke.

"Granted."

The assignment settled, Atami lowered his chin once again and then turned and left. Jogging to his longhouse, the smells of supper greeted him as he opened the door. Others were already eating and some looked to be finishing their bowls. Grabbing the biggest bowl he would find in the pile, Atami ladled as much stew as would fit from the clay pot, grabbed a wooden spoon, and found a place next to his father.

"Did you embarrass your family again today?" Nerkin asked in a playful voice.

"Completely. I embarrassed us so much he gave me another assignment for tomorrow," Atami managed to say between mouthfuls.

"Another?" his mother, Ziala, injected. "How are you going to fulfill your family obligations if you are always doing work for the chief?"

"Mate," Nerkin said in a calming voice, "it is an honour to be asked by the chief to perform tasks."

"Then why does it feel like he is commanding you when he asks?" Ziala gave her husband a piercing look before turning back to her bowl.

"What did he ask of you?" Nerkin turned back to his son.

"Twelve half hand-breadth limbs at least two body lengths long."

"Twelve?" Nerkin's head came back with the question. "How many is he sending with you?"

"One ox," Atami said through his food.

Chuckling, Nerkin smiled. "Obii will be glad to have the chance to run the plains with you." He lifted another spoonful of stew to his mouth.

"Maybe he won't want to go." Atami gave a small wag of his head. Nerkin laughed.

"That ox would follow you to the end of the plain and back. He looks heart-broken every time you leave without him." Nerkin took another spoon of food, chewed and swallowed. "Too bad he's not a woman."

Atami almost dropped his bowl, a small loss since it was almost empty. "That again!"

Nerkin swallowed and pointed with his spoon. "You are twenty-one season cycles old, five past the age at which you could take a mate."

Altaterra 63

"I've been a little busy or haven't you seen?" Atami rose, walked to the pot, removed another bowl of stew, and sat down a little farther from his father.

"That is an excuse," Nerkin said, waving his spoon.

Atami did not talk again until the bowl was empty. "Then maybe I think we have enough silly Redstone girls around here." Atami walked his bowl to the washing basin, cleaned it with the scrap of leather hanging over the side, and placed it in with the ones already cleaned. As he did, his father walked over to him.

"You need to fulfill your family obligation," Nerkin said in a low voice. "Look around. We only have two children in this home and it is by no way full. If we are to maintain any status in the village, we need more children." Nerkin paused a moment before continuing. "Besides, you need a mate to do your share of the longhouse work *and* it is stealing season."

"I do my share," Atami said, bouncing his finger on his chest.

"And are you going to do the hunting *and* skinning when the herds come back, at the same time? Besides, with all the requests from the chief, you are rarely home." The second statement was said with a huff. "I think he does it on purpose."

"Possessed by the Trickster, perhaps. Did anyone see any animals enter his lodge?" Atami took a breath and let it out as if to settle himself. "As part of my obligations, I left twenty poles at the side of the longhouse when I returned. I thought you might find them useful."

Nerkin took a breath. "You honour your family. But that does not fulfill your obligations."

Taking a breath of his own and letting it out while tilting his head back, Atami settled himself. "Fine. If I get back early enough tomorrow, we can go. But I'm not going to the Redstone village."

His father frowned and stared down at his son. "The circle ensures that blood is mixed for the strength of us all."

"Then we will go to the Horn village, or further. Not a Redstone girl."

"Your mother is Redstone."

"And you got lucky."

After a few seconds, Nerkin relaxed. "Fine. But we will have to leave early enough to be there at the proper time. And no lagging so we have to stay home!" He pointed a finger at his son.

"As my patriarch wishes," Atami said, moving his chin to the shoulder.

"And none of that." Nerkin pushed his son hard enough to make him take a step back. "You're my son. This is an event every father looks forward to." He broke into a smile.

"Yes, I know parents like to torture their children," Atami mumbled.

"When there is no war, who else are we going to torture?" A laugh accompanied the question.

Chapter Two

Waiting until they were more than one thousand paces from the village, Atami finally let Obii have his head. Letting out a bellow of joy, the ox shouted into the sky as he increased his pace to a full run. Sitting on the ropes he had wound around the beast before leaving, Atami leaned forward and laid his body on the ox's shoulders, feeling the muscles working inside the animal.

"My father was wrong," he told the animal. "You would not follow me across the plain. You would drag me behind you."

The ox bellowed in reply. With a head half as big as Atami's body and a mass three times that of the biggest prowler Atami had ever seen, there was no force he could apply that would make the beast do anything it didn't wish. But they had a bond that was only shared by those who raised their animals from birth. Of course the extra treats he had brought hadn't hurt either. Spending time in the trees gave certain benefits to those who performed the work and those they wished to indulge.

The trees Atami had chosen were some distance from the village and had not been visited for several season cycles. Given the number of branches he needed of the same size, such a location was required if he didn't want to visit several groves. With the ox pointed in the right direction, he could afford to let it run, though he kept track of its breathing. When the breaths started to become heavier, Atami suggested Obii slow down to a trot. Obii put forth no objection.

Sitting back up, Atami took note of their position and made a minor correction to their path. He also searched for terror birds and prowlers, though it was early and the chance of predators being out of their dens was slim. With none in sight, Atami scratched the ox behind its ears.

"No creature would dare confront the great Obii, would they?"

The ox softly bellowed in response, shaking his head up and down. It then huffed as it shook its head back and forth.

"Wanting a good fight, are we? Well, not today, my friend. I would rather avoid such an encounter and finish my task. Besides, my father has other plans for me." Obii grunted in response, causing Atami to laugh.

The tall trees might be visible for a great distance but it wasn't until they could smell the green of the patch that Obii became excited and increased speed. As they neared, Atami spied numerous patches of green grass under the trees, plenty to keep Obii busy while he felled limbs. Taking a quick survey of the trees, he selected those he deemed most likely to be useful and directed Obii to another location. The ox was only too happy to stop at the first patch of grass.

Dismounting, Atami removed the equipment he had brought and placed it between the ox and his selected trees. As his first business, though, he took the water skin and poured some water onto the grass that the ox was eating. Obii licked the water in a greedy manner.

"Let the grass have its gift also for what it is giving you," he admonished the ox, who didn't appear to be listening. He could see that some of the water was absorbed into the matting of the grass almost as fast as it fell, so he left the ox alone. "Stay away from my work, my friend." With a ruffle of the ox's head, he headed back to the equipment.

The trees here were not as wide as the one he had climbed the day before, making it easier to climb and promising smaller branches. The first tree provided four limbs of the required size. It also had one much larger whose end could have been used or may have had offshoots that he could have used, but Atami forced himself to concentrate. Before climbing down, he took note of Obii and searched for predators. A dust trail moving across the plain could have been a terror bird, but it was too far to tell what caused it. A look at the clouds showed no indication of rain and there was no smell of rain in the air, though he knew it would only be a moon cycle or less before clouds would start to form. The rains would green the plains and the grass would bring the herds from the north. Thinking of the life cycle reminded him of his father's words.

"No time to stare, Atami. Get the work done so you can fulfill your family obligations." He admonished himself with words in a deeper voice. Even in his father's voice, they still sounded somewhat hollow. Laughing at himself, he said, "Amazing what one will fear. Most would fear a climb to the top of these trees. I fear selecting a wife who cries for home all night long. Pitiful."

The second tree provided five branches. He did not bother to clean either tree's supply before climbing the third tree. With one tree left, it did not take long before he had enough for his obligation to the chief. Coming down, he noted that Obii had settled in the shade, twitching his ears at the bugs with his eyes closed. With the sun overhead, Atami decided on a break to eat but first took the water-skin over to Obii.

"Drink?" he said, waving the skin in front of the ox. In response, Obii tilted his head up and opened his mouth, allowing Atami to pour water directly into his gullet. Finishing off the skin, he patted the ox's muzzle as it closed and swallowed.

"Now my turn." Atami returned to the pile, removed a leather pouch and second water-skin, and moved to the deepest shade he could find. The pouch contained dried meat and dry cheese, both of which required water while eating. As he chewed he talked to the ox.

"I've cut down all the branches I need. Only need to dress them. We should get home in plenty of time." The ox mourned with his eyes closed. "I know, I know, you want to stay out here. But there are no cows here, are there?"

The question evoked a shake of the head from the ox.

"Don't act like you don't care, I know better. A big ox like you likes to have the cows around to appreciate him." In response, Obii let loose a long, high sound. "Not you too! It's bad enough to have my father bugging me about a mate to have you take his side." The statement was answered by a huff from the ox.

Atami waved a hand at the beast as he ate. "I know, I know, but you have it easy. At least the cows don't complain about missing their family and act like life is so unfair that they had to find a mate in another village. Why do you think I don't mind spending time in the trees?"

Obii shook his head, maybe to drive away flies and maybe for another reason. "So you have your own troubles? Well, I guess that could be true." Atami settled into a slump as he ate. "Okay, you may be right. We all have our own problems. And I could get lucky, I could get a good one."

The comment was followed by a loud huff from Obii.

"Thanks for the encouragement," Atami said, not hiding the snide nature of the comment.

With his rations, small to make sure he didn't get slow or sleepy, finished, Atami rose and dressed the branches. Their smaller size made the job easier than the day before, the hook on the axe easily slicing away the unwanted offshoots. All well over two lengths. Atami bundled the branches and tied a leader to each side. Done, he walked over to Obii.

"Time to go back to work," he announced. The ox huffed at him. "Hey, don't give me that. I could have chosen another ox to come out here with me."

The statement earned a glare from the ox as if daring Atami to do so. "Just saying," he said, holding up his hands. The ox looked away, huffed again, and then rose from the ground. It gave Atami a small head butt once on its feet. Atami responded by wrapping his arms around the ox's neck and hugging it.

"You know I wouldn't do that, don't you?" Obii's response was a low moo as it nuzzled his hip. "Come on, Father will be waiting."

The trip home was as uneventful as the one out, though Atami kept his eye on a far hill because of a feeling he could not dismiss. The brown, dormant grass did not prevent dust from being kicked up, even though the grass didn't tear under the ox's feet, just one indication of its toughness away from the rivers and lake. The other was that nothing Atami knew ate it when it was brown, which is why this time of year the prowlers and terror birds hunted near the rivers, making it the best time to harvest from the trees.

Riding the ox up to Knaake's longhouse, Atami dropped the branches in the delivery spot, led the ox away from the house, and then returned to await Knaake's attention. Knaake responded with unusual speed, examining each branch before turning to Atami.

"You have fulfilled your obligation this day," Knaake announced.

"Thank you, my chief. It is an honour to serve my clan."

"You will bring the same by the day after tomorrow."

Atami couldn't prevent a wide-eyed stare. "Three obligations in four days?" he said softly.

"Your clan is in need of your services," Knaake said in a stern voice.

Turning his head, Atami replied, "It is an honour to serve my clan."

As Knaake turned, Atami did a quick walk to Obii. "Looks like you will be needed again, my friend." Obii snorted and nodded his head.

With Obii cleaned and pastured, Atami made his way to the washing area outside of his longhouse. Two days of dust was his limit before feeling the need to wash. It came off easily enough. As the red-tan water ran down the trench cut into the ground, Atami hung the long leathers on a peg and washed the dust from one side and his sweat from the other. He paid special attention to his own arms and hands, making sure they were clean. Walking inside, he found his soft leathers and dressed.

"Good choice," his father said behind him.

"You did not raise a fool," Atami responded as he finished donning his upper leather. "Besides, I don't want something for my mate to complain about from the start." He looked for the ox grease pot.

"Good thinking," Nerkin said with a laugh and a slap on Atami's back that was a little harder than Atami would have liked. It wasn't the first.

"Do we get to eat before we leave?" Atami asked, applying grease under his arms and on either side of his groin.

"We'll eat on the way." Nerkin shoved a bag into Atami's stomach. "We leave now. Would not do to be late, would it?"

"It's a thought," Atami replied, securing the bag around his waist. As he walked, he grabbed a water-skin. When they were outside, he reached into the bag and pulled out a grain cake and took a bite. The heavy cake was unsweetened but was not as dry as the meat or cheese had been, being freshly made. A small amount of warmth still clung to the inside. "Mother make these for the trip?"

"She worries about you even though you have grown," Nerkin said with exhaled breath. "She is a mother."

"At least someone does." The statement was a mild accusation.

"If you had a mate, you would have someone else to worry about you," Nerkin countered.

"Let's hope so."

The pair headed west out of the village but took a slight northern bearing. The sun had not touched the horizon yet. Atami finished the cake and took one mouthful of water from the skin before swinging it to his back. As if knowing his son was done, Nerkin quickened the pace until it was a fast jog that covered ground at the speed of a lumbering ox. On his back was two spears with the red points crafted by the village Maker. The points were long and thin and rounded toward the shaft in the back. Thick in the middle, the spears could be used to slash if required. At the opposite end of the shaft was a small ball made of stone. Only a partial counter-balance, the stone did not weigh enough to prevent the spear from being thrown.

"You did not hand me a spear," Atami commented as he ran behind his father.

"You are catching a mate tonight. No spear is required for that."

"What if we are set upon by a prowler or terror bird?"

"You will get to witness how well I kill them."

After a few seconds, Atami added, "What if there are two?"

"Then I will get to watch one eat you." A small laugh followed the comment. Atami tried to kick dust at his father but their pace was too fast to allow the dust to catch him.

After an hour, the pair came to a crossing of two trails. Nerkin took the one that went the direction they had been chasing. Several more hours passed before lights passed on their left. Breath was preserved for running.

"The Redstones." Atami's comment was abrupt to conserve breath.

"Yes," was the only reply.

Several more hours passed. The moon made its way into the sky and the stars made themselves known to those below. No clouds passed overhead, not unusual for the time of year, though it meant the night could become cold fast. There were no clouds as far as they could see, across the plain or back toward the mountain spine closer to their village. Clouds could be angry, violent things that poured water as if from a pitcher and neither man missed them.

The night was full dark by the time they passed the Horn village marker stones one thousand paces from the village. The maidens' well was two hundred paces from the village, as they all were, and easy to find to suit its purpose. The bushes around the well had never been trimmed and only a minimal clearing surrounded the well, though a well-worn path ambled from the village to the well in nothing looking like a straight line. Nerkin stopped twenty paces from the well so they could catch their breath and breathe softer before approaching. He took the time to eat a strip of meat and drink from his skin. Atami only drank.

"Nervous?" Nerkin asked with some glee.

"Would hate to make this trip for nothing." Atami gave the skin to his father, removed the food pouch and gave that to him also. After examining himself, he also removed his knife and handed that over.

"Afraid she might attack you with it?" Nerkin smiled with the question.

"If I need a knife to defend myself, she will be well worth keeping."

Nerkin suppressed his laughter and led them to the bushes surrounding the well. It had a simple, stone lining only coming one foot above the ground. No one approached, so they settled in a place that showed signs of having been used before, convenient sections of brush being vacant at eye level. Atami crossed his legs with his knees high, placed his elbows on his knees, and settled his chin on his hands. Nerkin assumed a cross-legged sitting position and made the sign of the Maiden in the dirt. Both became as still as a stone.

The first wait was not long. Two young women that looked to have just reached mating age came down the path giggling to each other as they went. Each carried a water jug hung from a rope. Furtive glances were given to the area as they came to the clearing. After a look at each other, they walked to the well and lowered their jugs with the ropes into the water. Gurgling could be heard as air escaped the jugs. The glances and giggling continued.

Nerkin, with the slowest of head turns, caught Atami's eye, which rolled up in disgust and then looked away. When the gurgling stopped, the women raised their jugs, swung them over their shoulders, and hurried away. More giggling was heard as they left.

"That's exactly what I don't want," Atami said in a voice barely able to be heard.

"Hopefully there is more," Nerkin said in a equally low voice.

Before the giggling was far enough to be missed, another young woman approached the well. Her steps were long and purposeful, striding as if angry with the ground. Without pause, she came to the well and lowered her jugs. After a quick look around, she placed her foot on top of the jug and pushed it down. The gurgling increased in rate. As soon as the jug was full, she snatched it from the well and swung it over her shoulder in one quick movement. At a fast walk that neared a run, she made her way back up the trail, a smile on her face.

"Best left behind," Atami said.

"Probably her tenth trip. Has someone she favours in the village I would guess."

"I pity him." Atami resettled on the ground, shifting enough to prevent cramping.

The night wore on. The last girl had enough time to disappear into the village before another woman could be seen up the path. She walked at a normal pace as if fetching water for the longhouse. She was taller than the previous women, about half a head, and lacked the fuller hips of the other Horn women. Her hair was straight instead of waved and was tied together at the base of her head and allowed to hang loose lower down. As she neared the well, Nerkin turned to look at his son, only to see that he no longer sat in his perch. A smile spread across Nerkin's face.

Moving as silently as a prowler, Atami took one of the diagonal paths through the bushes that ended behind the woman. His deft feet avoided any rocks or debris on the ground, but as he grabbed the woman, his right arm bent at knee level to scoop her legs, he could swear that she gently leaned back into his left arm, settling her head against his shoulder. There was no resistance as he turned back toward the bushes, carrying her in front of him. When he had passed through the bushes and headed back to the path they had used to approach, the awkwardness of continuing to carry her in that manner became clear. Using his legs, he hoisted the woman over his shoulder as softly as he could manage. To his surprise, she seemed to assist in the manoeuvre as if expecting it.

With his prize secured, Atami made his way from the village with a gliding jog. Soon joined by his father, Nerkin took up a position behind his son as if guarding him from any approaching villagers. Being challenged was allowed by tradition but it almost never happened except in campfire stories and romantic hero tales.

Just before the village marker, Atami stopped and placed the woman on her feet in front of him.

"What are you doing?" his father said louder than a whisper. "A little more and she is yours for sure!"

"I will not take her is she if not willing." Atami looked into the woman's eyes. "What is your name?"

"The boy has lost his sense," Nerkin muttered.

"Thorea," the woman replied.

"Are you willing to come with me?" Atami asked without pleading or force.

"There is nothing for me in that village." The woman did not flinch as she said the words.

"You are older than the others," Atami said in plain comment.

"My mate died, killed by a prowler. As he was the youngest son and there were no others of the house unmated, the patriarch was under no obligation to keep me. Truth is I believe he did not like me, maybe thinking I was unlucky and caused the death of his son somehow. I am happy to leave. Do you find me undesirable now?"

"No!" Atami said with surprise. "Do you find me ugly and wish for another?"

"The light is not the best," Thorea said playfully, "but you appear handsome enough in this light, if a little undernourished. I can fix that."

"Come on, pick her up and cross the border. We don't have all night." His father's voice was insistent.

Bending down, Atami again picked up Thorea in front of him and carried her past the marker stones before placing her down again. Taking her hand, he led her away from the village.

"You do not have to hold onto me," she responded. "I will follow."

"I just thought it was a good idea for a while," he said, pulling her even with him.

"Am I your first wife?" she asked as they increased their speed to a jog.

"Yes." Their arms swung together between them.

"Why did you wait so long?" The question sounded genuine.

"I like to take my time doing things."

With a small giggle, Thorea said, "That is something a woman likes to hear."

Atami hoped she did not see his face turn redder.

Nerkin turned over again with a huff, ending up facing his mate next to him. She opened her eyes in a manner that indicated she had not been asleep.

"Will they never go to sleep?" Nerkin asked in a hushed, irritated voice, frowning.

As a smile grew on his wife's face, she responded, "Like father, like son."

As the frown was replaced by a smile, Nerkin put his arm around his mate and pulled her against his body.

Chapter Three

The next day when he awoke, Atami couldn't remember the last time he had slept so long past sunrise. Of course, after they bathed, there were things to be done. First he had to introduce Thorea to all of his family, one at a time in the formal manner of greeting. Of course they didn't hang around the longhouse and make it easy, and it was his responsibility to find them. That done, his mother, being the matriarch of the house, took Thorea to show her where everything was kept. Knowing his mother would take a while since nothing would be left out, Atami decided to be somewhere else.

With the women busy, Atami went to the village scribe so that Thorea would be recorded on the village scroll. Never taught the symbols used by the scribe, many remained a mystery to Atami, though some appeared obvious. His name place was occupied by what looked like an eye and a spear, a literal representation of his name, 'sure-thrust.' He had always felt it was a joke by his father.

"What is the name of your mate?" the man asked, his jaw quivering even when he wasn't talking, emphasized by the slack skin on his checks. Atami did not care to guess how old the man was, though he would have liked to know. The scribe had looked the same to him when he was a little boy.

"Thorea."

"What does it mean?" The scribe did not look up as he asked, his pen not having moved on the skin yet.

"Water plant."

The pen finally moved. First the man drew what looked like waves and then three leaves coming from a central stem. The movements were so sure and precise, they spoke of endless practice and a surprisingly sure hand for the man's age. The new symbols were placed next to Atami's, which appeared below his parents.

"What tribe is she from?" the scribe asked.

"The River tribe."

"Of course she is," the man said with a small laugh. Next to the symbols he had just drawn, he put another water symbol. "May your longhouse be blessed with many children."

"Thank you, honourable father." Atami made the head bow to his shoulder, placed a portion of fresh meat in front of the man, and left the longhouse. On his way to his next stop, he hoped Knaake was at his longhouse.

Stopping in front of the door, Atami waited the required ten breaths. When no one exited or entered, he banged his fist on the door three times and stepped back. It took twenty more breaths before the door opened but at least Knaake stepped out.

"Speak," Knaake commanded after setting his feet shoulder-width apart and placing his fists on his hips. Atami made a head bow.

"I have taken a wife. Her name is Thorea. The scribe has entered her name in the record next to mine." Atami made another head bow.

"You have fulfilled your duty to tell me." Knaake did not move or say anything for some seconds, then added, "You still have your task due by the end of tomorrow."

"It will be done, my chief."

"It is good I gave you two days." Knaake laughed at his own statement, though Atami did not. "You may go now."

Without hurry, Atami turned and made his way back to his longhouse. On the way back, every other person congratulated him on acquiring a mate. The comments were friendly, even if some had to remind him how long he took to find one. Some wished him a good feast. A few friends closer to his age gave him knowing looks, which he ignored.

Sure his duties were finished long before the house introduction had been completed, Atami made no hurry to enter. His slowness gave his father, standing outside, the chance to assign him duties that were needed for that evening's feast. Chopping wood was always done by the man who had just been mated, and of course the wood had to be newly cut. After that, he had to take thin branches and make the marriage trestle, just wide and high enough for them to sit under. How close they would have to sit was considered an indication of how well the new couple liked each other. Atami made his as small as he thought he could get away with. The trestle was covered by a prowler skin. Tradition said it was supposed to be a new skin that the man had just killed, but the likelihood of finding a prowler was so small that it would have been a waste of time to try and hunt one. With the prowler skin tied on, Atami selected some personal items to add to the display. Since they were to show his life, he added his hand axe and his knife, then attached the necklace of bones his mother had made for him. Last, he painted the sign of the Matriarch on both sides of the skin. Standing and staring at his work, he shook his head.

"What's wrong?" his father asked, having come back to inspect the trestle.

"It needs something else." Atami made a sweep of his hand in emphasis.

"Like what?" Nerkin twisted up his face in confusion.

"I don't know, it just feels not done." Atami tapped his chin multiple times, then his eyes lit up. "I know!"

Running to the river, Atami headed upstream for over a thousand paces until the water turned into shallow rapids. Heading into the water, he searched on the down-stream side of large boulders until he had a handful of rocks and then ran back to the longhouse. Picking up a hammer, he separated the stones into two groups and then started pounding one group.

"You are going to decorate your trestle with rocks?" Nerkin had walked up beside the large stone platform but not close enough to be hit by hammer or flying debris.

"I'm pounding them into two flat disks." The blows were steady but not fast.

"Why?"

"Because they will shine in the firelight, like stars."

Nerkin shook his head. "You have some strange ideas, my son."

"But my mate will like it." A broad smile grew across Atami's face.

"Oh," Nerkin said in an exaggerated manner and his head bent back and to the side. "Now I understand." He shook his head for a few seconds. "I wasn't aware you needed the help."

"I don't," Atami said with a shrug, "but it can't hurt."

"Oh yes, son," his father said in a sombre tone, "it can hurt."

Atami required no food before leaving on his task the next day. He had tried not to eat too much, anticipating other things later, but his mother had laced most of the food with honey and he couldn't resist. Thorea fared no better. The only consolation was that no one had shown moderation and many groaned as they went to their sleeping hides, the children being the greatest afflicted.

Heading toward the same trees as the last time, this time he took the larger branches and cut the wood required from them, either from their offshoots or from their end. The larger limbs he cleaned and bundled for his longhouse, placing those required to fulfill his assigned task on top. While the load was now heavier, Obii didn't appear to notice on the return journey. Because of the extra work, the sun was lower though, and the small rises to his right gave him a nagging feeling again. It was not long before the feeling became a young adult prowler following the ox at an easy pace. Atami pulled the ox to a stop.

"I'm not worried about you, friend," he said as he patted the ox while dismounting, "but I sure don't want to lead that prowler back to the village."

Obii bellowed in response.

"I know, you could make quick work of him, but I would have to unpack and repack you, which would take more time than I want. Stay here, I will be back soon."

With one spear in either hand, the one in the left held closer to the head, Atami walked toward the prowler. The animal stopped, crouched, and turned its head back and forth as if deciding what Atami was doing.

"I will not run from you, beast." Atami hefted the spear in his right hand to his shoulder, point forward. "If you do not run, I will kill you."

As if in response, the prowler opened its mouth wide and growled. The two long canines on either side of its mouth were displayed prominently. When Atami kept walking, the animal slunk down until its belly rubbed against the ground and took cautious steps toward its opponent, its body not rising with the steps.

At thirty paces, Atami stopped, placed one foot ahead and one behind him in a throwing stance, and waited. "You think the ox back there is a generous meal?" he asked the prowler. "Given the chance, though, he would stomp your carcass into the ground, which I am sure is painful. Your death you bring upon yourself."

At twenty paces the prowler stopped. Lower growls could just be heard from its throat. Posed, the two stared at each other. Atami made no moves, not even blinking. The cat returned the stare. The only warning of change was the growl becoming deeper.

With a full-throated snarl, the cat took two long steps and then leaped. At the same time, Atami threw. At the top of the leap the cat was met with the spear, point embedding into his chest, penetrating a hand-breadth of wood into his body. The throw was a little right of centre, causing the cat to spin to the left. His outstretched paw would have still reached if Atami hadn't moved as a consequence of the throw, spinning to his right.

Coming down hard, the cat stumbled, the embedded spear impeding his stance and movement. Letting out a high-pitched yowl, the cat fell to his right side and tried to grab the spear shaft with his teeth. His long canines prevented him from getting a grip and the actions only caused more blood to flow from his wound. As its eyes started to glaze, Atami walked up to the cat, still outside of its reach, with his second spear held with both hands. The cat weakly pawed at the air.

"You should have run when I gave you the chance." Atami stood, ready to react if the cat suddenly found its feet somehow. "You are not my first kill and I am sure not my last. I thank you for the gift of your hide."

Atami waited as the cat lost the power to move, slicing its throat after it had stopped breathing for good measure. Little blood flowed. Removing the spear, he used it to turn the cat on its back and then drove both into the ground nearby. Reaching behind him, he removed his skinning knife from the hair-belt around his waist. One more kick assured him that the cat was dead.

"A bonus to today's work," he said as he made the first cut. "Strange that I was given one to take home the day after my mating. It would have made a fine wedding gift. Guess this cat was just a few days late to his destiny."

When Knaake finally acknowledged his presentation of his task, he gave a short huff. "Took you longer this time, boy."

"Have I presented your request within the accepted time?" Atami asked without emotion.

Knaake looked up into the sky. "The day is not over yet. Are you getting slow after taking a mate?" A smile accompanied the question.

"There are only so many branches that can be taken without harming the trees." Atami talked still without emotion. "The greater number of wood requested, the farther one has to go and the longer it takes to retrieve."

Knaake glared. "I am not a child you need to instruct, boy. Leave! Your work is done."

"It is an honour to serve the clan." Making a head bow, Atami turned and walked from the longhouse, feeling Knaake stare the whole time.

"Who is next!" he heard Knaake bellow.

At the longhouse he was greeted by Thorea, a small amount of worry in her eyes. Not having taken the time to greet her after dropping off the hide and larger branches, he watched as she did a quick scan of his body for marks.

"I am unharmed, mate," Atami said in a soft voice.

"I would hate to lose a second mate so quickly." She looked up into his eyes. "I am glad you are unharmed."

"It would take more than a young prowler to harm me," he replied with a smile.

"Your thoughts may have been distracted and you miss the cat before it is upon you." Her eyes sparkled as she talked.

"Obii would never let that happen." His head gave a small shake.

"What, the cat getting close or your thoughts getting distracted?" A smile started to curl on her lips.

"Obii is not in charge of my thoughts."

Just then a large hand slapped Atami on the back. "Another kill, I see." Nerkin slapped his son on the back again. "You bless this family this day." In a softer voice he added, "Throw was a little off I see."

"The throw was where I intended it to be." Atami turned to face his father, preventing another back slap and possibly more bruises.

"I thought you might have been... distracted in thought." It was his father's turn to smile. Atami only huffed and walked into the centre of the longhouse. "Wash up before you eat. Prowler blood makes the food taste bad."

"That would be my task," Thorea said as she walked just behind Atami.

"Are you sure we will be done before supper is put away?" Atami did not turn to allow Thorea to see his smile.

"Other things can wait until later."

"Are you sure?"

"A mate knows these things."

Atami let out a small laugh. "If you say so."

Settled with a bowl of food, Atami listened to the talk around the fire. A conversation his father was having with several other men drew his attention. Thorea placed a gourd with water at his feet. Giving her a quick smile, he turned back to the conversation.

"He has not said what is he doing with the wood," Nerkin said.

"You know Knaake," Acves, Nerkin's cousin, replied. "He never tells anyone what he is doing until it is done. That way if he fails he doesn't have to admit to anything."

The comment brought low laughter from the other men but not Nerkin. "Say that in careful company," Nerkin said in a solemn voice, "and not outside of this house."

"All know I speak the truth," Acves said with a wave of his hand. "I hear that he has his Maker designing a new weapon."

"With all that wood? What would he need it for?" Nerkin placed his bowl on the ground. "So you think he is planning a war? With whom?"

"The Prowler clan, of course." Acves shook his head and took another ladle of food. Through the food he added, "You know he hates them."

"The Prowlers have too many warriors for us to attack." Nerkin swept his hand in front of him. "There is no way we could win a war with them."

"And that is why he is making a new weapon." Acves shook his ladle up and down as he spoke one word at a time.

"Then I hope he fails." Nerkin's head went down, staring at the floor. "The last thing this clan needs is to lose warriors, particularly now. The herds will be here within a month and we need every man we have."

"Maybe that is why he wants to attack now, before the herds," Hyrynen, Nerkin's uncle, put into the discussion. "Maybe he is hoping to kill enough warriors so the clan starves in the winter."

"It would be like Knaake to think that." Nerkin shook his head wider this time. "It is a dangerous game he is playing. He could end up making his own clan starve if things do not go as he plans."

"He would not go without food," Acves muttered through more food. The comment earned him a sharp elbow from Nerkin.

A soft hand on his arm caused Atami to turn to Thorea.

"Is everything good?" Thorea asked.

"Yes." Atami smiled at her. "The men are just talking. They like to sound like they know what is happening."

"But you are not worried?"

"I have you, why would I worry?" Atami touched his forehead to Thorea's. "Do not worry, you are not getting rid of me for years.

Besides, I think my mother likes you."

"I think she is just glad to have another hand around the longhouse." The comment came with a small laugh to release tension.

"Like I said, she likes you." Atami leaned forward so his mouth was next to her eyes. "Besides, I have something else for your hands to do later."

"As my mate wishes. I suppose I will muddle through somehow." She leaned her head against his.

"If that is muddling, I can't wait until you figure out what you are doing."

Chapter Four

Thunk! The spear hit the wooden target below the group of the others already thrown.

"You're lowering your shoulder," Atami said, putting his hands on both sides of Idula to rotate his upper body back. "Push with the shoulders but don't lower them. The prowler leaps at his prey and a low throw means you will become prowler food."

"Yes, Atami," the boy, Idula, said, his head dipped a little and his voice soft.

"Hey." Atami raised the boy's chin with his hand. "If you threw perfectly then I wouldn't need to be instructing you. In fact, you would be instructing me."

"I will never be that good," the boy said with a shake of his head.

"I hope you will. Someone has to look out for me in my old age." Atami slapped the boy on the back, not hard like his father, as they both laughed. "Now, retrieve all of them and go again."

As the boy ran to the target, he talked. "How do you find the courage to stand up to a prowler? I don't know that I could stand fast in front of one." The boy started pulling spears from the wood.

"When your choice is stand fast or die, it's not much of a choice. Besides, the fear shows up afterwards. What you have to avoid is not standing like a stupid wide-eyed herd-beast who doesn't even think to run."

Hearing movement behind him, Atami turned to find one of the young boys from Knaake's house approaching at a run. He only stopped long enough to announce, "Knaake has asked for everyone's ear," before running off again.

"What's that about?" Idula asked.

"We'll only know when we go. Lean the spears against the longhouse." Atami walked to the end of the longhouse to find others exiting and making their way. It only took a few seconds for Idula to join him. Giving the younger man a squeeze around the shoulders, they followed the others through the village. They found Knaake standing on top of a stump normally used for sitting that had been moved in front of his longhouse. At least half of the village had already gathered and the rest was not far behind. Atami's house stood together just as the other houses did. Knaake did not look at the crowd but waited until they settled down before addressing them.

"Ox clan! I have called you here to announce that our Maker, under my orders, has constructed a device to throw a multiple of small spears at once. We have done this to gain an advantage over our enemies, the Prowler clan, who have been our bane for generations. This tension must end and we will end it. We will end it. We will beat down the Prowlers to the point that they will no longer be a threat to us. How, you might ask? Follow me."

Jumping off the stump, Knaake headed out of the village to the south where a low plateau stood. As they neared, Atami could see what looked like a wooden box on three legs. Coming out of the sides of the box was two tapering pieces of wood. When he was closer, he could see a tendon string stretched between the extensions of wood and behind the box. He heard Idula give a grunt of confusion. Looking at the boy, Atami shrugged.

"Clansmen!" Knaake continued. "This device will take the place of several dozen spear throwers. It will cut down whole groups of Prowlers at one time. Observe!"

With the whole village watching, two men pulled the tendon string back, placing it over a peg. They then pulled the back of the box back against the string. Further on the plateau, Atami could see reed bundles about the height and width of a man. Knaake raised his hand. When it was lowered, one of the men pulled a rope that drew down the peg. With a low-key twang, the back of the box shoot forward. From the front of the box several dozen spears, shorter and lighter than normal spears, shot across the plateau. Coming down among the straw columns, the spears sank into and through many of the bundles, knocking some of them to the ground. Sounds of amazement went through the villagers. Knaake turned to the crowd.

"Three days from now I will take our warriors and attack the Prowlers. Every house must provide their warriors. The houses will attend me now so that a count can be taken."

As the crowd slipped away, the men walked toward Knaake. When Idula started with them, Atami grabbed his shoulder and drew him back. "You are not trained as a warrior yet. Go back to your home."

"But I can throw a spear," Idula protested.

Atami shook his head. "There is more to fighting than throwing a spear and the untrained will only be in the way of the warriors. Besides, someone must protect the village if all the warriors leave to attack the Prowlers. Can I trust you with our women?"

Idula's face looked hurt, but then he nodded his head and turned back to the village, his head hung lower than normal. Atami watched him leave.

"You can thank me when you are older," Atami said in a soft voice, unheard by Idula, before joining the other men.

The Scribe was counting the men when Atami approached. His finger bounced above their heads from one side to the other as he counted from higher on the hillside. When he stopped he announced, "Fifty-four."

"Then fifty-four men shall meet me here in two days for our attack on the Prowlers." Knaake gave the group a grin.

"Fifty-three," Nerkin announced.

The comment drew Knaake's attention. Glaring at Nerkin, he said, "Is there a reason for someone here not to attend the wishes of his chief?"

Nerkin braced his feet as if expecting a fight. "My son has just taken a mate. He has not passed the period from which he is exempt from war. Unless you wish to defy tradition, he will not be going."

"Father," Atami said quietly, only to have the back of a hand in front of his face.

Knaake gave his shoulders a minor shake and moved his tongue in his mouth, and then said, "Fifty-three it is. You will all bring your weapons, water, and food for the trip. Any who do not appear will answer to me. Go, prepare!"

Nerkin herded his son away from the crowd, his look demanding silence as they walked. Once out of earshot, he finally spoke. "I will not have Knaake violating tradition. More importantly, I do not wish to risk my son on Knaake's foolish war."

"But his new weapon…" Atami started.

"Wars are not won by weapons, they are won by men. Men who are willing to stand and not run when spears are thrown and axes are swung. Men who will not cower at the sight of their own blood and continue to fight."

"I am willing, Father, you know that!"

"Yes, I do. That is why I wish you to stay here. The Prowlers are fierce warriors and I have no confidence in Knaake's weapon. If it does not work, I worry that things will not go well for us. You are my only child and I will not see you killed for Knaake's foolishness. No argument."

Atami bowed his head. "Yes, Father. I will respect tradition and do as you say. I am sure my mate will be relieved."

"She is a fine woman. Treasure that one, my son, and have many children."

"I will do my best, Father." Atami's words were sombre.

"Now, help us prepare for war. If we are to go on this foolishness of Knaake's, we should be as prepared as possible. And I have to see if I still fit in my war leathers."

Three days later as Atami watched the men leave, an ox pulling a wagon loaded with the spear thrower, Thorea came up behind him and took his hand. She leaned on his shoulder and intertwined her arm with his.

"You father is a brave man, he will come back to us," Thorea whispered into Atami's ear.

"I hope you are right. Everyone knows Knaake is a fool. I don't know why he is still chief."

"Because none will challenge him for his place?"

Atami huffed. "Of course you are right. My father could take him, I am sure, but he refused. He said he did not want to divide the clan. I hope it wasn't that my mother talked him out of trying."

Thorea let the silence hang a while before speaking. "Then you would be the son of a chief. That would be a large responsibility?"

"You don't think I would make a good son of a chief?" Atami's brow furrowed as he asked.

"Look how long you took to conquer a mate." Thorea smiled with the accusation.

"And should you not be happy that I did?" Atami turned to face her.

"I'm just saying." Thorea swayed as she spoke. "Wouldn't it have been embarrassing for the chief's son to wait so long?"

"The chief's son would have even more responsibility than me. Maybe I would have taken even longer before finding a mate. You should be glad that I rescued you from the Horn clan." Atami put his arms around Thorea and drew her to him.

"I am ever so grateful, my mate." She snuggled into his arms. "What can I ever do to show you how grateful I am?"

"I have a few ideas." The words came with a knowing smile.

The warriors of the Ox clan stood one hundred paces outside the marker stones of the Prowler village in a crescent shape. Knaake's new weapon was hidden behind the tallest warriors. Knaake stood in front, watching the Prowlers take up their position at the edge of the village area. The Prowlers, at least eighty in number, had walked out of the village in a confined group.

"Are they carrying something on their backs?" Goazi asked, straining his eyes.

"It doesn't matter," Knaake said with a dismissive tone. "Grouped together, they will only be a better target for the weapon. Soon there

Altaterra   89

will be much fewer of them standing."

"But why would they stand like that? It is not normal."

"I said it doesn't matter. Is the weapon ready?"

"Yes, my chief."

"A few moments more."

A few moments later, the Prowlers settled into their positions and started the yelling that proceeded a fight. Axes and spears waved in the air as the sound echoed off the barren plain. All other life became silent. The Ox clan warriors didn't answer, as instructed.

Knaake took a deep breath. "Part!" The warriors in front of the weapon moved to the side with quick steps. "Release!"

At Knaake's shout, not only was the peg pulled but the Prowler warriors brought their hands that did not hold weapons around their bodies. In them were mats of woven sticks that covered their upper bodies. Grouped tightly together, the mats left little of the warriors exposed for the spears. When they reached the group, most of the spears stuck into the mats, though a few did pass between the mats to the warriors beyond. The impacts finished, the warriors dropped the mats, yelled again, and started to run at the Ox clan.

"Sound the attack, my chief," Goazi said to find Knaake staring at the Prowlers.

"It didn't work," Knaake said in a low voice. "How did they know? How could they have known?"

"Sound the attack, my chief!" Goazi's voice became more insistent.

"How did they know?" Knaake continued to ask. "What do we do now?"

"Ox clan!" Goazi shouted. "Attack!"

Chapter Five

The change in the direction of the wind brought a scent that Atami could not identify. It was more of a feeling than a smell, as if sorrow could be carried on the wind, and caused a chill to settle into his bones. Standing up from the leather work he had been doing, he looked around. Not seeing anything out of the ordinary, he walked around the longhouse, scanning the horizon. A small dust cloud appeared in the distance. Watching the cloud, it became people dragging themselves across the plain. As panic spread inside of him, Atami ran toward the group.

"*Obii!*" Atami shouted as he ran. "*To me, Obii!*"

Joining footsteps were ignored as Atami rushed toward the group. Faces became clear and he searched for his father's. None of the warriors were free of cuts or bandages. Passing through the too small crowd, Atami found his father. Even with one arm wrapped in the remains of his war leathers, his father assisted another warrior whose leg was wrapped in the other half of his father's leathers. Blood was pooled on Nerkin's head and he had a defined limp.

"Let me take him, Father." Atami rushed to remove the man from his father's arm and support the man himself. Relieved of the burden, Nerkin almost fell over from shifting his balance. Looking around quickly, Atami spotted Obii ambling toward him, slowing to avoid the mass of men. Atami led the man to the ox, helping him mount before turning back to look at his father, who had stopped where

Atami had left him. "Take him home, Obii." Atami patted the ox on the shoulder, trusting him to obey as he ran back to his father.

"Lean on me, Father." Atami took a place under his father's shoulder and wrapped his arm around his waist. "One step at a time."

It was only a few steps before Ziala appeared, tears forming in her eyes. She placed herself under her mate's other arm, pushing herself into his shoulder for support or someone's comfort.

"Help the others," Nerkin said in a weak voice.

"They have families too. We help you, my mate." Between the two of them, Ziala and Atami made almost normal progress with Nerkin. The journey to the longhouse still seemed to take a lifetime. Atami watched the other families helping their warriors. None looked unhurt.

"Too many are missing," Atami said. "Where is Knaake?"

"He was taken," Nerkin said through a wheeze. A drop of blood fell from his head and onto Atami's.

"Why did they let you go?" Ziala asked.

"I don't know. Maybe because they had Knaake? There are more on the trail, I lost track of them."

Ziala gave a glance to her son. Without words, she communicated her meaning. The sun was going down and prowlers would be out, attracted to the scent of blood. "We will get all home we can," she said as she turned away.

With Nerkin safely in the village, Atami turned back to the others, helping those who went the slowest. Obii came back and he placed two more men on the beast's back and led it into town. That task done, he rode the ox onto the plain back the direction the men had come. As he crested the first rise, the sun just touched the horizon. Stopping the ox, he looked over the plain. He could hear the prowlers howl in the distance, most likely arguing over their prizes. Tears ran down his face. Obii bellowed his challenge to the world, voicing his willingness to brave the dark and predators for whatever his companion wanted. For a moment Atami wanted to kick his heels into the ox and charge across the plain, daring any prowler or terror bird to defy them. But his hands were empty of spears and there were men in the village that needed him.

"Let us return home, Obii." Openly weeping, he allowed the ox to have his head. Before he realized, it brought him to the door of his house. Dismounting and giving his friend a hug, he buried his head into the ox's neck for a moment. "You are a true friend. Keep the cows safe." With a final pat, he turned into his longhouse. Waiting just inside the door was Thorea, wringing her hands. After only a moment's hesitation, she rushed into his arms, wrapping hers around him.

"I was afraid you would go after more," she said into his chest.

"I was tempted. Obii would have gone with me." He wrapped his arms around his wife.

"That ox is as stupid as you are."

"We were raised together." Atami nuzzled his nose in her hair.

"By who, a stupid cow?"

The comment caused Atami to laugh and raise his head. "My mother better never hear you say that."

"I wasn't talking about her."

He pushed her away with gentle hands. "I must take a count of who is here and who is not."

"Is that not someone else's job?"

"Who else is there?" He took a quick look around the room. "Find out who is missing from our house and how hurt are those who returned. Can you do this for me?"

"Of course, my mate. I will do it right away." She looked surprised at the question.

"I will return as soon as I can. Make sure no one goes outside. Prowlers might have followed the wounded here."

As he turned from Thorea, she grabbed his leather vest. "Be careful, my mate, and make sure you return to me."

Selecting a spear from the wall, Atami grinned. "I will. No prowler will want to mess with me tonight."

As he went from one longhouse to the next, Atami made a mental list of those who had not returned. The list got longer with each house and not many of those who had returned would be on their feet soon. His heart grew heavier with each name. Bognor, Yolnu,

Kijiri, Zale, Lamana, Rhata, and Stiputa had not returned. When he made it home, he learned that Acves and Kalla were also among the missing. All had been fine warriors and would be missed by their households and the clan. At each house he warned them of the danger of prowlers outside. Most nodded at the wisdom of his advice though a couple looked at him as if wondering why he was advising them.

"Let them be mad," he told himself as he left one such longhouse. "It is better they are reminded and we lose no one else this night than not to be angry with me."

In his own longhouse there was plenty for all to do. The women tended the wounded but bloodied clothes and bandages had to be cleaned or discarded, furniture had to be moved to make room for the attendants of the wounded, broth had to be made and heated, and beds were placed next to the wounded. Herbs were brewed to help treat the wounds and quiet the moans of the injured so they did not disturb the other wounded or the family members. Children who had never seen the effects of war had to be consoled or distracted. The fire was made larger than normal so the wounded would stay warm. Atami had no idea how late the night was before he reached his bed. As he sat, Thorea brought him a bowl of broth.

"Shouldn't we save that for the wounded?" he asked.

"It will do no good for you to lose your strength."

Nodding to her wisdom, Atami drank the warm broth to the last drop and handed the bowl back to her. Satisfied, she stood back up. "Now get some sleep. You will be needed in the morrow."

"You sleep sometime too," he directed.

"When those attending the wounded sleep, I will sleep."

Atami chuckled. "If you try to out stay my mother, you will lose."

"She will most likely tell me to go to bed. Until then, I will assist as possible. Sleep well, my mate." She planted a kiss on Atami's forehead and turned to walk back into the busy end of the house. Atami thought of a comment, found it inappropriate, and turned to his bed.

Chapter Six

The next morning, Atami found Thorea curled up next to him fast asleep. Managing to rise without waking her, which he took to mean she was deeply tired, he went to the water bucket and washed the night away. Little activity occupied the longhouse, though he saw his mother awake and tending to things. With as much quiet as he could manage, he retrieved the few things he needed, found some dried meat, and went outside. To his surprise, the sun had already cleared the mountains to the east.

"Getting soft in your old age," he muttered to himself.

"I'm not getting old," Idula answered, some confusion in his voice.

"I was talking to myself." Atami chuckled at the boy, who was attending to his chores. "Has anyone checked on the oxen this morning?"

"Not that I know of."

"Then go out and make sure we lost none last night. Don't approach any hurt or dead, just come tell me how many."

The young man looked at the wood in his arms with a question. Atami waved his hand to tell him to put it down. With a grin and some haste, Idula placed the wood back on the pile and ran toward the basin where the oxen slept.

"Oh, to be doing anything except firewood duty." Atami chuckled to himself. Walking around the longhouse, Atami surveyed it and the village but could detect nothing that would indicate prowlers had visited the night before. It was happy and sad news. As he completed the trip around the longhouse, he noted several people looking south toward the plateau. Turning, he noted a faint cloud of dust and a flag that was just visible. Grabbing a spear, he hurried toward the flag, joining others in the process. Among them were the four members of the village council that could still walk. His father and Nephel were still recovering. Being the son of the patriarch of the house, Atami could represent their house according to tradition. When that thought ran through his head, he remembered that Nephel's son had not come back the previous night, sending sorrow through him again. While Zale had not been a close friend, he felt sad for Nephel and his house. Looking at the group who walked to the plateau only emphasized their losses in Atami's mind.

It did not not take long to see that the flag belonged to the Prowler clan. At least it was the white flag of parley and not the red flag of war. Further war against such a diminished clan would have brought dishonour to the Prowlers but that didn't mean it hadn't happened in the past. Atami joined those in front, his spear point toward the ground. At the head of the parley group stood Sar with the flag-staff in hand. Next to him stood Knaake, arms bound behind his back, legs tied together at the knees far enough to allow him to walk but not run, and a large bruise on the top left side of his head. Knaake stood with his head bowed and his shoulders bent forward. Sar, standing straight and tall, waited for those approaching to reach the plateau before speaking.

"Ox clan. Your chief has foolishly made war on the Prowler clan. He thought his weapon was a secret but a foolish tongue betrayed his secret and we were prepared. Now he has cost your clan lives and weapons. The Ox clan makes very good weapons and we thank you for them." The comment caused a low laugh to rumble through the Prowler clansmen. "We have generously allowed your warriors to return to your village."

The Ox clan members held their tongues. Argument would have been cause for more violence even though all knew what Sar had done.

"In further generosity I bring back your chief for ransom. Let those on your council come forward so we can discuss the price."

A sigh went through the Ox clan as if a burden had been placed upon them. The four members present looked at each other without envy. One glanced to Atami with an unspoken question. While it might have just been a question about his father, he took it as an acknowledgement of his acceptance as a member of the council and stepped forward two paces and stopped.

"You can keep him," Atami said in a clear voice. He heard those behind him gasp and watched Knaake's head jerk up to stare at him. "He has cost our village lives, resources, and time that we can little afford to lose. He has acted selfishly, not in the best interest of the clan. In this he has demonstrated his inability to lead our clan. Why would we want him back?"

As Sar's expression turned to mirth, Knaake spoke. "You are not on the council, you do not speak for the council!"

"What has been said has been said," came from behind Atami.

"My father lay in his bed," Atami continued. "My mother attends the wounds he took in your war. Who knows if he will rise again. As his only child, I am now the council's representative of our house." Turning around, he addressed those from the village. "But more than that, I feel I speak for all in our village. Are there any who thought this war with the Prowlers was good? I hear none. Did Knaake take words from the council to decide if war should be waged? My father spoke of none. Nine of our village died and yet here is our chief, bound before us, without wound or loss of limb."

Atami turned back to Knaake. "Does this lack of wounds show his bravery in battle? The chief is supposed to lead his men. How do you avoid any cuts of spear or axe? If you were so skilled, why did we not win? Explain this to me and I will withdraw my words."

Silence took the plateau as both clans waited for Knaake to speak, but after waiting, Knaake took a deep breath and bowed his head again. Atami waited even longer, but no words came from Knaake. When Sar shuffled his feet, Atami spoke again.

"Our *chief* condemns himself with his silence. Sar of the Prowler clan, take him and subject him to whatever justice you see fit for the suffering he has forced upon your clan. The Ox clan no longer claims him."

Looking pleased with himself, Sar said, "So I shall. Give my sympathy to those families that lost warriors. Tell them I hold their fallen in highest regard and hold no grudge against them."

"And the Ox clan holds no grudge against the Prowler clan. We thank you for your kindnesses." Atami gave the man a head-bow.

Sar grabbed Knaake by the arm and spun him around. "Come, *chief*, we shall find something entertaining to do with you."

The members of the Ox clan on the plateau barely dared to breathe as the group of Prowlers and Knaake walked south from the plateau, waiting until they were much farther than earshot to speak. Atami exhaled and inhaled a deep breath. Exhaustion invaded his muscles and bones and thoughts of his bed filled his head. Turning around, he found everyone looking at him. It shocked him and his eyes scanned back and forth across the faces.

"What are you looking at?" Atami asked.

"We now have no chief," Jacu, one of the members of the council, said.

"And may the wind take him. We are better off without him." Atami swept his hand in a wide gesture.

"But we now have no chief," Jacu repeated.

"So? Let the council ask another to be chief, as is tradition." Atami searched the other council members, who looked uncertain.

"But only half the council still stands, not counting you of course."

"So let the families pick those to represent them on the council, at least for one meeting. Is that so hard?"

Jacu turned to the other council members. They spoke in hushed tones to each other for a few moments. As they all nodded, Jacu turned to those gathered. "We will have a council meeting tonight when the sun is gone to discuss who will be offered the position of chief. Let each family send who they will to represent them."

The crowd broke up into groups based on family. Several people took glances at Atami while they talked. Shaking his head, Atami made his way back to his own longhouse, ignoring the others. "Let them think as they wish," he told himself. "I care not what they think."

In the village, women and children stood outside the front of the longhouses. As the men drew near, they huddled in groups, speaking in low tones before moving into the houses. Atami noted several more glances his way, making him wonder how long the looks would last. His mother stood outside their own longhouse. He gestured to meet him inside. To his surprise, she did as he asked. She watched all come in and closed the door before speaking.

"What happened?"

"Sar brought Knaake to ransom him," Atami said in a calm voice.

"And what price did he set? Will we be able to pay it?"

"We told Sar to keep him."

Ziala's eyes went wide, then she turned to the side a little as she kept her eyes on her son. "Was this your doing?"

"Yes, it was." There was sharpness in Atami's voice. "He cost this village the lives of good men needlessly. He deserves whatever they do to him."

"And what about a new chief?"

"The council will meet tonight to discuss it." Atami's voice had changed to flippant.

"And you will represent our family." Ziala's tone was that of a statement and not a question.

"Me?"

"Your father is in no shape to go. You are his son, you will go." The tone became more insistent.

Atami huffed, looked around at nothing in particular, and then sighed. "I guess I have to be the one to go. You should come with me."

"*No!* Women do not attend the council." Ziala shook her head violently.

"But there have been women on the council before, so we are told."

"That is different." Ziala poked her son in the chest with a finger. "If I went, it would cause others to doubt anything you said were your words. If Thorea went, it would be the same. You must go without me."

"But I am not going alone," Atami countered.

"Fine, take another man with you. But take no women. You will look weak and they will not listen to your words."

"Fine." Atami looked at the ground. "I hate these kinds of things."

"As leader of our family, you better get used to them."

"Father will recover. Even if he can only use one arm, his wisdom will still be able to lead this family."

"The patriarch must be able to fight and you know it. Yes, your father will continue to bless this family in other ways. Take his council when he gives it. But if he is not fully himself, you must be the patriarch. It is what he would want." Ziala grasped both of her son's arms.

"Of course it is. Not that he ever asked me if it was what I wanted."

"He shouldn't need to. Now go clean up for the council meeting."

Atami's head came back. "But it is not until tonight."

"Clean your clothes too, and your hair. Have Thorea comb it neatly. It never hurts to look your best at a council meeting." Ziala gave his arm several slaps.

"Mother!"

The council was held around a large fire in the centre of the village. Atami took Rfala with him. He was the largest warrior that could walk without wavering. By the time they arrived, most of the families were already there. Taking the location occupied by his father in the past, Atami nodded to those around the fire. Rfala stood behind him, two axes in his belt and a spear in his right hand, point down. Other warriors stood behind their representatives. Goazi stood behind Knaake's uncle, who was much older than Knaake. Even though he had wrappings on his arm, leg, and across one eye, Goazi showed no indication of pain or weakness.

It did not take long for the rest of the families to join. Most were older than warrior age. One representative, Allo, was even younger than Atami, a boy whose face was still smooth. The implication almost made Atami weep. Jacu spoke first.

"We all know why we are here. We have no chief. Our village must have a chief before anything else can be done. I know we have lost many but we must choose from those who are left, but only the family representatives can speak who should be chief. We will now hear names."

The fire crackled as people paused. Several heads turned toward Atami as if they expected him to say something. Even though he didn't, the faces didn't turn away.

"Why are you staring at me?" he finally asked.

"We expected you to put forth your name for chief," Gudagi, one of those who stared, said.

"What? Why would I do that? I am not full grown. Any of the true warriors could challenge me and win the position. I would not hold it for a season cycle. What would be the point?" Atami gave a full shrug and spread his arms.

Several around the fire chuckled in agreement. Others shook their heads. Atami was sure at least one around the fire looked relieved. His head spun at the idea that others had expected him to put forth his own name, not being able to imagine how much pride a man would need to do that. Even though he wanted to put forth his father's name, he knew better. His father would be even less able to defend himself than Atami.

The silence hung in the air as all stared at each other. The voices that finally spoke were soft and tentative.

"Our village is vulnerable. We need our best warrior."

"We lost our best warriors. How can we choose?"

"Maybe we should have a challenge."

"And risk losing more warriors? That is madness."

"Maybe we have been choosing a chief wrong," Goazi's voice boomed over the fire.

Jacu stared at the man. "Only representatives can speak."

"My family honoured Dalketh by naming him our representative, but he is old and does not speak much, and hardly at all in groups. Before we came, he told me to speak for the family if I felt I should, and I do now. We have always chosen the strongest warrior to lead our clan. Look where that has taken us. Warriors constantly think of fighting. We should not be fighting now, we should be finding other ways for our people to survive, to feed ourselves, to make the things we need. Maybe the one who should lead us should be he who thinks more than fights."

"And who do you say that would be?" Jacu asked.

"I name Atami for chief." Goazi's voice boomed the statement.

His head spinning, Atami did not even hear the reactions around him. When his mind came back, he began to wonder if Goazi was setting him up, naming him chief so someone would challenge and hurt him in revenge for Knaake. Goazi had never acted like Knaake, but they were family.

"And how do you expect him to surmount any challenges, as he has already stated?" Jacu asked.

"I will be his champion," Goazi proclaimed. "Any who would challenge him must fight me."

Atami's head spun to the point he almost fell over. No one had ever volunteered to champion someone from another family, it wasn't done. And for that offer to come from a rival family was unthinkable. Surely some evil plot was being hatched. He silently prayed to the Sky Gods that another name would be put forth.

"You would champion someone from *another* family? And not your own?" Jacu's voice was filled with disbelief.

"I will champion whoever the council thinks is the smartest chief we can name. I have spoken a name. If there are others who one thinks would be better, let them speak."

A quick idea went through Atami's head, enabling his tongue. "I name Astreba."

"You can't name Astreba," Jacu snorted. "She is a woman."

"Goazi wanted someone smart. She is the smartest person I know." Atami didn't like the reaction of those around the fire.

"No. We are not naming a woman chief at this council," Noctu said firmly. "We would be the laughing stock of the clans. It is a foolish suggestion."

"Atami is just trying to distract you from himself," Goazi said. The comment brought laughs from those surrounding the representatives. "You see how smart he is?" The second comment brought even more laughs and some slaps of approval.

"Enough of that, this is serious business," Jacu scolded. "Atami's name has been put forth. Are there others?"

"Chebucto," was spoken. Atami noted it was the representative from Chebucto's family.

"Are there others?" Jacu asked. After some silence, he continued. "If any wish to speak to either of these names, let them speak now."

"I voice for Chebucto," Atami said immediately, bringing even louder laughs from those watching. "He is a good man," he said in defence.

"Yes, but is he up to leading our clan?" Daketh said, surprising all. "He is old. I am old. Let the young take charge of things."

It took a few minutes before others spoke but the comments held little difference from each other's. The same person would seem to speak for and against the same idea. Some repeated what others had said as if they had not already been spoken. Atami could not determine what was being decided, if anything. All he could do was wait for the voices to die away and Jacu to take control of the meeting.

"We will now show our choice. We will side for either Atami or Chebucto. You can only side with one. All those for Chebucto raise a hand." Only Atami's and Allo's hands went up. "For Atami?"

"Do not worry, little one," Goazi said as he laid a hand on Atami's shoulder. "You will have no one to worry about from this house."

"What about the other clans?"

"I can protect you from everyone." Goazi laughed.

"I feel so much better. It would serve you right for someone to make a challenge just to pay you back for getting me into this situation."

"They would have to wait until I was healed and then no one would challenge me. I did not challenge Knaake because he was of my family and it would have been dishonourable."

"And if one day you decide to challenge me?"

Goazi huffed. "I saw how much Knaake had to suffer through because he was chief. I do not want to suffer until I am old."

"You make it sound so tempting."

As Goazi walked away, Rfala joined Atami, speaking low. "I am glad I do not have to fight him, hurt or not."

"You would do that for me?" Atami asked.

"No. But if you were patriarch, you might order me to."

"That," Atami said as his eyes lit up, "is good to remember."

Chapter Seven

Only coals remained of the fire the next morning. Waiting, Atami stood next to them for the council to arrive. It didn't take long. When a chief called a meeting, it was considered an insult to be late. He looked at the group huddled around him.

"Well met this morning." He tried to put on a genuine smile but it was early for too much forced emotion. "First we must settle the question of the new council." He held up his hand. "I know each family was there but I want to make sure we have the people we need and who want to be there. Do not be offended by any questions. I will not know if I don't ask."

Tentative looks greeted his glances. "First, I need to know if Dalketh's family wants him to stay on the council."

"No," Goazi said. Dalketh nodded his head. "While honoured, Dalketh does not feel he can be good council. He says he almost fell asleep last night and thinks he will only fall asleep again."

"Are they proposing someone to the council?" Atami asked.

"They are still discussing it." Goazi emphasized the word 'discussing' as if distasteful.

"Then I will be over there right after this meeting to announce my selection, providing a choice has not been made by then."

Goazi huffed. "Not much to worry about there." Goazi gave a head-bow. "It is the right of the chief to choose his council."

"Thank you." Atami made the abbreviated head-bow. "Secondly, we were all honoured to have Allo at the meeting last night, but if we are honest, he is too young for the council."

All could see Allo deflate in relief. He opened his mouth to speak but then held his tongue.

"They only sent him to nominate Chebucto so he won't have to do it himself," Jacu said, drawing a few stares for the comment.

"Whether that is or isn't true doesn't matter. I would be happy to have Chebucto on the council and will tell him myself. Are there any others that wish to leave the council? The reason does not need to be stated and it will not offend me." Atami waited for more than a while but none spoke. "Fine. We will meet again tonight. There are things that need to be attended to right away."

"What about your own family?" Jacu asked. "Who will represent them since you are chief?"

"I will ask my father to be on the council for our family. It should help him heal faster to have something waiting for him. I will be taking over his duties in our family until then anyway and I believe we will be too busy to make new decisions before he is ready to attend."

"Busy?" was voiced by several.

"You will find out tonight. You may now go back to your families."

As people left, Rfala walked up to Atami. "Are you sure your father will agree to be on the council? He has declined before."

"And not have the chance to give me advice in front of the whole village? Why would he miss that?" The frustrations of a child with their parents filled the question.

"He has always preferred to give his advice in private." Rfala looked concerned and not convinced.

"Don't worry, if he refuses I will tell him that I will then name Mother as our representative."

Rfala let out a laugh that was followed by more that continued even after they turned and walked toward their longhouse. "Please, let me be there when you say that. I have never seen his face so pale as it will become."

The first meeting going faster than he expected, Atami had to wait a short while until it was an appropriate time to go to the other longhouses. Having not eaten before the meeting and not trusting his stomach to behave, he now ate the boiled grain his wife brought him. It was flavoured with broth and herbs similar to but different than his mother made. He gave a questioning look to Thorea.

"I will prepare my mate's meal as I deem fitting." She gave him a smile and sat before him, producing a bowl of her own.

"It's good. And it's good to have something different every so often." Atami nodded his head as he spoke.

"Food, yes." Thorea's tone was more serious.

"I thought we were talking food." Atami grew a smile of his own. "I have not had enough of the other to complain yet."

"As long as we are only talking about food." She gave him a serious look, at which he laughed.

The meal completed, Atami rose and made his way to the door. Rfala rose also and looked toward him. Atami waved him off, which didn't make Rfala happy, but the warrior sat back down. Thorea held the door open for him.

"Be safe, my mate," she said.

"If I am not safe in my own village, I am safe nowhere." He gave her another smile.

"But you are chief now."

"If the chief is not safe in his own village, he needs to leave that village."

"I would go with you." She gave him fast, small nods.

Atami reached out and put his hand to her cheek. "I know you would."

Walking slowly, Atami made his way first to Goazi's longhouse. Even outside he could hear the heated discussion inside, making him wonder if they had been told of his intention to name someone to the council if they had not decided. Beating on the door with his right palm three times, he waited to be welcomed. All discussion stopped inside. Small feet hurried and the door was opened. Half the family stood just inside the door.

"You honour us with your presence, our chief," Padana, the matriarch of the longhouse, said with a head-bow.

"You honour me by your welcome," Atami said, making a short head-bow. Some of those inside reacted to the gesture, something Knaake had rarely done.

"And to what do we owe this honour?" Padana asked, stepping back to give him room to enter.

"Have you decided on a council representative?" Atami's question was greeted with silence and swapped looks between the house members. Standing without moving, Atami waited for a reply. Fighting nerves, Padana turned back to Atami after silent communication with the other house members.

"No."

"Then I wish to speak to Astreba." Atami walked three paces into the house.

Confused looks went back and forth as Astreba walked through the throng. She was about the age of Atami's mother and was the wife of Yolnu, Knaake's cousin. She wore the black of a widow around her shoulders and was barefoot, per tradition. Her face had the clear features of a Redstone woman.

"How may I serve, my chief?" Astreba asked with a head-bow.

"You can represent your family on the council."

Gasps sounded for those who found enough breath to make any noise. Padana looked the most shocked. Astreba was the most composed.

"You do not wish Goazi to be on the council?" she asked.

"He will have enough duties and I will need your wisdom on the council. Do not tell me I am wrong, I know you have a keen mind and see everything that goes on. We have much work to do and the council members will be very busy outside their own longhouses." The comment appeared to give Padana something to think about. "I need those who can get things done quickly and not let themselves be bullied by the words of others."

Astreba gave a suppressed laugh. "I will take your words as a compliment."

"And so they are intended. Do you accept your appointment?" Atami did not waver his look from her.

"As my chief wishes, I will represent our family on the council."

She made another head-bow.

"Good. We will meet tonight at the customary time. I will have tasks for all."

"Tonight then."

"Thanks to your house for allowing me to visit. I am sorry I do not have time for other hospitality. I have other things I must attend to now." Atami turned and walked from the house. The door was closed, but not before he could see that most were still as shocked as they had been before. Once the door was closed, he laughed to himself as he walked. "That was more fun than I expected."

Giving short greetings to those about, Atami made his way to the other longhouse he needed to visit. There was not heated discussion behind this door when he knocked. Chebucto was on the other side of the door when it opened. He made a head-bow before speaking.

"Welcome, my chief. How may my house serve you today?"

"I have come, Chebucto, to ask you to represent your family on the council. Will you accept?"

"As my chief wishes, I will accept this honour." Chebucto made another head-bow. "I will admit, I was surprised to learn that you intended to ask me."

"Why is that?" Atami tilted his head to the right a little with the question.

"Your father and I have agreed on so little over the years." A small shrug accompanied. "And you intend to name him to the council, or so I am told."

"And do you think I would let him run rampant with it?" The question was answered by a small huff of mirth. "Besides, you are a clever man. Our village will need the advice of such men for as many season cycles as it takes to make us strong again, which I hope will not take more time than we are allowed. I will meet you at the council fire tonight." Atami gave a small head-bow.

"As my chief wishes," Chebucto returned with a full head-bow.

As the door closed, Atami turned back to his own longhouse, going over in his mind all the things that needed to be done. The fact that they had lost no cattle was good, but he was afraid they would be vulnerable to theft. Any plan that he could imagine would take more workers to handle the cattle. "Maybe we were lax anyway. There are many places where we may have become lax. And we have to prepare for the herd-hunt, and winter." His head went back and his eyes went up. "Thank you Knaake for leaving me with such a hard season."

Back at the longhouse, people were busy, but Atami did not let that stop him from assigning tasks. "Rfala." He motioned the warrior to come over to him, walking toward him at the same time. "We need a full count of spears and axes. All of them, even the hidden ones people keep. I also need a count of those who can throw a spear with skill and those who can dress a stag on the plain."

"Preparing for the hunt?"

"Yes, but also taking stock of what we have. I then need to know how many we have to train in spears and axe. Chebucto will be around tomorrow for the numbers."

"As you wish, my chief." Rfala made a head bow and left. Atami found his mother.

"How is Father?" he asked.

"Resting easy." She gave a small smile with the statement.

"How long will he be down?"

"It matters what you want him up for." Her face started to turn stern.

"Walking. Sitting and talking." With success, Atami did not react to his mother.

"Oh." She appeared to ease. "A week, maybe, if he heals well and doesn't try and rush things."

"Make sure he doesn't." Atami shifted his weight. "Tonight I am going to ask someone to take a stock of the village's supplies. With the loss of a dozen warriors, we will not harvest as many stags as we normally do and I want to know exactly how bad off the village is going to be."

"If we do not harvest as much meat, I have a few ideas of what else we can gather." Ziala's finger came up into the air.

"Good. We will most likely need it, but first we must do the herds, for meat and for leather."

"You know, with fewer warriors we will need less meat. Not that I want fewer warriors, I am just saying." Ziala shook her hands in the air and waved her head.

"That is truth but I am sure they would bring in more meat than they would eat."

"Ha! You have never watched them eat." Patting her son on the shoulder, she said, "I will have a full count made of our house and determine how many days we have and how much we need."

"Thanks, Mother. Now, where's Idula?"

"Outside, probably throwing spears. That boy is anxious to prove himself."

"He has plenty of time to do that." Atami turned and made his way outside. Indeed, Idula was throwing spears at the prowler target.

"Not bad," Atami said as he approached. "Keeping your shoulder up, I see."

"Yes," Idula replied with excitement. "I am doing much better."

"Good, but I need you to do something else."

Idula stopped, turned, and straightened. "Of course, my chief."

"Don't know if I'll ever get used to that," Atami said more to himself than to Idula. "I need you to go to the Redstone village and tell the chief that I wish to speak to him, tomorrow when the sun is high if possible. If not, a day very soon. Tell him you need an answer right away and have to return here immediately."

"Y... yes, of course." Idula hesitated a few seconds and then asked in a low voice, "What is it about?"

"You don't need to worry about that. He will either meet me or not, but it is a friendly visit. Make sure you take a spear with you."

"Of course, my chief." Idula regained his composure.

"Leave right away, don't wait."

Without further words, Idula grabbed a spear and a water-skin and ran off. Atami watched the boy go. "I sure hope nothing happens to him or I will feel awful." He shook his head. "Wonder if I will ever get used to that also."

Atami looked around. No one was telling him what to do. No one had assigned tasks for him to complete that day. No one was staring at him wondering why he wasn't doing something. It felt good, but it felt strange. A few days before, all sorts of people could have commanded him to do something. Today, no one could, at least he didn't think so. His mate was still a question in that regard. He could decide what he wanted to do and when. He looked at the longhouse and then looked off toward where the oxen were pastured. Switching views between the two several times, he thought while he did, but then sighed and turned toward the pasture.

"Things that must be done before the things that I would like to do, Father would say. Sounds like poor advice to a clan chief to me, but hey, what do I know. I am new at this chief stuff. There'll be plenty of time, right? Who am I kidding."

By the time the sun was high, Atami was back at the longhouse. After a small refreshment, he found a bowl, filled it with water, found soap, and placed them in an enclosed area behind the longhouse. Then he found Thorea and took her to the enclosure. She gave him a questioning look.

"Sit there, with your head back over the bowl." She complied and Atami poured water over her hair, draining it back into the bowl and working it into her hair. Once it was soaked, he rubbed soap on her hair until it had lathered.

"You are washing my hair?" Thorea asked with a little giggle.

"Yes, I am. My mother always told me if I wanted children, I should wash my mate's hair." Atami spoke easily as he worked the soap among her hair.

"I am pretty sure your mother knows how children are made, seeing she is a mother. What did you father have to say about this... family secret?"

Atami rinsed his hands in the bowl and then started bringing water up to Thorea's hair to rinse. "He said that mother just didn't like getting her top leathers wet."

Atami's hands stopped their motions and he went silent. Thorea tilted her head back slightly and looked at him.

"My mate, did you just figure something out?" A smile grew on her face.

"I guess I know now why he always washed her head in here."

Atami's hands slowly started moving again.

"You know," Thorea said, looking away, her voice wistful and her hands starting to move, "I would hate to not continue your family traditions." She started to undo the toggle from the loop at the top of her upper leathers. "I was welcomed into this family, you know."

Atami started to scoop water faster onto her hair. "That depends if you want me to finish washing your hair."

"My mate!" Thorea said with fake shock. "Are you saying I might distract you from your work?" The second toggle escaped its loop. Two-handed scoops of water doused Thorea's hair.

"Distract? That seems a poor description to use."

"What? You mean I might do more than distract?" The third toggle fled its prison.

The answer to the question proved to be "Yes."

Short of breath, Idula returned that evening. His skin looked dry and dusty, so Atami made sure the boy had some water before speaking. "The chief of the Redstones said he would meet with you tomorrow."

"Good work. Get some food and rest." Patting the boy on the shoulder and walking away, Atami made a list in his head of who he would take to the meeting. Goazi would insist on going, he was sure. Sure his age would be an issue, a couple members of the council who wouldn't slow them down to show his support in the village wouldn't hurt. Not Astreba, though, that would be seen as a sign of the village's weakness. Shaking his head in frustration, Atami moaned. "So many things to worry about."

In his longhouse, Rfala entered during the meal. Atami waved to him to sit and eat, though Rfala only took a small portion required for courtesy. He ate the contents of the bowl before speaking.

"I have made a count of all the weapons in the village. I was surprised at how many were hidden and I reproved those who had hidden them for doing so. Sadly, we have many more spears than those trained to use them, but not enough axes if we were to go to war. We will require the Redstones to make more."

Swallowing before he talked, Atami nodded his head. "I am

speaking with the chief of the Redstones tomorrow. Hopefully I can talk to him about a trade. We need to train more spear-men. How many do we have that can be trained?"

"A dozen. But they will not be trained in time for the hunt." Concern showed on Rfala's face.

"It can't be helped, but I have a thought about what to do for that also." Atami went back to eating.

"Do you wish me to start training the boys?" Rfala asked.

"No, I will do that. Tomorrow, tell them to meet me in the training field at first light in three days. They can at least get a feel for the spear before the hunt and not be complete prey if we run into cats or birds. If I can make a trade tomorrow, you will be making the new axes. Everyone knows how keen the edge on yours is."

The comment brought a smile to Rfala's face. Atami marvelled in his own mind how easy it was to make people feel good with what he said now that he was chief, unlike before when he was looked on with distaste by the chief. It felt wrong.

"If my chief does not need me, I will go my way."

"Yes, go. Give your mate someone to talk to." Atami chuckled with the comment. It brought a pained expression from Rfala.

"She has waited all day to see me. I am sure she will be reciting well into the night about *everything* that has happened to her today." Standing, Rfala appeared weary already as he moved away from the fire.

"At least his mate still likes to talk to him," Thorea said into Atami's ear as she leaned toward him.

"She likes to talk to everyone. I do not know how her throat is not dry from all the talking she does." Turning to look at his wife, Atami's eyebrows rose. "Has she not bent your ear before?"

With a small shrug, Thorea turned back to her food. "I have no time for such things. I am the wife of a chief."

Not able to prevent laughter, Atami shook his head. "I see you use your position well, my mate."

"One must act in the way one's position in the village demands," she said with ease. It made the laughter continue.

Chapter Eight

The sun had started to warm the land after burning off the light mist that had kept the dust on the ground during their travels. Atami stood two spear throws away from the Redstone village marker with five others, three warriors and two council members. The council members looked nervous up close. He hoped they did not appear that way from a distance. The warriors stood proud, spear butts planted on the ground and tips high, one behind each of the other members of the group. As the sun reached its zenith, men walked from the village in their direction.

At the head of the group was Zlopol, the chief. He was as large as Knaake had been, maybe twice Atami's weight, and came bearing spear and axe and a headdress of feathers. Atami furrowed his brow at the man's attire but then recovered.

"Why is he dressed so?" Goazi asked in a quiet voice behind Atami.

"We will find out," was Atami's answer.

"Greetings," Zlopol said in an uncertain voice after stopping two spear lengths from Atami. "You are now the chief of the Ox clan?"

"Yes. Knaake was taken in a raid on the Prowlers. I was named chief in his place." Atami searched Zlopol's face, not liking what he found.

"I had heard that Knaake was gone. I would have expected the village to pick a chief who was... taller." The implied insult was not hard to find.

"I was chosen by the elders to do what is best for the village." Waiting for Zlopol to breach the subject of the visit was a custom Atami was finding frustrating.

"Before saying your purpose, I find myself wondering if I should even be talking to such a chief as you. As far as I know, you are unproven. How can I face a chief as equals if he is unproven?" A smile crept onto Zlopol's face.

Pausing before speaking, Atami stared into the man's eyes as he spoke. "I did not know it was your opinion that counted when *our* village chose a chief."

Zlopol huffed. "Choose who you want. Choose a woman if you want." Laughing at his own jest lasted a while as Atami stood in silence. None of those standing behind them joined in. Settling down, Zlopol continued. "Your clan lost a lot of men in that foolish raid. Now they pick a chief who is puny. Your clan is weak and the others will take what is yours. Who knows if you will survive. Why shouldn't the Redstones be the first to benefit?"

"You want to make war on us?" The statement was barely a question. Atami stood his ground but braced for the response.

"I have no wish to kill your people when I can then raid them again in the future." Zlopol smiled with his mouth but not his eyes.

"So you propose a chief-fight."

"It is better. Only one dies." Zlopol scanned those accompanying Atami. "Choose who you want. That big one there. Or a woman if you wish." More laughter. "It will make no difference."

"You choose the time and place." Atami had not flinched.

"Tomorrow, when the sun is high, halfway between the villages." Zlopol's shoulders settled as his hands grasped each other.

"I will choose the weapons."

As Atami turned to leave, Zlopol interrupted. "What weapon should I bring?"

"I will bring the weapons," Atami said over his shoulder.

Scoffing, Zlopol shouted, "An unfamiliar weapon will not help you, small one."

Not stopping when he reached his followers, Atami started a

determined, quick-paced walk that could not be called running. Goazi, with his longer legs, caught up to him without needing to run. "Do you wish me to fight for you?"

"No. A chief must fight his own battles." Atami's voice was hard.

"He is much bigger than you," Goazi said with concern.

"Then I will pick a weapon that negates his size." Atami took a dozen hard steps before talking more. "Why must everyone be violent? Why can they not work together?'

"It is not our way," Goazi replied with ease. "It never has been."

"Then our way needs to change. Where has our way gotten us? How many generations has our village been the same, life been the same, the hungry time been the same, fighting been the same?"

With a shrug, Goazi said, "It is how we live. How else would we live?"

"Without hunger? Without fear of the cats or the birds?"

"How do we do that?"

"That's what I would like to find out. But I am sure it is not taking from each other at every opportunity."

It was Goazi's turn to scoff. "Tribes form and are gone. It has always happened."

"Maybe it's time it stopped happening."

The next day, Atami and Zlopol both arrived with the required six witnesses. Atami's looked nervous while Zlopol's had the attitude of young boys on a frog hunt. Wearing his battle vest, Zlopol walked halfway between the groups where Atami stood, waiting, no weapons in his hands. As the witnesses formed around them, they clapped to signify the closing of the duelling circle. Zlopol chuckled to himself.

"I, Zlopol, chief of the Redstone clan, challenge the chief of the Ox clan to a chief-fight. Do you accept or do you concede?" Zlopol's voiced bellowed more than required for all to hear.

"I accept," Atami answered in a normal voice.

"I fight for my clan. Do you fight for your clan or do you pick another?"

"I fight for my clan."

"Then the chief-fight is called and started. Let no man interfere or enter the circle under punishment of death. The fight will be to the death or until one man's yield is accepted. The Ox clan chief has the honour of picking the weapons but I see none. Do you choose to fight unarmed?" Zlopol grinned. "You are brave. Foolish, but brave."

"I do not fight unarmed." Reaching behind his back, he pulled out two short, curved knives, presenting them in his palm. "You may have choice of the weapons."

"Skinning knives?" Zlopol picked one up with his thumb and forefinger. The knife looked half as large as it should be for his hand. "You expect me to fight with this?"

"I chose the weapons, as agreed." Atami spun the other knife into a ready position in his hand.

Looking at it with furrowed brow, Zlopol threw the knife to one side. "This is no weapon."

With a quick step and a flash of his weapon, Atami made a shallow cut on the back of Zlopol's arm, enough to draw blood but not enough to cause a real injury. "Looks like a weapon to me," he said as he took a step back.

His face turning red, Zlopol glared at Atami as he balled his fist. "You think you are clever unarming me, but this will not save you. I will crush you with my bare hands."

Zlopol's fist came down toward a crouched Atami's head. Atami slid to the side of the swing, spinning forward to pass along Zlopol's left, his head barely above the man's waist. As he passed his opponent, Atami sliced with the knife, point first, across the back of Zlopol's leg, and continued past, halting just out of the man's reach. A roar came from Zlopol and his body bent toward the injured leg. Pivoting on his good one, he turned toward Atami, his face grimaced and his fists clenched.

"I will crush you slowly. You will feel the pain of your life ending!"

Zlopol lunged at Atami but slower than the time before, favouring the injured leg. Again, Atami side-stepped the attack, this time scraping the blade on the inside of Zlopol's left arm as it passed. Again, blood flowed, not enough to kill Zlopol but enough to cause continual drops to hit the ground. Another roar, this one from frustration, sounded.

"If you wish to bleed me to death," Zlopol said through heavy breaths as he again turned, "you will have to bleed me much more than that. I have a lot of blood."

This time Atami moved first. Faking a move to the left that drew Zlopol's arms in defence, Atami dodged around to the right, grabbing the back corner of Zlopol's vest, and swung himself onto his back. As he did, he reached around Zlopol's neck and drove just the tip of the blade into the left of Zlopol's neck just past his jugular vein, enough to catch in his muscle but not enough to cut the vein. As Zlopol went stiff, Atami placed his mouth near Zlopol's ear.

"And how much blood will you lose if I cut the vein in your neck?"

Stiffening his body, Zlopol answered in a soft voice. "I will still kill you before I die."

"Then we will both be dead and our villages will both lose a chief. I have no wish to kill you but you must now make a choice. Die, or the Redstones become our ally."

"Ally?" Zlopol said, talking so as to move his neck as little as possible.

"You are still Redstone and we are still Ox, but we help protect each other from other clans that would make war on us. We can sit around each other's pots and not fight, we can help each other during the herd harvest, and we can trade on friendly terms. We do not try to take from each other, we work together, from now until our clans are no more."

"But we are not Ox clan?"

"No. I have enough problems with my own people, why would I want yours?"

The comment made Zlopol start to laugh, but it was suppressed by the increased pressure from the tip of the knife. "And what do we get if I agree?"

"First, I don't take the blood price from your village." Atami could feel the reaction in Zlopol's body that the statement caused. "Secondly, you get to live."

"Living is good."

"And third, you get our help as much as we get yours. You are not conquered, you are friend."

"You do this because you need it for your village to survive." Zlopol's tone was one that believed he understood the situation.

"I do this because we must stop feeding off each other if we are going to do more than just survive. My clan is weakened and the Redstones are not among the strongest of the clans. Together we would form a strong tribe, one strong enough to scare any from attacking us. Agreed?" Atami pushed the knife in a noticeable amount for emphasis.

"Agreed," Zlopol said with a hurried voice.

Backing the knife out of the wound, Atami slid from Zlopol's back and walked around to face the larger man. Throwing away the knife, he held out his right arm. In response, Zlopol held out his to grasp Atami's elbow. Atami's hand did not reach Zlopol's elbow but he grasped the arm where he could. Murmuring could be heard from the witnesses. Blood mixed into the grasp as if to consecrate the agreement.

"Let all here testify," Atami said in a clear voice, "that the Ox clan and the Redstones are now brothers of different villages. Those who attack one attack the other."

To muttering voices, Atami released his grasp and addressed Zlopol. "Now I can talk to you about what I came to your village for. The herd harvest."

Looking at his hand after feeling his neck, Zlopol talked without looking at Atami. "What about the harvest?"

"Both of our villages have a limited number of spearmen. Because men must protect those gathering from cats and birds, it limits our harvest. But if we harvested side by side, there would be less each of us has to protect and more that could harvest meat."

"So," Zlopol said, looking at Atami while contemplating the idea, "we would harvest our meat and you would harvest yours, but we each would only have to protect one side of the harvesters."

"Yes." Atami stood still while allowing the time for Zlopol to think.

"That is a good idea. And since we now trust each other, we do not have to worry about the other stealing our meat." Zlopol's head nodded up and down as he talked.

"Or anyone else."

Chuckling, Zlopol rubbed his neck again. "They will be so confused they will not know what to think."

"The rains are coming faster than normal. I say we leave in five days. Agreed?"

"Sounds right. Your hunting grounds or ours?"

"Yours are better." Atami permitted himself a smile.

"That is true. We will meet on the way in five days."

"Done." Atami waved at Zlopol's neck. "I would let it scar."

"Of course."

On the return to the village, Goazi walked with Atami. "That was clever."

"Thinking will always win over strength." Atami took a few steps before adding, "At least most of the time."

"It is unfortunate that you forsook the blood prize." Goazi looked up as if he had something in mind.

"It would have weakened their village and not strengthened ours enough at this time. We would have both been weak and the other tribes would have just considered me lucky. This way we are both strong."

"Yes." Goazi's head bobbed up and down. "We have doubled our warriors. That is good. I do feel hurt that you did not ask me to fight for you." The tone of his voice did not sound hurt.

"Would you have won?" Atami asked with a chuckle.

"Of course! I always win," Goazi replied in a good-natured voice.

"Until you don't."

"That is something I will not have to worry about afterwards."

"But *I* would."

"The reaction of the tribe?"

"The fury of your mate!" Atami corrected.

"That is why I fight to the death. I don't wish to ever tell her I lost." Goazi's head went back and forth in small, quick motions.

"She would avenge you," Atami said through a laugh.

Altaterra   121

"Increasing my shame." The sigh was the verbal element that accompanied Goazi's shoulders sinking.

"Don't worry, you will be dead. You'll never know."

"Oh, don't doubt, she will make sure I know. If not while she is alive, then forever when we are both dead. That is not how I wish to spend the afterlife."

Slapping the taller man on the back, Atami let out a laugh. "Let us postpone the afterlife as long as possible." Bending closer, Atami asked, "What is the reaction from the others?"

"They are still making sense of what you did. It will take time, but I think they will understand."

"Good, because I do not have the time to explain it to them. We have a hunt to organize and four days to do it."

A heavy sigh came from Goazi. "That means a bath."

"Don't worry, my friend, it will not kill you." Atami inhaled deeply through his nose. "Besides, you could use one."

"I don't mind being clean, it's the cold water I don't like. It makes things… shrink."

"Better than having a fish bite it off," Atami said in a playful voice.

"That would have to be a big fish." There was a hint of defensiveness in Goazi's voice.

"If you say so, I will trust your word."

Goazi stopped talking and stood straighter as they walked.

Five oxen each pulled a skid while people ran beside them just as the sun made its way above the spine of peaks to the east. Most skids had four people in them, older women, hide skinners of the kills, who had been given the honour of riding to the hunting site. In the lead, Obii had six women in his skid and Atami riding on his back. He loped along as if he did not notice the extra load. A recent rain had the land smelling of the fresh grass, which soaked up the sun and water from the mud. The smell drew all the small creatures out of their burrows, from insects to the small, tan-haired, pig-like animals that dotted the plain with holes big enough to cripple an ox that wasn't careful. At intervals, Atami would stand on Obii's back and scan the countryside. No terror birds or cats could be seen but they were several hours from the hunting grounds. Several leagues away he could see the Redstone people angling toward their path. Sitting back down, he glanced at Goazi striding next to the ox.

"Is it too much to hope that the birds and cats eat their fill before we get there?" Atami asked.

"Have they ever?" Goazi shot back.

"No, they haven't." Face sagging, Atami adopted a grumpy appearance.

"Maybe they are lazy and wait for us to kill it for them?"

"The beasts would, wouldn't they? If we had enough spear-men I would organize a hunt of them too at the same time." Atami's voice held bitter overtones.

"That would be a good idea if we had the men and the skids to carry the spoils."

"Some day, my friend, some day." Atami's words drifted off as he spoke them.

"Is that part of the better life you spoke about before?"

"Yes. Imagine the plains without the fear of the birds and cats."

"I can't." Goazi shook his head. "They have always been there."

"That does not mean that some day they will not."

"It does not mean that some day they will," Goazi countered. "Sickness has killed many before."

"That is true." Atami huffed. "If it kills us, then I hope the birds and cats that eat our dead bodies die of the sickness too."

Laughing, Goazi asked, "Then who would live here?"

"The herds, I guess."

"They would eat all the grass and then die from lack of food."

"So only fish in the rivers?"

"Then it would be called the Fish Plains." Goazi laughed at his suggestion.

"That would be confusing. Maybe others would come looking for fish that walked on the land." Atami's brow furrowed with the idea.

"That would be something to see. I wonder if they would taste different?"

Laughing at their musing, the Redstone people drew closer at what appeared to be an ever-increasing pace. It was not long before the two tribes ran side-by-side. Atami greeted Zlopol in as formal a manner as riding an ox would allow and received a greeting in return from the running Zlopol.

Atami spoke in a voice loud enough to be heard over the grunting oxen and falling feet. "I give you the honour of being first in the herd line."

"You are most gracious," Zlopol called back. "Your ox appears to enjoy the run."

"He likes to demonstrate his strength." Both men chuckled at the ox's expense, who took no notice of them. "How will you signal a volley?"

Pointing to his head, Zlopol shook the feathers of his headdress back and forth.

"Ah, that is what that is for. They do not scare the herd?"

"They are not terror bird feathers so the herd ignores them."

"Clever." Atami looked ahead and to his right, again noticing the cloud of mist coming from the ground. "It seems the herds are early this year. They are already passing the hunting grounds."

"Then we won't have to wait for them to appear," Zlopol said with a shrug.

It took another hour to reach the hunting grounds. As the ground dropped off in front of them, the clansmen were presented with a wide river valley raised on both sides. A river flowed on the far side of a basin. As the water swayed back and forth along its path, a belt of herd-beasts at least twenty animals thick wound its way along the river through the tall grass for as far as the eye could see in either direction, a river of beasts next to a river of water. Low grunts could be heard from the beasts as they moved, to complain or encourage those next to them, or both. The smell of wet beasts and manure filled the valley air. On occasion a beast would stop to drink or take a mouthful of grass, but most only walked and grunted. Pregnant females could be seen among the herd. These would not attract spears, but the young bucks with a head of antlers would be a favourite target. The rise of land on either side directed the herd at their fast walk in a south to southwest direction. The river would end in the marsh next to the ocean far downstream where the beasts spent the winter. The wet ground of the marsh made the beasts harder to hunt, though not impossible. Seven months from now, the well-fed beasts would travel back north in small groups instead of this mass.

As the warriors spread out on top of the ridge and to the south, Goazi gave an arm-wave to Atami. "Good luck on the hunt. May we have much meat for the next year."

"Stay safe," Atami replied as he shook his own arm. "The line looks thick this year."

With a head turn a little to one side, Goazi gave Atami a questioning look. "Are you sure you want to put Idula with the warriors?"

"He is too small to drag a dead herd-beast by himself." Atami's face became a grin. "Besides, did you see the joy in his face when I told him to take a place with the warriors?"

"Do you think he is ready to take his place with the warriors?"

Waving at the dispersing men, Atami replied, "Place him near the top of the rise where the grass is shorter. Another warrior will be near enough to help if a cat or bird does approach him. I do not think he will run from a beast."

"That is what I am worried about," Goazi said through a sigh as he turned to check on the men's placements.

Slowing the pace of his group, Atami let the Redstones pass in front of them to take a position downstream. The butchering camp was set along the downward slope of the hill as the spear-men carried weapons and ropes through the grass in a low-crouching approach. Zlopol wasted no time getting near the undulating herd line, only the feathers of his headdress visible above the grass. Taking a quick look to his right at his own men showed no heads above the grass. When all movement through had stopped, Atami looked to the headdress feathers.

The sound of the camp being prepared could still be heard when Zlopol's feathers twitched forward. Giving a long whistle, Atami rose, took one step, and threw his spear into a herd-beast in front of him. The line of spear-men performed the same motions almost in perfect unison. Spears sank into the sides of herd-beasts, most falling within a few steps of being hit. A couple penetrated the flanks of beasts who ran that much faster along the herd. One with a Redstone spear fell in front of the Ox clan spear-men but a couple more continued downstream, no chase given. As the line of beasts swayed away from the attack, the spear-men ran forward with ropes that were placed around the antlers or heads of the downed beasts and pulled the fresh meat up the hillside. They were met by others, two or three, who took the ropes from them while handing them a new one. The river of beasts did not stay away long as if the flow had no memory of the attack. Taking up their positions, the spear-men waited hidden in the grass for the next signal. When the herd-beasts resumed their original path, the signal was given again.

As he handed off his fourth kill, Atami heard a deep bellow from the top of the ridge. Obii stood on the ridge south of the line of warriors, looking at the herd and issuing one bellow after another.

"There he goes again," Atami said with a shake of his head.

"What is he doing?" asked the spear-man next to him.

"Issuing a challenge to the leader of the herd-beasts."

"Why? Does he wish to take females back with him?"

"Because he can and he's Obii, the mighty ox." Atami's eyes grew wider as he watched. "It appears one has answered this year."

Further downstream, a male herd-beast walked up the ridge. He was larger than those they had been hunting and had antlers with too many points for Atami to make an accurate count. The herd-beast issued a return bellow higher in pitch but no less determined. Scraping his hoof on the ground, Obii's bellow became more energetic. The herd-beast answered again, also scraping the ground.

"They can't be serious," the voice of the spear-man said from behind Atami.

"I would say they are," Atami replied with a chuckle.

Both beasts lowered their heads and charged, taller herd-beast versus more massive ox. Atami thought he could feel the ground shake beneath him. As they neared, Obii managed somehow to place his head between the antlers of the herd-beast, hitting his opponent forehead to forehead. The sound of the impact echoed through the valley. The herd-beast was thrown back over his rear legs to tumble twice down the hill before stopping himself. While he lay prone, Obii issued his loudest bellow yet, raising his head in triumph. It took a moment for the herd-beast to rise on unsteady feet and perform a slow walk back to the herd. Obii strutted back to the other oxen, prancing at times.

Atami laughed. "Well, he finally got his fight. He will be insufferable the rest of the day. Come, we must return to the hunt."

More beasts fell to the spears. The size of the herd made killing the animals easy to the point Atami sent several spear-men back to help with the processing. By mid-afternoon the sleds were starting to become full with meat still waiting to be processed. After two more volleys, Atami called a halt to the spear-men and then returned to the camp. Atami found Goazi.

"Any problems?" he asked the warrior.

"Surprisingly, no. We have seen a few cats and birds from a distance but none have come close. Strange." Goazi rubbed his chin with one hand.

"Maybe they don't know what to make of us." Patting the man on his back, Atami added, "All the better, my friend. We have abundant meat and hides. Have your men eaten?"

"Only what they were carrying when they got here."

"How about you?"

Staring down at Atami, Goazi frowned. "Do you think I could carry enough to settle my appetite?"

With a laugh, Atami shook his head. "I will have someone make sure everyone eats before the return journey. We don't need a warrior distracted on the way."

"That is true. Will the Redstones go with us when we leave?"

"They look to be as far along as we are, so I expect they will be ready, maybe even before us. Unless some warriors wanted to help process the beasts?" Atami gave the man a sly look.

"A warrior dress an animal? Never. That is woman's work." Goazi huffed as he talked.

"Unless there is no woman around and you are far from the village."

"That is different," Goazi said as he raised his chin. "That is roasting, a long-standing tradition."

"But you still have to dress the kill." Atami put emphasis into the words.

"We don't talk about that." Goazi looked off into the distance.

By the time the beasts had been processed, the smell of dead animals permeated the area. The whines of the cats and squawks of the birds could be heard in the distance. Everyone worked faster with those sounds in their ears. As the sun started to reach out to the western edge of the landscape, the clan travelled back to the village. The Redstones had left a few minutes before the Ox clan so the passage of their sleds kicked up dust for the Ox clan to bathe in as they travelled, whatever water that had been on the ground long since burned off by the sun. Atami stood at the top of the rise until the whole clan had passed before bringing up the rear of the column. Idula stood next to him.

"Go!" Atami commanded, waving his spear.

"You should be at the head of the people," Idula said in a small, squeaky voice that was forced out through pursed lips.

"I sent Goazi to the front and he argued enough with me about it. Now do as your chief says and go guard the meat. I can't leave until you do."

Taking in a breath, Idula sighed and ran after the column. With a shake of his head, Atami followed. "And here I thought people were supposed to listen to their chief, not argue with him. Besides, there is less dust back here."

The easy jog Atami used to follow the sleds felt good after crouching all afternoon stalking the herd. The wind came from the south, driving the dust to the right, though the smell of meat and hide still reached him with a vengeance. "Is it asking too much for it to come from the north on a hunt?" he asked himself. "Of course it is. At least it isn't cooking and making me hungry. But then maybe I would run faster."

After an hour, Atami heard a reoccurring squawk that kept getting louder. A turn of his head revealed a red and yellow-feathered terror bird following the column and getting braver by the minute. Stopping, he turned to face the animal with his spear in his hand and his arm behind his body. The bird was taller than he could reach his arm into the sky, a full adult. When he turned, it stopped for a moment, swayed its head from side-to-side several times, and then started a cautious advance. Every few steps it would raise its head and bellow a challenge before lowering it again and advancing. Atami stood motionless and waited.

When the bird was within fifteen paces, it stopped again, spread its wings, and raised its head with a ragged squawk. The response from Atami was a quick launch of his spear. Without time to react from its position, the bird took the spear in the upper chest. As the bird collapsed, Atami turned and ran back toward the column without watching the bird die. "I hate to leave the feathers," he muttered to himself, "but the meat is more important."

He hadn't gone more than a couple of dozen strides when another bird crested the small hill to the left, this one with red and blue feathers. Moving his second spear to his throwing hand, Atami quickened his pace to get between the bird and the column as it took long strides over the hill. This one took a more aggressive approach, head down and no stops to intimidate. Atami had just reached a position parallel to the bird when he had to stop and pull back his spear. The bird made a straight approach and was less than ten paces when Atami threw his spear. The impact at the base of the neck was not an instant kill, but it caused the bird to slow and thrash. Weaponless except for his knife, Atami again did not watch but hurried to join the others. As he reached Idula at the back of the column, the boy was watching the bird while striding forward.

"It dropped," the boy said.

"Good. Spears."

Idula handed both spears in his possession to Atami.

"Too bad we have to leave it. Blue feathers are not common." Idula's voice had a wistful tone as his head turned back.

"Someday. Run to the front and tell Goazi that any more speed that he can get from the column would be good." Taking deep breaths, Atami recovered from his increased exertions.

"And leave you?" The boy sounded concerned.

"Go! Now!"

The shock of the sudden increase in volume caused Idula to raise his head but after a quick look at Atami's face, he took off at a sprint toward the head of the line. Several people had turned their heads to see what was happening, but only saw Idula pass them. Their interest did not last more than a few seconds, saving their energy for the trip home.

Breathing in the smell of dead meat with a small mixture of manure, Atami shook his head. "Still arguing with me. Guess I will have to figure out how to stop that. But then again, he is young."

In a couple of minutes, the pace of the column increased a little but not a significant amount. Atami shook his head but said nothing to anyone. A quick glance behind him showed no pursuit but that did not make him feel more comfortable. He was joined by two more spear-men who took up positions ten feet away on either side of him.

"Goazi sent you?" It was more of a statement than a question. The spear-men did not reply, just continued to scan the land for threats. "Don't get in my way."

The sole visitor they had for the rest of the trip was a cat and it stopped when it saw the three armed men. Appearing to think better of its chances, it turned away, heading toward the hunting grounds.

Everyone visibly relaxed when they entered the village. The sky was dark, lit only by thousands of tiny stars, but the meat and skins still had to be moved into the longhouse that had been prepared to receive them. With many hands, the work went fast. The ceremonial washing was next, a practical matter given that everyone smelled of dead meat and blood. No one was shy about stripping off their leathers and placing them into the wash pits that had been filled with water before they left. Bars of soap lining the edges of the pits were used and passed on to the next person. As the water in a pit started to turn colour, it was abandoned for another. As people left the pits for their longhouses, the crowd grew thinner and thinner. Atami watched, waiting for all others to bathe first. He was joined by Thorea.

"Always the last, I see." She smiled at him as she stood an inch away. "That is not the action of a chief."

"It is the action of this chief. I am not their ruler, I am their leader. A leader must be able to put his clan before himself when needed." Standing with his arms crossed, the statement came out as a proclamation. He let a few seconds go by before speaking again. "Besides, has your nose not told you how bad the people smell?"

Laughing, Thorea placed her hand on his shoulder until her laughter stopped. "And here I was thinking you were waiting to have me in a pit by yourself."

"Don't you know how bad you smell right now?" Atami replied with a playful voice and a smile. It was rewarded with a punch to his shoulder.

"Shall I speak about you?" Thorea turned her face away from Atami.

"If you wish." A shrug went with the words.

"You smell worse than the ass end of your ox." The words had the force of truth with them.

"And you would want to be with your mate when he was in such a condition?" Surprise filled Atami's voice.

"I would do anything for my mate if he asked," Thorea said in a quiet voice.

"And it is appreciated," Atami said, tilting his head toward her, "but I would not want to conceive a son in such a condition."

"What about a daughter?"

"Not a daughter either."

"Then I guess it is a good thing you don't have to worry about it." The statement hung in the air for a while, then Atami's head came up and he looked at Thorea with wide eyes, mouth open. She turned her head with slow intention. "I guess your mother's advice was right."

"Do you know if...?"

"Too early."

"But you will tell me as soon as you know?"

"Of course."

"Wait." A finger came up and wagged from Atami to Thorea. "Can we still... you know?"

A chuckle was the first reply. "Of course we can. Don't you know?"

"No. I mean, I have never been a father before."

"Well," Thorea said, looking back at the pits, "you better be ready."

Chapter Nine

The mood the next day while everyone was processing the meat was high. As the smoke house filled with smoke, sections and strips of the meat were hung from poles. The choicest portions went into cooking pots, no one willing to take the chance that they would go bad or be stolen by animals. Livers were put into a brine. The skins would only be touched when the meat was done, with antlers, sinews, and hooves the last to see attention. Only four warriors stood guard around the edge of the village with Goazi in charge.

Atami cut long slices of meat to be hung and turned into jerky. Because the meat lost so much volume when used so, not much of the animals were allocated. While also assisting those carrying carcasses from the longhouse and sections to the smoke house, Atami wasn't done cutting strips until the sun was setting. Food during the day had been dried fruit, raw vegetables, and old bread soaked in milk. The evening meal of boiled and seasoned meat felt like a yearly feast. Old stories were repeated, particularly those that embarrassed someone present. All laughed and took it with good cheer while enjoying the meat. Full and tired, Atami shuffled to his bed mat. He was soon joined by Thorea.

"Leaving before someone tells an embarrassing story about you?" she asked with playfulness.

"They already did," Atami said as he closed his eyes.

"They did? I missed it? Who was it so I can ask them to repeat it for me?" Thorea grabbed his arm as she spoke.

"Pay more attention next time." Rolling over to his side, Atami turned his back to his mate. "I am going to sleep."

"You're no fun." Thorea gave him a small shove before her voice took a defiant tone. "Fine, I'll just ask your mother." Atami responded with a fake snore. "You'll see. I'll have more stories about you by morning than you knew existed."

"Good luck. I'm sure I've heard them all, even the ones that didn't happen."

Leaving in a huff, Thorea walked back to the gathering. When she had left, Atami said to himself, "She doesn't know Mother very well, does she? She would never tell embarrassing stories about her only child and chief." He was silent for a moment. "I hope."

It took another day to process all the meat. Once done, fat was stripped from the hides and rendered. The hides were stretched between the longhouses so the ropes could be tightened when needed. Smaller boys climbed the sides of the longhouses to fasten the ropes to the poles of the houses, pulling with both hands and their feet pushing on the support poles to stretch the hides as tight as possible. Each boy grinned as he worked. Because there were so many hides, a couple of girls climbed the longhouses to help, drawing frowns and divisive comments from the boys and a laugh from Atami.

"Why shouldn't girls help?" Thorea asked. "Some are bigger and stronger than the boys of the same age."

"Tanning is a man's work and this is the first 'man' job the boys are given as they grow. They must first learn to process a kill before they are allowed to make one."

"But a girl could do everything a man could do, even learn to throw a spear." Thorea's tone was firm.

"And what would men do?" Atami turned to face her instead of the work. "They would stay home all day and lay around, telling the woman to do everything for them."

"They might try," Thorea protested.

"Oh," Atami chuckled, "they would certainly try. And they would remind the women that only men could be warriors and defend the village."

"But women could be warriors." Thorea's back straightened and her voice took a haughty tone as she spoke.

"Men would never risk it." Shaking his head, Atami turned back to watch the work. "One male can impregnate many females but a lost female cannot be replaced by a male."

"So we are only here to have your babies?" Thorea's voice expressed concern at Atami's attitude.

"No, I am saying that there are things you can do that we can't and those must be protected to preserve the future of the clan." No words passed for a moment, then Atami added, "Besides, you make a bed cozy. I don't wish to lose that."

The response was a fist to the shoulder, not a hard hit. It was followed by Thorea's shoulder leaning against his. "Maybe I don't wish to lose it either."

"Then you agree."

"That's not what I meant."

"Too late, you agreed." Atami rocked up onto his toes and back down.

"Men can sure be stubborn sometimes," Thorea said with a sigh.

"Us?" Atami scoffed. It earned him another punch.

When the work was completed, the village resembled a huge hunting camp. The hanging skins provided shade through most of the day. The smell of smoking meat was everywhere, even inside the longhouses. It would soon have competition from the tanning pits, but only if someone walked downwind from the village or the wind changed to an unusual direction. Most of the villagers spent large parts of the day guarding the meat or skins, which was a great reason to rest after their exertions.

Atami thought of more duties for himself than anyone else, the first to find Rfala, who was taking a turn guarding the smoke house. As Atami approached, Rfala jumped up and struck his chest in greeting.

"What does my chief require of me?" Rfala asked.

"Have our tools and weapons been counted after the work?" Atami put most of his weight on one leg as he looked up at the man.

"They have been counted. There were some that had to be thrown away, more than I would have liked, but the red stone only lasts so long. We were waiting a while after the hunt before approaching the Redstones so they can replace their own losses, which they would tell us they have to do anyway."

"What about the black stones?"

"Hmm, yes, they could be used. It would take longer to make weapons and tools but they would last longer. I think we are in most need of knives and those we could make out of the black stones, but it would take more time." Rfala pushed his lower lip up against his upper lip and rotated his chin in a small circle as he talked. "The rains may have washed some of the softer stone from the black ones, making them easier to harvest."

"Do we have the tools to harvest them?" Atami asked the question with directed concern.

"Yes, we keep them separate just to harvest black stones. They are red stone themselves that Chebucto does something special to. He will be glad to have the change to make things from the black stones again."

"Prepare a party. We leave in two days. Better to start sooner than later." Atami turned to go, cocking his head as if to remember the next things on his list.

"Yes, my chief. It will be done." Rfala stayed at his post while Atami walked away, talking to himself.

"I guess that means we bring Obii. Not like that ox would let me leave without him. I must speak with Chebucto."

Chebucto was easy to find. He was at his longhouse doing something with the knots for the ropes holding the hides to which Atami gave a questioning look but said nothing about. With a shrug, he announced himself. "Chebucto, I have need to speak to you."

Turning, Chebucto waited for Atami's bow first before executing his. "What does my chief come to me for?"

"We need to gather a party to visit the black stones in two days. You are required, of course."

"Ah! Not one to sit around, I see." A pleased smile rose on Chebucto's face. "Are you choosing the people or am I?"

"You can pick who you think is best. I will have the supplies prepared except for your tools and anything else you think you need to gather the stones. How many people will we need?" Atami shifted from foot to foot as he spoke to the elder.

"I will need four besides myself, plus whoever you think is required for protection. And at least two ox drivers."

Looking up as he counted, Atami's headed nodded with the numbers. "That will be eight, plus a couple of warriors, so we will say ten. We will gather in the morning just after sunrise in two days."

"As you say."

Bows were exchanged again. Atami left, doing more thinking than watching those around him. "Two oxen for the stone, another for the supplies. That makes eleven people. Too bad the meat will not be ready by then. What else?"

Two days later in the early morning, Atami was watching Rfala pace back and forth between hitched oxen, supplies, and people, never reaching any destination before turning to the next. Unable to contain his laughter, Atami approached Rfala.

"Take it easy," Atami said, putting his hand on the man's shoulder. "I am sure you remembered everything. If not, so be it."

Rfala tried to relax a little. "I don't know why you put me in charge of this. I've never done anything like this before. I mostly just train fighters."

"Because you haven't done this before, that's why." Atami's grin grew broad.

"So you are torturing me," Rfala said with a huff.

"No, I am widening your experience. Now you know you can do it." Atami's arms went out to demonstrate his words.

"Chebucto helped a lot," Rfala said with resignation. "But I'm still worried."

"You did fine. Let's get moving." With that said, Atami walked over to Obii and jumped on the ox's back. Obii pawed at the ground and shook his head up and down. "Yes, yes, I know, you want to go. Let me make sure everyone is ready."

Standing on Obii's back, Atami scanned the group. There was some last minute fussing but that would continue until they left. Drawing in a breath, he announced, "Okay, let's get moving. The sun only stays in the sky so long and we have a long way to go."

His bottom had just hit Obii's back when the animal started working up to a trot. The near-empty sled made light skidding sounds until it hit the grass outside the village. The fields were still green from the rains. Eager as the ox was to run, Atami had to slow it down to a pace the other animals could maintain. Rfala ran up alongside.

"I wanted to ask," Rfala said with ease as he jogged, "why are we leaving so soon after the hunt?"

"The green grass will make the sleds easier to pull when they are full. Plus we need less feed for the oxen." Atami patted the spears loaded into the holder on Obii as if to make sure they were real.

"But we have all that meat in the village. Isn't it a tempting target?"

"Everyone has lots of meat at the moment. What would they do with more? Where would they store it? It would go bad before they could eat it."

"This is true. Unless they just wanted to be cruel and take ours."

"Waste of men and time."

"I think some chiefs are willing to waste men and time."

"Maybe, but with their bellies full of meat I think they would choose to sit around and drink fermented milk."

"Yuck!" Rfala's face contorted. "I hate that stuff. Tastes awful."

"I agree. They say you get used to it." Atami shrugged.

"I suppose you could get used to drinking ox piss but I wouldn't want to do that either," Rfala said in a serious voice. The comment drew a loud laugh from Atami, throwing his head back as he rode Obii.

"So now we have two things we never want to pass our lips," Atami said when he had recovered from laughing.

"Oh, there are more, I am sure."

"I am sure also, but let us dwell on more pleasant thoughts."

After a couple of hours of riding, Atami dismounted and passed back through the train of people and oxen. Some people were riding on the sleds, but it did not look like a comfortable ride. Every bump no matter the size sent them off their seat and back down. Nodding his head at what he found, he made his way back to Obii but did not remount. Rfala gave him a look.

"Not riding?"

"It can be hard on one's butt," Atami answered, trying to sound nonchalant.

"Not much padding on Obii?" The small snicker that came with the question gave a hint that Rfala knew the answer.

"Nor in those sleds either, I would guess."

"Unless you are sitting on a sack of something soft."

"Did we bring anything soft?" Atami turned his head while contorting his brows.

"Not really. I find it much easier to assume the pace of the oxen and just run beside them."

"Yes, but Obii thinks I should be riding him for some reason. An issue of pride, I assume."

"Who knows what oxen think," Rfala said with a dismissive tone, "if anything at all."

"Sometimes I would like to."

By the afternoon of the second day, they had reached the spine of short mountains that defined the eastern boundary. While not very tall, approximately fifty meters, the sides of the mountains were sheer and steep as if they had been pushed up from below with great force to form a wall. The cliffs were also now eroded by wind and water so that the tops looked spiked and jagged and the sides were full of long gullies from the rain. At the base at their destination was evidence of digging where an outcrop of black rock came up from the ground. It was the only black rock within eyesight the whole trip and was so low to the ground that it would be easy to miss from a distance. Atami stood and stared up at the cliffs.

"First time?" Rfala asked.

"Yeah," Atami said without looking away from the cliffs. "Not like any other rock I have ever seen. Not even as tall as the trees."

"You thinking of trying to climb it?" A small laugh accompanied the question.

"I don't see any way to climb it. Not even cracks to use." Atami continued to scan the wall of rock. "Has anything ever come over the rocks?"

"Besides birds? No. How would it?" Shrugging, Rfala turned to help set up the camp.

Approaching the wall of rock, Atami reached out and felt its smooth surface both up and down and side to side. "It's like someone put it here on purpose. But how could they?" He shook his head. "There is so much we don't understand or even try to." He turned to watch Chebucto's crew removing tools and approaching the black stone vein. Leaving the wall, he gathered the oxen and moved them onto nearby grass. Before he left them there, he patted Obii.

"You'll protect them, won't you, boy?" He received a grunt in return. "I know, I don't need to ask, but I do." Walking back, he said to himself, "Now for three days of nothing to do. Hmm, maybe I'll go hunting, if any animals are here instead of the river."

The hunting was poor, mostly ground burrowers, but it kept Atami busy. On the second full day as he was returning to the camp site, he looked up at the jagged peaks above it, watching for any birds hovering over the camp. Small flying birds were not a danger like the terror birds, but could be a pest. Plus some had beautiful feathers. As he walked and looked, the figure of a man stood up on top of the peaks about forty paces from the camp, causing him to drop his kill and stare. The man was tall, muscled, and wore strange skins that covered his whole body. More important, he carried a spear strapped to his back. Forgetting the kill, Atami ran to the camp and waved at Rfala, who ran out to meet him.

"Bird or cat?" Rfala asked as he neared.

"Neither. Man," Atami said through his panting.

"Which tribe?"

"None that I have seen before. Gather the fighters."

"Where is he?" Rfala asked as he turned.

"On top of the mountains."

The comment caused Rfala to stop and turn. "What? How?"

"I don't know. We need to find out. Go!"

Not able to see the man so close to camp, Atami walked back onto the plain while Rfala gathered what fighters they had. The man had been joined by another who did not carry any spear that Atami could see. The man was older and had something slung on his back, some kind of bag. The man in charge was giving directions to others that did not reach Atami's ears.

"Of course he is in charge," Atami said to himself. It only took a moment for the other three to join Atami, who led them in an arc toward the location of the strangers but with enough room to avoid spears if they were thrown. "Keep your spears upwards," he said as he ran. "We do not know how big of a tribe they have, so do not act hostile."

"Do we act friendly?" someone asked from behind.

"I didn't say that," Atami answered.

Standing on top of the ridge, Kaitja never took his eye off the men running around the plain below them, even when helping the rest of the party up the back of the ridge. Soon enough he gave that job to Xitano and proceeded to take another rope out of the supplies.

"Are you going down there?" Robterns asked, a small shake in his voice.

"It would appear to be the next step." Kaitja tied one end of the rope around a rock projection.

"They're armed," Robterns' assistant, Perral, said as she pointed at the four men below.

"So are we, at least two of us." Kaitja threw the other end of the rope over the side.

"Not great odds," Perral said.

"We're here to explore, right? There is no village here so they are here for some other reason. Maybe they are here for the metal you're looking for." Kaitja turned to Xitano. "Stay here. Do not descend unless I tell you to." Worry filled her eyes. Kaitja tilted his head. "Someone needs to be here to help me back up and cover my retreat, if needed. Don't let anyone else down until I say so."

"We didn't bring a linguist," Robterns said to no one in particular.

"A what?" Kaitja asked, turning back to the rope.

"Someone good with languages."

"There is more than one?" Kaitja's jaw came up and to the side with the question.

"There were many back on Earth. One was sufficient here and there was no reason to maintain others, though some can be seen in the records. Few can translate them." The wistful look Robterns' eyes got during his musings appeared.

"I'll do my best." Grabbing onto the rope with both hands and facing the cliff, Kaitja started his descent to the ground. After ten meters when no spears impacted him or the cliff face, he relaxed a little. "Maybe they are as curious about us as we are about them."

Once on the ground, Kaitja pulled out his spear and held it as the men he faced did. They were clothed in leather shirt and shorts that were loose enough to allow movement but not enough to get in the way. Their skin was darker with a reddish tint, but the ground also had a reddish tint so that may not have meant anything. Their hair was tied back behind their heads and they had no beards, making him glad he kept his shaved. Their spears had non-metallic points and each had at least one knife and what appeared to be an axe at their belts. Kaitja walked halfway to the group and stopped. Off to his left, he heard what sounded like cattle but did not look away from the men. Three of the men were at least as large as he was, the one in front was smaller.

"Practical for fighting as a group," he said softly to himself. When the smaller man started toward him, he was surprised. "Send out the least missed?"

As the shorter man neared, Kaitja could see the intelligence in his eyes and nodded. The man stopped about two meters from him. He looked to be around twenty but that was a guess based on his experience with his own people. While smaller, the man's frame held lean muscles that spoke of hard work and a few scars that told of a tough life. After he stopped, the man said something in words that meant nothing to Kaitja. With a sigh, he began.

Pointing two fingers of his free hand to his chest, Kaitja said, "Kaitja."

It only took a couple of seconds for the man to respond, though still with a heavy accent. "Atami."

Waving back at the cliff, Kaitja said, "Human."

Using the butt of his spear, the man drew a oval and then an arc through one end of the oval. "Guara pleme." The man then waved to Kaitja's left. When Kaitja looked, he saw three rather large bovines near the cliff twenty meters away.

"Cattle herders?" Kaitja said, squinting his eyes. "That can't be right. Somehow they identify with their beasts." Kaitja turned back as the man spoke again. It was just a single word, but the exaggerated shrug conveyed the meanings.

Placing his free hand flat about his eyes, Kaitja pivoted his head. "Searching?"

"Om?" Again the man shrugged.

Lowering the tip of his spear and pinging the head, Kaitja said, "Metal."

The spear point drew a keen look from the man. No metal showed on the man's clothing or accoutrements, giving Kaitja little hope that the man even knew what he was talking about. The tip of the smaller man's spear was a red, sharpened, flint-like material that looked like tool stone to Kaitja. Kaitja pinged the tip of the his spear and then waved his hands at the cliffs behind him. The gesture drew a chuckle.

"No," Atami said.

"Well, at least that word seems to be universal." Kaitja made an exaggerated shrug. Atami pointed toward the cliff the direction he had come. Turning back to the cliff, Kaitja shouted, "I'm going to need the professor."

Even from a distance, Kaitja could see Robterns descend with giddy anticipation. "I hope he doesn't fall," he said to himself but then saw that the rope had been tied around the man's waist and legs.

"Good thinking, Xitano."

"There is another on the cliff with a spear," Rfala said from behind Atami.

"I see. Thin. Maybe this man's son?" Atami squinted for a better look.

"Not a son," Rfala replied in a serious tone.

"A girl? Are you sure?" Atami's head swivelled back to look at him.

"No bulge." Rfala gestured in a curved motion near his waist.

"That would be strange. Maybe they have plenty of women." Atami turned back forward.

"Maybe they could spare a few," one of the warriors behind Atami said, a hopeful lilt in his voice.

Atami scoffed. "I don't think that one would just let a stranger carry her away."

"It might be fun to try," the man replied.

Atami watched the new man descend the cliff. He was older and thinner and did not carry a spear but had something hanging from his belt that looked a little bigger than his hand. "Not a warrior," Atami commented. "Must be an elder."

When the man who called himself Kaitja turned back from talking to those on the cliff to Atami's group, Atami made a 'follow me' gesture with one hand and walked toward their camp in an unhurried manner. He could hear the uncertain steps of his group behind him.

"Where are you going?" Rfala asked. When Atami didn't answer, he added, "Why bring them to camp? They could be dangerous."

"In camp," Atami replied in a calm voice, "there will be even more of us and only one of them who can fight, so I think we will be safe."

"What if the others come down?"

"I think they are scared, plus this man in charge only asked for the one."

"Look! Up on the cliff." Rfala only pointed with a quick jerk of his head. Turning just enough to see, Atami noted the girl with the spear following them along the cliff.

"Keeping their leader in sight. She is loyal."

"They raised the rope too," Rfala added.

"Cautious." Atami could hear the strangers talking behind him. The older man's tone was like a child going to the river to find shiny rocks. The crunch of their shoes, which covered all of their feet and their lower legs almost to the knee, was different from the sandals his men wore. He could also hear the swish of their pants as the legs rubbed together, a new sound. "Do you think the different colours they wear mean something?"

"Different tribes?" Rfala said.

"That would be unusual, maybe bad for us. I noted the two with spears wore similar clothes."

"To show rank or position?"

"Could be. I can't figure out what they are made from."

"There are plants from which you can get fibres that can be woven, such as the reeds in the river, but it would take a river of reeds to create such clothing." Rfala shook his head at the thought.

"Maybe their reeds are bigger."

Their approach to the camp with the strangers had not gone unnoticed. All were there standing and watching. Atami gave them a gesture to stay calm as he walked past them to the cliff side. Continuing until the strangers would have plenty of room for access, he gestured at the stones and said, "Black rock."

"Obsidian," Robterns said without pause.

"So they came here to harvest obsidian for tools, I assume." Kaitja glanced back and forth to see if anything else of interest was nearby.

"Yes. But it's unusual." Robterns put his elbow into his left hand and stroked his five-day old beard with his right hand.

"Sounds practical to me." A small bit of confusion was present in Kaitja's voice.

"No, not that." Robterns waved his hand back and forth in front of him. "The fact that obsidian is here is unusual. From what I have read, obsidian is formed in dormant volcanoes, and if this is a volcano, it is the biggest one I have ever heard of. We couldn't see another mountain range while standing on this cliff or the one previous so we are talking maybe hundreds of kilometres wide. Plus it wouldn't be so flat, more bowl shaped like where the town is." He drew in a deep breath and let it out.

"So what are you saying?"

"It's almost like someone put it here for them to find. Unless the gorge we came through was formed by some geological process that I don't know about, like a river of magma, but that would have to have been thousands of years ago, if not tens of thousands."

Head slowly turning to look at the older man, Kaitja's head tilted and his brows came down. "Are you saying someone designed this planet the way it is?"

"It makes sense." Flipping his hand, Robterns turned to Kaitja. "Nothing we have found on this planet corresponds to what our records say is normal for planets. Look at our valley. Perfect for agriculture but nothing to develop further. If it is a delta, there should be some mineral deposits washed down from the mountains, but there is nothing, not even gold or silver. Then those same mountains are filled with dangers as you ascend that do not exist in the basin, making it appear that someone didn't want you leaving. If we hadn't salvaged the few machines we had, there is no way we could have developed weapons to defeat those dangers. And then you have two jagged rock spines in between these two areas, almost like someone wanted to keep them separate."

"You are just drawing a conclusion that fits what you see without knowing the truth," Kaitja said with a huff.

"A scientist looks at the facts. Our area is humid and rainy, this one is dry and barren. Two totally different environments basically right next to each other? Populated by two totally different sets of human?" The strength and excitement in Robterns' voice rose.

"You sure they are human?"

"Yes, I am. Some native tribe from a thousand years ago or more, but there are too many similarities for them to be different evolved species."

"If they evolved on similar planets, wouldn't they be similar?"

"Not this similar. Change the skin colour and dress one properly, they could walk down the street without drawing notice."

"So where does that leave us?"

"We have to find out more about them."

"You mean go to their village?" Concern started to fill Kaitja's face.

"Yes. They seem friendly. And learning more could tell us about our own past."

The shuffling of feet behind him made Atami aware of people's nervousness as the older stranger's voice got louder and more animated. "Settle down," he said over his shoulder.

"What are they talking about?" Chebucto asked.

"I don't know but I don't think it's about the black rock. They don't seem to have much interest in it." Atami remained in his stance as he watched the strangers.

"Good. That means more for us," Chebucto said.

"Did you see his spear?" Atami asked. "I think it is made from rock better than the black ones."

"Awww," Chebucto said. "So you are hoping to trade with these strangers."

"Why not? If their spear tips are as good as they look, they would be very useful and give us standing with the tribes."

"If they didn't attack us to take them away," Chebucto countered.

"They wouldn't. It's too new, they would be cautious, giving us time to acquire many." Giving those behind him a hard look, Atami turned back to watch the strangers talk.

"We need to take some readings on this side of the range," Robterns was saying.

"You don't have to take them right here, do you?" Kaitja asked.

Laughing, Robterns replied, "We're not looking for obsidian, though it would make nice jewellery. Maybe these people would want to trade."

"The short one was looking at my spearhead. I am sure they

would trade for some of those, but I doubt the city has any extra to trade them."

"That would be counter-productive. We came here looking for iron, not to trade it away. But if there was volcanic activity here, there may be ore. I'll go back and have Tarn bring down the equipment." Robterns turned without waiting for a reply.

"I'll try to tell their man what we are doing." Shaking his head at Robterns, Kaitja walked toward the group of tribesmen that had been watching them. Inhaling deeply, he straightened.

"We," he said, indicating himself, "are going to bring down," he put his hand up and toward the top of the cliff and then down toward the ground, "some people and equipment to look," he bent his head down to look at the ground, "into the ground," he pointed. The man he was talking to turned his head to watch Robterns for a moment, then brought his gaze back and nodded before turning to his own people and talking.

Kaitja left them, following Robterns to the base of the cliff. He did not hear the strangers following him but checked on them once there. The group was in conversation, some smiling and chuckling. He noticed two glanced up and followed their gaze to where Xitano was standing.

"Great," Kaitja said to himself. "Here she draws that kind of attention. I hope that doesn't mean trouble later."

With only modest trepidation, Tarn came down the rope with the survey equipment strapped to his back. "You have to give the boy credit," Kaitja said to Robterns, "he's getting better at rock climbing, though I doubt he has done much before this trip."

"He's a good lad. He doesn't get enough credit back at the academy but he will make a good engineer. Not afraid to take risks, either." Robterns looked up as Tarn made it down the last few feet. "Good job. Set it up over there. Let's see what we have here."

More people came down the rope while Tarn expanded the tripod that held the ground sensor. As fascinating as it was to watch, Kaitja turned to attend to the tribesmen who had followed but kept a respectful distance. The ground sensor held their attention. After a few moments the short leader started a slow walk in their direction.

"We should be able to get a better signal here," Robterns said behind him. "The ground is flatter and there isn't any of that annoying shale that was on the other side, which in itself is strange, but I'm not arguing against it."

When he came close to Kaitja, the short man pointed at the ground sensor. Kaitja pointed at the instrument, then his eyes, and then to the ground. The man gave him a confused look but then his face contorted as if considering the statement. "I know this is probably beyond your comprehension but maybe you will understand once we have a readout."

The ground sensor beeped as it worked, which got the short man's attention. Small red dots raced across the screen, settling into a picture in a gradual manner from top to bottom. It took almost ten minutes for the display to complete. Kaitja joined Robterns, who shook with excitement, at the machine.

"You see! You see!" Robterns pointed at a large display he had unfolded from the bottom of the instrument. "It's huge!"

"What is it?"

"Ore deposit. Massive." Robterns' hands went wide as if he was showing the size of a fish.

"Where?"

"Forty-five meters underground, about a quarter kilometre to the north." Robterns' left arm waved as he talked.

"What kind?"

"I can't be absolutely sure, but whatever kind it is will be useful." Robterns' hands flipped in the air as he talked. "Unless it is radioactive, that is, but there is no indication that it is. We would need to take a sample but we don't have the equipment to drill down that far. It would be quite an enterprise, and a big one at that, but well worth the effort. We just have to get the town council to agree."

"I'll leave that to you." Kaitja looked up into the sky. "Day's been pretty used. We don't have time to make it back to the mountains today."

"We can't leave!" The pivot Robterns made was a blur. "We just discovered another race of humans living on this planet. We need to investigate!"

"We came here to search for metals." Kaitja's voice emphasized every word.

"And if there are any, they would probably know." Robterns' eyebrows went up as if they were smiling.

"Not from the equipment they are carrying," Kaitja countered.

"I doubt they would know how to refine the ore if they found it. To them it might just be shiny rocks. If we can communicate to them what we are looking for, they can tell us where it is." Straightening his back, Robterns added, "And as leader of this expedition, I say we go to their village and find out."

The display brought a huff from Kaitja. "Leader, right."

"You sir, if I need to remind you, are here as scouts and trailbrazers, nothing more." Robterns' chin rotated to the side and up an inch.

"Next time we encounter a mountain cat, I'll be sure he knows who to go talk to." Waving at the machine, Kaitja added, "You've found what you are looking for, what else do you want?"

"If there are ore veins at or much nearer the surface, collecting the ore would be much simpler. And these people do not look like they are capable of mining operations, so any ore they know about will be easy to gather. We at least need to take samples back with us of as many different sources as possible." Turning back to the others, Robterns announced, "Pack it up, Tarn. We're moving."

Shaking his head, Kaitja looked up to the top of the cliff at Xitano. "Leave the rope tied off and bring the rest of the gear down."

"About time," she said back, not loud but loud enough to hear. "I was wondering if you were going to leave me up here."

"You may wish I had later." He took a deep breath that came out as a sigh. "Now to try and convince our new friends to invite us."

"They seem to be excited," Rfala whispered to Atami.

"Yes. Whatever that... thing... is they set on the ground seems to have them excited."

"What do you think it does?"

"I think it looks into the ground."

"What? How?"

"I don't know, but the way they are pointing it would appear so."

"They look for rocks under the ground. How would they get them?" The contortion in Rfala's face could be heard in his words.

"Another thing I don't know, but if they are able to do that, they would be good allies." Atami watched the strangers. "We should take them to our village and make friends with them."

"Do you think that is safe?" Rfala asked in a cautious voice.

"Do you see any weapons on them besides the two spears?"

"No, but if they have things that can look under the ground, who knows what else they have?"

"I wish to find out." Atami had just resettled on both feet in preparation for walking over to the strangers when he noticed the lead stranger coming toward him. He planted himself in a firm but comfortable stance.

The one who called himself Kaitja started talking slow and making motions. One motion clearly mentioned their group, another Atami took for travelling, one for searching, and then there were some that might have been mountains or something with peaks. During the speech Atami tried to associate words with the motions, like 'we' and 'looking' if he was correct. When the man had stopped, Atami made his own speech and gesture.

"You come with us to our village?" He made gestures framing a long house with the last word. To his surprise, the man smiled and nodded right away. Turning his head a little toward Rfala, he asked, "Do you think we were saying the same thing?"

"I don't see any tents on their backs so maybe they are just looking for a place to camp."

The man Kaitja again talked, using 'plemea', the word Atami had used for village, and making jumping motions with his hand.

"Two days," Atami answered, holding up two fingers.

"Do you think he understands 'days'?" Rfala asked.

"We'll find out."

"Some of their people do not look like they are up to a two-day run."

"We might have to let them ride."

"Chebucto won't be happy about that."

"I'll use Obii. He can't complain about me using my own ox."

Part Three
New Beginnings

Chapter One

Robterns stood from the skins where he had been lying on the ground and exercised his sore muscles as far as they would allow. Every motion was accompanied by a groan. As he came forward from bending back, he sniffed his arm. His shoulders gave an involuntary shake as he did. When his eyes opened, he noticed Kaitja coming toward him.

"Must we sleep on these smelly skins?" Robterns asked.

"It would insult our host not to. Besides, you were too tired to set up a tent last night." Kaitja handed him a crude ceramic cup filled with liquid. "Try a little first. I think it is the local version of coffee."

Taking the cup, Robterns took a small sip, made a face, but then finished draining the cup in a slow manner. He gave a sigh when finished. "I've had worse."

"Really? Not sure I want to know." Kaitja chuckled with the statement.

"How long have you been up?"

"Everyone else has been up for at least two hours. Excited to look around, I guess." Kaitja took back the cup.

"Two hours? And you let me sleep?" Indignation crept into Robterns' voice.

"You needed it. There's food in the pot over there if you want to eat." Kaitja's head nodded once to the right.

"Think I would like to catch up with everyone else first." As he moved to his feet, Robterns' hand went to his hip. "Not a smooth ride here for sure. Think I would have rather walked."

"Then it would have taken at least three days instead of two." Kaitja followed Robterns as he left the longhouse.

"I guess these people have no idea what a horse is. Shame." Lifting the covering flap, Robterns walked outside.

"Or they ate them all."

"Ate them?" The jerk of Robterns' head and body to look at Kaitja showed less weariness than professed.

"That is what people back on Earth initially did, so I'm told, before they decided they could be ridden. The beast-master told me."

"Barbarians!" Robterns huffed.

"So was everyone at one time."

Walking into the centre of the village, Robterns did not have much time to look around before being called by Tarn. "Professor! Professor! You have to see this." Tarn waved at Kaitja to join him.

"Let's go see what the boy found," Robterns said after an intake of breath. Kaitja followed, looking around to see if anyone took notice of where they were going. None in the village seemed to care.

Travelling around one of the longhouses to the back, the men were greeted by racks of spears, tramped ground, and targets some ten meters further away. The targets were made of shafts of wood tied together and displayed the dents of spear-point impacts. Robterns gasped as he looked at the targets, walking closer in steps of fascination.

"Do you know what those are?" Robterns asked in a daze.

Walking toward the targets also, Kaitja asked, "Are they actually that size?"

"Yes, they were, at least on Earth." Robterns pointed at one target, then the other. "A *Brontornis*, or similar species, otherwise called a terror bird, and the famed sabre-tooth tiger. Both prehistoric predators. Amazing!"

"Do you think they actually have those... things... here?" Fear filled Tarn's voice.

"Why else use them for targets?" Robterns shrugged while examining the pictures. "The detail! Amazing. Look at the colours of the feathers."

"I've seen some of those on the men around the village." Kaitja ran his fingers over the spear holes near the vital parts of the body. They were deep. "These throws would have definitely done a lot of damage to these creatures, maybe even killed them."

"If these people have to deal with this, they certainly are fearsome warriors. Just standing up to a terror bird was an act of bravery." There was plentiful conviction in Robterns' voice.

"Or getting your head bitten off by one," Tarn commented.

"But that also means there must be other animals to eat, herbivores of some kind." Robterns tapped his chin with his finger. "Meat must make up most of their diet since I have seen few domestic plants. Maybe something we can trade to them."

"Trade?" Turning his head, Kaitja looked confused at the shift in conversation.

"Yes, trade." Robterns' voice got animated. "Not only metal, but can you imagine being able to examine one of these creatures? So many questions that may be answered from Earth history. Or just the chance for people to see something of Earth that we couldn't bring with us, a connection to our previous home."

"That's one connection I only want to see dead," Tarn grumbled.

"Of course, boy, they would be too dangerous alive. At least until we have much more capabilities." Robterns waved the comment over to Tarn with one hand.

"I, for one, am not carrying one of those things over the mountains on our return home. We have enough to carry with all your equipment, not to mention any ore samples." The words were hard and determined from Kaitja's mouth.

"But at least some feathers! It would be a start." Shaking his head back and forth, Robterns smiled. "Besides, wouldn't you like a sabre-tooth tiger pelt for your bed?"

"I am in no hurry." Kaitja glanced behind them. "Someone's coming."

As they made their way back to the spear racks, they were joined by Atami and a smaller, younger native that had not been in the group they first encountered. Atami smiled at them as if in acknowledgement of their recognition of the purpose of the range. Words that were said meant nothing to Kaitja, but the gestures that accompanied them were a clear invitation to test his skill. Nodding, Kaitja moved to the most tramped bit of ground and drew his spear from its back harness. Atami also picked out a spear from the rack. With a bow, Kaitja swept an arm down range, inviting first throw to their host.

With a small shrug, Atami lifted the spear into position, settled, took two steps and launched the spear at the terror bird target. A short flight later, the spear embedded itself into the centre of the chest of the bird and stuck fast.

"Good throw," Kaitja said with a small nod at the smiling man. Raising his spear, Kaitja took one step and made his throw, ending with his back almost parallel to the ground. The spear flew with almost no arc and hit the target with a thud, shaking the target as if to threaten its standing position. Embedded right next to Atami's, the spear point was fully embedded into the target. When Kaitja turned back to Atami, he was greeted with wide eyes and admiration.

"He seems impressed," Robterns said.

"More by the spear than me, I suspect," Kaitja replied.

As he talked, another spear flew past them to their right. The spear embedded itself into the same target in the same location but not as deep. Everyone turned to find Xitano approaching.

"Mine was from farther away," she said in a playful mood. A smile appeared in the blink of an eye on Tarn's face.

"We're not here to show off," Kaitja said.

"Really?" Xitano asked. "I thought we wanted to impress them."

"Then impress them by taking the spears out of the target," Kaitja replied. The command brought a sigh and a look from the top of Xitano's eyes before she proceeded to the target.

Atami was talking again. He pointed at Xitano, then Kaitja, then held his hand flat about chest high while he talked. Turning his head to Robterns, Kaitja asked him a question with his eyes.

"I think he wants to know if she is your daughter," Robterns said, suppressing a laugh.

Turning back to Atami, Kaitja shook his head and said, "No."

Again Atami asked a question but this time he held his hands together on his chest. His eyes, though, made it clear he didn't expect a positive answer.

"I have no idea what that means," Kaitja said, a little frustration in his voice.

"He's asking if I'm your wife," Xitano said, throwing Kaitja his spear.

"You speak their language?" Robterns said in shock.

"Picking up a few words here and there. You just have to listen."

Vigorously shaking his head, Kaitja again told the man, "No." It brought a thoughtful look from Atami, and then a shrug. "My wife," Kaitja said as he turned back to the centre of the village. "Stars forbid." That brought a laugh from Tarn, who received an elbow to the back from Xitano for the response.

"I have to check in with my people, see how much they've learned," Robterns said as he walked with the group.

The statement seemed almost prophetic as they rounded the longhouse, because two of their group, Dalia and Oberns, were walking toward them at a fast pace, excitement in their eyes. When both tried to speak at the same time, Robterns shushed them with his hands and took a breath before saying, "Dalia?"

Through breaths, Dalia talked fast. "The reeds in the river have a starchy root that the people here harvest and eat. There's not enough to be a staple of their diet. But look at this." She held out her clenched hand and then opened it up. Inside was white and brown kernels. "Rice! Or close enough. The woman I talked to made a vague gesture where they gathered them but it has to be along the river somewhere, like a lake. They have baskets of this stuff and more empty."

"Interesting." Robterns picked up a kernel and examined it closely. "Indeed, a variety of wild rice. Maybe there is more food around here than at first we thought."

As Robterns mused, Oberns fidgeted in place. Sighing in annoyance, Robterns looked at the man and said, "Yes?"

In answer, Oberns held out his hand and opened it to reveal a small, shiny nugget. It was quickly snatched by Robterns.

"Where did you get this?" Robterns demanded.

"They find it in the river. They pound it into shapes for jewellery, but they do not value it much," Oberns answered.

"What is it?" Kaitja asked.

"Silver! Do you realize how valuable this would be for those trying to maintain our circuit boards and electronics? We could make new solder! Invaluable!" Robterns' voice was loud with excitement while his hands flailed.

"Calm down, idiot," Kaitja said in a hushed voice. "You'll ruin our negotiating position." That said, he turned to Xitano and winked, smiling.

For a moment Robterns was reproved, but then he recovered when he saw the smile on Kaitja's face. "Kidding aside," he said, "point taken. Still, we need samples to take back with us to test for purity and content."

"Then I guess we better decide what we are going to trade them for these 'trinkets'," Tarn said.

"I don't think that will be hard," Robterns said with a dismissive tone.

"Don't be so sure," Kaitja said. "They aren't as unsophisticated as they seem."

Turning back to Oberns, Robterns said, "Get as many samples as you can without trading something for them. Search the river to see how common they are." Oberns turned back toward the river and left the group. Dalia pocketed the rice.

"Had enough surprises yet?" Kaitja asked Robterns.

"Enough? This is wonderful. I haven't had so many interesting things at once in… ever. We need to have someone stay, live with them. Who knows what we will find." Robterns' energy had not diminished.

"But we are not prepared to do that on this trip." Kaitja's voice was insistent. "No one here has the supplies for such an endeavour and it should be discussed with the council at least."

Robterns' eyes and head rolled up. "The damn council. Why do you want to condemn us to delay after delay?"

As the men argued, Tarn tapped Xitano on the arm and nodded

over his right shoulder. "I think you have admirers."

Sighing, it was Xitano's turn to roll her eyes. "They've been following me all day. You'd think they've never seen a girl before."

"If you would happen to observe, my dear," Tarn said with a smile, "the other girls don't look anything like you. They're not carrying a spear, for one."

"Yes, very domesticated." Scorn lined the comment.

"So you are, what's the word, exotic?"

"And for my punishment I get four little puppies following me around? No thanks."

The group consisted of four young men, all appearing to be in their late teens, but one, Idula, was shorter and younger than the rest. They huddled together, not hiding their glances or their hushed conversation, which became more urgent and was accompanied by shoulder nudges between the boys. After a few moments of this, Idula spoke in a somewhat louder voice with his head held up, turned, and approached Xitano and Tarn. Stopping about a meter from them, he took a sideways stance, put his right foot out pointed forward, his left foot in a bracing position, and held out his hand, palm flat and sideways, his elbow bent below almost in a handshake position. He smiled at Xitano and said a unknown word.

"What's he want? To dance?" Tarn asked.

"I think he wants to wrestle," Xitano replied.

"Why? Wait, I could guess why, though it's hardly appropriate," Tarn mumbled.

"To test my strength, I'm guessing."

Xitano walked forward and put out her right foot. The boy moved his so that they met at the outer edge of the feet, each foot next to each other. Holding out her hand, it was grasped by the boy around the base of the thumb.

"Quo?" the boy said.

"It's your funeral."

Slowly, the force from the boy's hand increased, trying to push Xitano over his extended foot. While he looked a couple of years younger and was several inches shorter, he was strong for his age. It took less than half a minute before each contestant was straining against the other, Xitano making minor adjustments to her stance and arm to resist the increased force. It became clear that she was not going to be able to push the boy over with his greater bulk, firm stance, and greater experience at the game. But she could prevent him from pushing her over by using her longer leverage. Of course, the contest couldn't be left in stalemate.

Once both contestants were straining as hard as possible, Xitano pushed the boy's hand up and over his shoulder. Taking a step forward with the left foot, she pushed his hand past his back, bending it backwards and causing his back to bend. With wide eyes of surprise, both of Idula's feet came off the ground and he crashed onto his back, Xitano letting go as he fell.

A howl of laughter along with pointing fingers came from the three boys watching. One laughed so hard he bent double. Brushing her hands together, Xitano went back to Tarn.

"Was that fair?" he asked.

"He didn't explain the rules so if it wasn't, it's his fault," she said easily. She turned back to see Idula lifting himself from the ground, protesting to the laughing boys. "He's probably saying I cheated but I doubt it will matter when they tell the story."

"He lost to a girl. He'll probably be really embarrassed." Tarn looked at Xitano's eyes, which smouldered. "For his culture, that is."

"He's young," she said with a shrug, "he'll get over it. Besides, the others didn't even try."

That evening at supper, there were multiple discussions happening at the same time among the scientists. Each spoke about their specialty and the things they had learned around the village, none lacking for conversation.

"They sound like a bunch of excited chickens," Xitano muttered.

"What did you expect?" Kaitja asked.

The native closest to them made a questioning look with his face. Xitano looked at him and said, "Cluck, cluck, cluck, cluck," in rapid succession. The man laughed in response.

"You're good at communicating with them," Kaitja said between bites.

"I'm told that there used to be many different languages when we first arrived on this planet," Tarn said, "but they've all been lost but one and aren't spoken by anyone, just appear in some books. I'm afraid we have lost any skill in dealing with other forms of speech. If we do come back, they may ask Xitano here to tag along to interpret."

"So they can all stare at me more?" Xitano shook her head. "No thanks."

"First you get no attention," Kaitja teased, "and now you complain about too much. You're hard to please."

"I get all the attention I want," Xitano said in a flat voice. She didn't look at Tarn, but he smiled.

They were joined by Robterns and Dalia. Neither carried bowls of food but looked too excited to eat. "Dalia was telling me that the villagers kept asking the women something they do not understand."

"They are probably asking which of the men are their husbands," Xitano interjected. "Haven't you noticed that any female more than about fifteen appears to be married off? The braids around their head are a dead giveaway."

"How'd you discover that?" Dalia asked.

"I've had my share of admirers," Xitano said, looking at her food and smirking.

"Really?" Dalia's face changed from surprise to reproved embarrassment in a few seconds.

"I have also counted at least three different strains of females in the camp," Xitano continued. "If you look closely."

"Strains?" Robterns asked.

"Different tribes," Kaitja stated.

"That explains what one was trying to tell me," Dalia said, reanimated. "I think it was a story about going down to a well to get water and being taken by their future husband."

"Mixing the genetic pool between villages." Robterns's head bobbed up and down as he talked. "Smart. Prevent inbreeding. Do you think they steal them?"

"If it is a ritual," Kaitja answered, "then it's probably standard practice between the villages."

"To be whisked away by a total stranger? Eww." Dalia shivered.

"Who says they are strangers? If the villages meet at times during the year for festivals or something, the young people may take a liking to each other and arrange a time to meet." Kaitja continued to eat while discussing the matter.

"Oh! How romantic!" Dalia got misty-eyed and blinked rapidly.

"Assuming the right young man carries you away," Kaitja said without looking at the woman.

"Spoil-sport." Dalia pouted at him.

"Have either of you bothered to notice," Kaitja went on, "about the lack of children around the village? The number is much lower than one would expect."

"So a low birthrate among the villagers," Robterns said in a thoughtful voice.

"Yes. It would explain their preoccupation with the women's marital status."

"What would cause that?" Tarn asked. "The low birth rate, I mean."

"Environmental factors more likely," Robterns replied. "Something in the food source, or just genetics maybe."

"Aren't there some natural poisons that would cause that to occur?" Kaitja asked as if he knew the answer.

"Yes." Robterns nodded. "We better take samples of the water and soil with us to be tested. If someone is going to move into their village, they'd better be prepared."

"That counts me out," Xitano said, placing her bowl on the ground.

"It would take long term exposure," Robterns said with a sigh. "Years. We have nothing to worry about."

"Still," Xitano replied. Her silence was full of meaning.

"If low birth rates are common," Kaitja continued, "then these people will be looking for allies for their village. I have also noticed more women than men of adult age. That has to be dangerous if the other villages are aggressive."

"A dangerous lifestyle?" Robterns asked.

"Or war, or those creatures we saw pictures of, or who knows what. If we could move a few Arms to this village, they could learn from the men here about the surroundings and the nature of the relationship between villages. I find it hard to expect that their chief would object to more armed men."

"The river does appear to be at a high mark," Dalia added. "Don't exclude floods in your reasons."

"Hmm," Robterns mused, hand to chin. "That may be our way in. Of course we would want to send capable people, not new trainees. We could swap them out after a year to report back what they have learned."

"Explaining the arrangement to them would be the hard part." Kaitja went back to his food. Several pairs of eyes turned to Xitano, who must have felt their pressure because she looked up from staring at the ground.

"Hey," she said, her hands coming up in protest. "I don't know that many words. Besides, Kaitja here seems to be able to talk to them pretty well with his gestures."

"Either way," Robterns said, looking away, "it would have to be approved by the council. Not that we have an abundance of weapons. Recent events have made sure of that."

"Priorities," Kaitja muttered. "I know a few that would be more than willing to take a turn out here. Since we don't have much to worry with the Infected anymore, they are looking for a challenge."

"I am sure the council members would be uncomfortable losing anyone at this time." Robterns took up a bowl and played with it. "Plus we don't want them coming here just so they can hunt sabretooth tigers."

"Weak women, and I am talking about the men and women on the council. They act like scared children half the time." Raising the bowl to his lips, Kaitja drank the last of the fluid.

"They remember hard times before you were born," Robterns said, his eyes still downcast.

"With ore discovered in the mountains, we don't need inaction, we need to use the opportunities found. People who stare at the past too long die of inactivity. We need the metals, we need the fresh blood, we need people who will get off their butts and lead." Kaitja's bowl came down with a slam, drawing momentary attention from the villagers and the rest of their party. When nothing else happened, they looked away.

"I agree with you," Robterns said in a low voice. "But getting the people in power out is never easy or swift unless you are going to shed blood and no one will tolerate that."

"There has to be other ways. I have been on the mountain for two decades and nothing has changed in the city in that time."

"Except that more machines are broken and more information is no longer available," Tarn put in with a grumbling voice. "I see more of them go down every year and we have nothing to repair them with. The last may stop working in my lifetime. Where would that leave us?"

"You would have to live on your wits and your charm," Xitano teased while shoulder-bumping him.

"Well then I'm fine, but what about all the other engineers?" Tarn shot back. It brought an exasperated look from Xitano and a tickle to the ribs.

"He's right," Robterns said, sounding depressed. "We lose more every year. We must turn things around fast."

"Then worry about how to change things back home instead of how to get people stationed here." Kaitja found one of the water gourds and took a long drink. "Without that, everything we find here will be meaningless."

"And since when have you been interested in how things in the city are run?" Xitano asked.

"Why do you think I live on the mountain?" Kaitja said with a casual voice. "I'm going to get some sleep."

Chapter Two

"I can't believe we're leaving already." Xitano was standing next to Kaitja, watching the scientists pack their backpacks. "When we first got here I thought Robterns would never leave, and it's only the third day."

"I think he's anxious to get back to the city and ask the council for a real expedition to this village, and maybe the others, though I would hate to assume that the other villages will be as friendly as this one. We haven't even seen any travellers while we were here."

"In three days? You're expecting a lot. We didn't see travellers in my village for weeks at a time." Xitano scanned the area. "What bothers me is I don't see that little pest around."

"The young man you told me about?"

"Yeah. He's never been far away until now. Makes me nervous not to know where he is." Her brow furrowed deep.

Kaitja laughed. "Maybe his chief sent him on an errand so he wouldn't bother you."

"That's the thing. I think he's a favourite of the chief, like a little brother or something, though he lives in a different house. I just hope he doesn't try to give me something dead as a going away present."

"Maybe he will bring you one of those pig-like things they hunt but leave it alive so you can take it home." Kaitja's mouth was almost bursting with laughter while he talked.

"The professor called it a tapir, whatever that is. How would I get it over the mountains, anyway? Did the professor get his samples?"

"A baby one. Yeah, I believe he did." Kaitja shifted his weight to his other foot. "Traded the locals with a couple of cups, two plates, a mirror, and a couple of shirts."

"What he get in return?"

"Rock samples, seeds, an obsidian knife, a pelt, some feathers, and some jewellery."

"So they traded junk for junk." Xitano shook her head.

"I'm sure both sides thought they got a good deal. Oh, and he gave the chief a few rations, including some hardtack."

That caused Xitano to laugh. "Did he tell him to soak it before trying to eat it?"

"I'm sure they'll figure it out."

"Are the scientists going to ride in a sled again? I don't see one." Xitano stretched her neck to look around.

"Nope, we're all walking. I think they want to look for more samples along the way to take back." Kaitja turned to find concern in Xitano's face. "Don't worry, I told them they had to carry whatever they pick up themselves and if it slows us down, it gets tossed."

"Hauling those packs up the cliff will be hard enough as it is," Xitano said with a huff.

"It's going to take us three or four days to walk back. We'll find out what is precious to them and what isn't." The statement was made with firm confidence.

A moan from beyond the village edge was followed by shaking ground as Obii lumbered into the village. Searching, he found Atami, pranced over to him, and bellowed at him. Atami said something to the ox, which was answered in a more insistent bellow.

"That ox is as bad as a dog," Kaitja all but spit out. "What did that guy do, sleep with it when it was little?"

"He might have," Xitano laughed. "Be good at keeping you warm."

"And if he rolled over and flattened you like a pancake?"

Another insistent bellow came from the ox. Atami threw up his hands and petted the beast, who rubbed his nose in Atami's chest.

"Great," Xitano said, "we just acquired a pack animal for the scientists to have carry their stuff. So much for limits."

"Look at it this way. At least they won't be slowing us down as much now." Kaitja turned to find Robterns approaching him. "You ready yet?"

"Once we get the packs on the animal there, we are ready to go. Mighty nice of it to insist on joining us." Robterns' grin was broad.

"I don't think he likes to miss much." Kaitja lifted his pack and swung it onto his back. "We'll go at a fair pace, but we're not stopping for a person who wants to investigate something. Someone gets distracted, they have to make the time. Since you have something to carry your packs, that shouldn't be much of a burden to anyone, but I don't want them wearing themselves out."

"Don't worry," Robterns said with a chuckle, "we have enough to keep us occupied for quite a while. It'll have to be something special to encourage someone to wander off."

"Which can be dangerous here. Remind people of that." Kaitja gave the older man a stern look.

"Will do. The village is only sending three men with us, the chief and two others. They all look capable of protecting us if we stay together."

With the packs rapidly being attached to a rope harness on Obii, Kaitja took a deep breath and said, "Then let's go. We're wasting daylight."

Three days later, the group made the cliffs and the location where they had descended. Even though he had worried about the scientists slowing them down, Kaitja had been surprised that all of the group had managed to keep together. Not that the pace had strained the natives at all, but they had shown patience with the group, enforced by their leader.

Stretching, Kaitja called Xitano over to him. "I will go up the rope first and help the others. Tie their packs to the ropes I throw down. I mean to make them pull their own packs up the cliff. We'll see how many can accomplish that."

"They've been spoiled letting the ox carry them," Xitano all but spit out. "About time they had to do some of the work."

"We have a long way to go still. Don't be bitter yet. Once they are back in the city, you can say whatever you like." Removing a thin rope from his pack, Kaitja tied one end to the top of his pack and looped the other through his belt. Giving the larger rope dangling from the cliff a firm tug, he started his ascent.

While the cliff was steep, it still provided small footholds to assist the experienced climber. "Makes one think this will not be too hard for the others, but one never knows. I hope none panic and forget to climb. I guess we better tie them to the rope in case the worst happens."

Planning on how to get people and goods up the cliff occupied Kaitja's mind while climbing. It was all the more reason that when his head reached the top of the cliff, he was surprised by a small, reddish face that greeted him.

"Ba!" Idula said.

"What the…" Cursing, Kaitja finished bringing his feet onto the top of the cliff, the rope being tied to a peak above where one would stand. "What do you think you are doing here?" he asked the small native.

"Idula fadu." The boy grinned with effort.

"Shit. I have no idea what that means." Leaning over the cliff, Kaitja shouted down, "Hey, Xitano, I found your shadow."

"What?"

With one hand on a rock, Idula leaned over the cliff and waved. "Ba! Idula fadu!"

"What! Stars no!" Xitano cursed under her breath. "Who invited him?"

Atami started to talk in a loud but non-shouting voice. Kaitja assumed he was ordering the boy down since he pointed at the ground, but the boy was having none of it. Finally, Atami threw up his hands and mumbled to himself.

"Guess you won that argument," Kaitja said to the boy, who grinned in response. Taking the rope from Kaitja's belt, Idula started pulling up the pack. "At least he makes himself useful."

Tarn was the first one to follow. He managed to climb the cliff with almost no help. When he made it to the top, Kaitja couldn't help but comment.

"I must say, you are in better shape than when we started this expedition."

"I was always a shape," Tarn said with good nature, "maybe just not the one needed at the moment." Unslinging the three ropes he had bought with him, Tarn led Idula about two meters from Kaitja, threw the ends of the ropes to the ground, and handed the boy one.

Ignoring the other two, Kaitja went back to the job of helping people ascend. Unencumbered, most had little trouble making it up the cliff with his help. The exception was Robterns, who had to be all but lifted up due to his nervousness and tentative motions. When he made it to the top, he had to sit down for a while, holding his head in his hands. "That was nerve-racking," Robterns said. "I don't wish to do that again."

"You were never in any danger," Kaitja said as he watched Xitano climb. Looking up, he waved at Atami and his men watching from below. They waved back, but did not leave until all people and ropes were hauled up to the top. "I wonder if he was expecting that kid to change his mind?"

"We could only hope," Xitano said.

"What's your problem with the kid?" Kaitja asked.

"He talks all the time," Xitano said one word at a time.

"Should give you a good chance to learn their language." Her only response was a stare. He added, "Might as well use the time constructively."

"So when we get back they can ask me to go with them and continue to learn? No thanks." Xitano turned and picked up her pack, descending the other face.

"I don't think she wishes to be a linguist," Robterns said, standing from his rock seat.

"I guess not. You ready?" The question was a mild accusation, missed by Robterns.

"No time like the present," the man responded in a cheery voice.

People, as they and their packs had been brought to the top, had started their descent as soon as possible to make room for the others coming up. Idula, carrying only a water-skin and a small pouch, picked up the pack Robterns headed toward, slung it on his back, and followed the others, giving Robterns a broad smile.

"How very nice of that young man," Robterns said.

"He's just trying to make sure we don't send him home," Kaitja mumbled.

"Why would we send him home? This is a great opportunity to learn about his people and their lands. If was can teach him to speak our language, he will be a wealth of information." Robterns took tentative steps down the curved slope.

Kaitja followed behind. "If he can find the right words to describe what he knows. Since he only knows things in his language, finding them might prove difficult."

"True. Nouns will be easy but verbs and descriptive words will be more difficult. We'll find a way, though. Plus he will be a great asset in convincing the council to send a more permanent expedition." Robterns raised a finger to the air, almost slipping as he did so.

"Just be careful what you feed him. If you didn't notice, the food in the village was pretty plain. It probably won't take too much sugar to make him sick."

"Ah, good point. Much like feeding wild animals hay and oats, I expect. Though, I would think one bout of stomach trouble would teach him."

"Don't count on it. Our beef might even be too rich for him."

"Don't worry, I am sure people will be very interested in keeping him healthy."

"I'm not worried, just suggesting."

"The whole existence of more primitive humans on this planet makes me curious." Some of the tension left Robterns' body as the slope became more gradual. "Our own history is lost for some inexplicable reason, though I am sure there are records somewhere. Why would they erase it? Now these people look to have come from a much older time period, thus all of their stories about their origins, if they exist, are not more than fables now. Most likely not reliable or applicable. But the fact that humans from a different time period co-exist indicates a very interesting idea."

Robterns slid on some rocks but recovered, Kaitja's hand hovering just above his shoulder while he did so. As he withdrew his hand, he said, "I don't see any interesting questions."

"The question is," Robterns said, pointing up, "are there more humans from different time periods residing in different locations on the planet? Imagine a Greek society, or a prehistoric one, or one we don't even know about. That could prove very interesting."

"How would any of those help us?" Kaitja asked.

"Well, we don't know until we visit them, do we? Who knows what they have discovered or developed in their time here?"

"And we probably couldn't talk to them anyway," Kaitja said with a scoff.

"At least we would have a reason to learn," Robterns countered. "What if they have developed the capability to make bronze, or even iron? Trade might be very beneficial."

"In my experience, benefits go mostly one way and less the other." Looking at the base of the peaks, Kaitja could see that some of the group had reached the bottom and waited for the rest. Xitano was already there. "I don't know if you should share your thoughts with the council. It might scare them."

After smacking his lips, Robterns cleared his throat. "You are most likely right. The council is made up of timid nitwits who hate anything new. It's almost like they are hiding something. Do you think they know more about our past than they are saying?"

"Would not surprise me in the least. People like keeping secrets." The ground was now almost flat.

"Do you keep secrets, Kaitja?" Robterns asked in a playful voice.

"No, of course not," Kaitja answered in a flat voice.

"Or so you would say if you did, right?"

Two days later, they stood at the base of the opposite mountain range. The path up the mountain cliff they had used before was obvious, though none of the scientists looked at it with joy.

"We will camp for the night and start the ascent fresh tomorrow," announced Kaitja. Heads nodded all around and Xitano came closer.

"I could take a couple of packs up before dark. It would speed our ascent tomorrow."

"Only those without food in them. And have that boy take a couple up also." He hitched his thumb at Idula.

"Sure. Put him to work. Good idea." Xitano moved to where the packs were being piled. "Hey," she said, giving Idula a shake. "Come with me."

As Xitano sorted through the packs, Kaitja made sure the camp was set correctly and a fire was started. Several of the scientists had learned the skills during their travels, able to do most things required. The men liked starting the campfire, acting like boys in the task. It drew derisive remarks from the women.

First up the mountainside, Xitano made sure the ropes they had left were secure and ready for use the next day. Idula did not use them as he ascended, more interested in the rocks that made up the mountainside. Looking with care at the top before cresting the ridge to make sure they had not been visited by another mountain-cat, Xitano picked a place out of the way to store the packs.

When Idula made the top of the ridge, his eyes went wide when looking at the green plants. Setting his packs down with little thought, he approached the sparse grass and bushes, looking in wonder at their blue-greenery instead of the reddish-brown of his homeland vegetation during half of the year, going so far as to lick the leaves and taste a few.

Laughing at her companion, Xitano slapped his shoulder. "If you think those are something, follow me," she said with a wave.

It only took a few minutes to head high enough to provide a view of the valley below. Idula's intake of breath made his amazement clear.

"Ee verriv!"

"If that means green, yes it is, and all year long." Xitano pointed as she talked. "The river coming in over there spreads out and forms a delta, or it did before we changed some of the flow. Of course we haven't changed all of it yet, but I expect that in another couple hundred years all the land will be tamed, as they say, for farming or whatever we intend. We don't have enough people yet to worry about needing all the land."

It was not clear from Idula's demeanour if he was even listening. Staring as if lost in the scene, he didn't move or form words for several minutes. Pointing, he found his voice.

"Guara omk da?"

"Yes, we have our own cows, but so much more than just them. Sheep, horses, goats, chickens, ducks, geese, pigs, to name a few."

"Huh?"

"Don't worry, you'll see." Turning, Xitano started back to the cliff. "Come on, there'll be plenty of time to explore tomorrow."

When Idula faced her, a hurt expression covered his face. "Idula na ha?" he said, pointing at the ground.

"No." Xitano shook her head. "Cats, wolves, other things that would eat you." She made clawing motions with her hands.

Idula moved his hand to his back, only to find no spear held there. With a sigh that resulted in drooping shoulders, he followed with plodding steps.

"Don't worry," Xitano said with a shake of her head as she once again headed to the cliff. "It will all be here tomorrow."

The next day Idula couldn't get up to the top of the mountain fast enough, even though they made him carry a pack. With the path being easier than the smaller range, Kaitja had no compunction making some the scientists carry the rest of their packs. His assurance that it was only two thousand steps did not seem to make the scientists feel better about the climb. They found Idula examining the leaves he could find, feeling, smelling, and tasting.

"At least there are not poisonous plants this high," Kaitja scoffed as he watched the boy.

"I would hate to lose him before we get to the city," Robterns commented.

"Or someone to carry your pack?" Kaitja replied with some disdain.

"I would carry two packs if that was required to get him to the city," Robterns replied, nose raised in the air, "but since it is not, I find no reason to not have him carry one. Just practical."

Kaitja gave him a stare and a scoff. As he turned he noted Xitano, the last person to ascend, cresting the ridge, Tarn waiting for her and giving her a smile as greeting. She returned the smile, then put on a serious face as she retrieved the ropes from the slope. Tarn stood by, taking a rope as she disconnected it and storing it. She saved the last one for her own pack, throwing it over the top of the pack with practised ease after winding it into a coil. Giving Tarn another smile, they both started toward the rest of the group. Kaitja turned east and walked through the group. Some looked tired but he ignored them.

"Let's go, people. The sooner we are down the mountain, the better."

Taking a place next to Kaitja's side, Idula pranced as they went down a faint trail left from their previous travels. The boy seemed to have no problem following the trail.

"You probably have plenty of experience tracking animals on your plains," Kaitja said, gesturing at the trail.

"Kai!"

"I'll assume that means yes and not trail. You should be walking with Xitano, she would understand you more."

"Xitano." The movement of eyelids up and down accompanied the name.

"She's taken, you know. At least I'm pretty sure, though I have never known a young man not to dream." A chuckle passed through Kaitja's throat. "I can't wait to see your reaction to the girls in the city. Of course they will be more domestic than Xitano, though I am assuming what attracts you to her."

A critter scurried across the ground ahead, causing Idula's head to jerk in its direction. "Om?" the boy asked, pointing.

"Squirrel."

Idula made motions with his fingers toward his mouth, a question in his eyes.

"No, not normally. Not me at least. Very little meat." Kaitja pinched his fingers close together without touching. Idula's only response was to shrug.

As Kaitja walked, he heard grumbling from the scientists behind him. The sun had been high when they made it to the top of the mountain and several hours had passed since then. "I suppose we should stop and let them rest," he said to the boy next to him. "They're probably hungry. How about you?" Idula made no response until Kaitja pointed at him and then rubbed his stomach. Nodding his head with enthusiasm, Idula's eyes went wide and a smile rose on his lips. "Of course," Kaitja said with a chuckle, "boys are always hungry."

Halting in a small clearing was greeted with sighs of relief and people flopping onto the ground. Kaitja made his way to one of the food packs and took out enough for four people. Giving one portion to Idula, he took two to Xitano and Tarn, who were close by.

"Why don't you take point when we restart," he said to Xitano as he handed her the food.

"Why? Wait, that kid has been up there with you, hasn't he? Must have been since he wasn't with me." She shook her head and looked at Kaitja with suspicion. "You're tired of listening to him talk, aren't you? Been asking a lot of questions? Asking what everything is? Tasting every leaf that comes along?"

"That doesn't matter." Kaitja dismissed the questions with a wave. "I need to talk to Robterns. He's got a lot of strange ideas about what we found. I'd like to know how much trouble he's going to cause."

"What's that have to do with us?" While Xitano looked confused, Tarn, behind her, looked concerned.

"You remember the ruckus that last time we were in the city?"

Xitano's eyes narrowed. "I never was sure what it was all about."

He took a quick glance at Tarn, who turned as if to hide from the conversation. "I don't think the council told the people everything they know," he said to Xitano as he watched Tarn sneak off. "Robterns thinks this new information will cause drastic reactions from the council. It has to be connected to what they found in that mass grave."

"Why do you care? You live on the mountain, not in the city." Xitano still looked confused.

"Why do you think I live up on the mountain?"

"Because you wanted to be alone?" The question was a tentative one.

"Because I couldn't stand the politics of the council ruining the city, that's why." Kaitja's lips pressed together as he huffed.

"So you cared too much?"

"It prevented me from bashing their heads together."

The comment brought a laugh from Xitano. "Now that I believe. So what's different now?"

"Now there's an innocent kid in the middle of it and I'm not going to allow them to stick him in a dark hole just to keep it quiet."

"So you think *I* would let them stick him in a dark hole?" The question was asked with some surprise.

"Well, keeping you out of jail is another consideration." He gave the girl a small smile.

"Oh, I see, just looking out for my best interest." The words were said with disbelief.

"You are my apprentice, you know."

"*Was* your apprentice." Xitano emphasized the first word.

"Fine. Understudy. Assistant..."

"If you say minion I will stab you." The look on Xitano's face attested to the truth of the statement.

"Whatever you want to be called. I have to talk to Robterns." That said, Kaitja walked away.

"Wait! I... darn." Xitano kicked the grass.

All of Idula's reactions were small compared to his reaction when he saw a horse. Their friendliness only added to his wide-eyed fascination. He examined the animal as if buying it, from mouth to haunches. He paid particular attention to the mane and tail, admiring the texture of both, laughing when the tail flicked at him. The horse didn't mind the attention.

"Guara?" he asked.

"Horse," Xitano replied. The journey down the mountain had been a long one and darkness was settling in.

"Hooorse," Idula repeated.

"Horse," Xitano said, not prolonging the 'o' sound.

"Horse." Idula grinned.

"We'll ride them tomorrow down the mountain. We've used enough supplies that there should be enough horses for everyone to ride." The statement seemed to mean nothing to the boy but Xitano didn't bother to explain. There were ten tired scientists to deal with. Idula remained with the horses until the food was ready.

Everyone ate, but only Xitano and Kaitja examined the tack right after the meal. Idula went with them and watched, able to saddle a horse on his own after watching the process only a couple of times.

"He seems impressed with the hitches," Xitano said to Kaitja.

"Doesn't surprise me. They had no real metal in the village and the hitches have to be iron, if not steel. Tool stone would never hold up."

"They could have used wood."

"With those huge beasts they used? It would break in no time."

"You'd just have to make it thick."

"Really thick. You realize we have an extra person with us and I doubt the boy will want to walk when everyone else is riding." Kaitja gave her a sideways glance.

"He's not riding with me. I'll ride with Tarn and he can have Tarn's horse."

"Put an inexperienced boy on a horse by himself?" Kaitja huffed. "Fat chance. He needs to ride with someone so we don't end up chasing his horse down the mountain."

"Well, then he can ride with one of the scientists, but not me."

"Fine. Ask around and see who volunteers."

A volunteer was not hard to find. Kaitja made the scientists convert their own backpacks to ones that could be placed on the pack animals. The next morning he didn't help them mount either. Robterns was the only one who had trouble getting on and Tarn went to help him. With the horses following Kaitja's stallion, there was little for the scientists to do but stay in the saddle. With the faster pace, they made the next village by nightfall, a sight welcomed by all. Of course Idula was the centre of people's curiosity, to the thrill of girls and the resentment of the boys. His muscular and mostly bare torso didn't hurt the girls' interest either.

"I think we are going to have to get him some proper clothes before much longer," Robterns mused to Kaitja.

"Someone may have some for sale if you ask," Kaitja said as an off-handed remark. "Start with a parent of one of the girls would be my suggestion."

"Hmm. I'll have to see if we have any money in the group." Robterns patted his pockets as he talked.

They slept in the small town hall, packed from one side to the other. Idula looked confused, his gestures asking about the small size of the building and something else no one could figure out. The scientists seemed happy to be inside for a change. Kaitja and Xitano slept outside to allow more room for the others and, as for Xitano, to avoid Idula and Tarn fighting over sleeping locations. The drama brought chuckles from Kaitja, which brought scowls from Xitano.

The next morning, the whole party seemed chipper. It helped that they slept in later and had an abundant breakfast prepared by the village women. By the time they mounted the horses, most were smiling and eager to get to the city, once again speaking about the trip in an animated fashion.

Robterns joined Kaitja at the head of the column. "Fine day for a ride."

"The weather seems agreeable," Kaitja replied, "though we would have to travel even if it was raining. The village couldn't support your group for long."

Giving the man a pout, Robterns said, "Must you always be negative?"

"Only when the situation calls for it, which happens quite often." Returning a strained smile, Kaitja gave the horse a gentle kick to encourage it to move. Robterns followed and continued to talk.

"Our little friend seems to be taking to horses quickly."

"They did ride their oxen back in their village."

"And the horse is so much easier and more comfortable. Believe me, I know." Robterns adjusted his position in his saddle. "Did you see that they actually stood on their beasts while they were moving?"

"Probably a demonstration of skill by the men. A matter of pride."

Altaterra   181

"And more comfortable than sitting on them, that's for sure. My bottom still hurts just thinking about it." Robterns rubbed his back as far down as he could while seated. "I wonder if there were horses originally on those plains. The pictures we found indicated that they most hunted what appears to be an ancestral form of elk."

"Do you think they hunted their horses to extinction?"

"I find it hard to imagine, but if their ancestors didn't see the utility of the horse, they may have. Or they could have been much smaller and thus less useful."

"I have seen villages use large dogs as pack animals."

"True. If they were smaller, maybe they were easier to hunt."

"Is this what you do all day?" Kaitja asked, turning his head to look at the older man, whose eyes wandered inside their sockets. "Speculate about things you have no way of proving?"

Head turning toward Kaitja, Robterns twisted his mouth. "What else am I to spend my time doing while sitting on a horse that knows his way home?"

"How about something more practical?"

"What do you spend your time thinking about?" Robterns' half-smile and eyes indicated that he thought he had caught Kaitja in a trap.

"Mostly I watch everything for your safety. Doesn't leave much time for idle musing." The ease of that statement deflated Robterns' mood. "I want to know what you are going to do with the boy when we get to the city."

"Him?" Robterns shrugged. "Keep him in the centre. I'm sure we'll have plenty of questions for him as soon as we teach him to speak our language. I've been thinking about who to give that job. We have several teachers that could, though I am not sure whether to use one who does children or who teaches adults because..."

"Send him out to play with kids," Kaitja interrupted.

"Kids?" A small jerk and furrowed brow was Robterns' physical reaction.

"Yeah, little kids. They'll chatter at him all day and enjoy explaining everything to him without judgment. He'll have to learn the language to keep up." Kaitja maintained his eyes forward as he talked.

"Interesting idea." Head bobbing, Robterns mumbled to himself.

By noon, they had made it to the base of the mountains. Idula was an expert at riding the horse by then, always wanting to make it go faster. On the winding mountain trails that was not advisable, but once they reached the plain he looked confused at why it wasn't allowed. The horses did break out into a gallop for a while, which assuaged him some.

"If you put him on a horse by himself, I could take him for a run," Xitano offered in a grumpy voice as she pulled her horse up to Kaitja's. "It would stop him from bugging everyone."

"He'd probably fall off and hurt himself and then we would be in trouble with Robterns," Kaitja replied in a voice her grumpy equal. "Plus it won't go over well with those back in his village."

"How would they know?"

"Who do you think is going to do the translating on the return trip?" He gave her a 'didn't-you-think-of-that' glance.

"I thought they would learn his."

"First he has to learn ours in order to teach someone his, and I don't know if Robterns can restrain himself that long." The comment brought a laugh from Xitano.

"You're probably right there."

As they rode to the city, visible even from this distance, the road improved with every kilometre until it became a proper dirt road instead of a worn path. The organized farm fields did not extend this far but that did not stop a few from setting up homesteads, those who wanted to live far from anyone else. Where there was a homestead, there were cattle or other grazing animals. It was Idula's first look at a domestic cow. He didn't seem impressed, gesturing at how small it was. He did recognize ducks, though not chickens, sheep, or pigs. He also seemed impressed with the variety of crops being grown and wanted to taste them, even the ones that weren't ripe. His face showed amazement at the size of the fields.

"Never seen so much food in one place, I imagine," Robterns commented.

"I didn't see any planted fields around the village," Kaitja said, "so

I expect not."

"It would have been nice to see where they harvest the rice from but I think it was out of season."

"And the villagers have little time to waste on visitors." The statement was said as a flat fact.

"With how close to the edge of disaster they live, I expect not. If we can establish trade with them, though, that should change. Once they are more secure, I am sure we can get more information out of them. Maybe they even know about other, shall we say, settlements?"

Squinting, Kaitja looked at the man. "The way they reacted, I doubt they know of anyone else. The cliff we crossed is not an absolute barrier but with their primitive tools, it's effective enough. I would guess there is a matching set of cliffs on the other side of their basin, to keep them encased or at least encourage it."

"Like a cage?" Eyelids going up, Robterns's voice became more animated. "What an intriguing idea. Almost like what they used to call a zoo."

"A what?"

"A place where they would keep animals so people could see them. That was when people did not live in the wild with the animals. Not only were they there to be seen, but they would also breed and study the animals."

"So we are here to be bred like cattle? I can't believe that. Where are our owners if that is why we are here?" The horse Kaitja was riding side-stepped past a rock, separating the men by another two feet for a while. Robterns brought his horse back closer.

"It's fantastic and of course I can't prove it, but it would be one explanation. As to where our keepers would be, I have no idea. We've had no contact with anyone else for three hundred years until the ones we have just met, and they obviously don't have space travel technology and couldn't have brought us here." As Robterns finished his speech, his eyes brightened. "Do you think that is what the council is nervous about? They know something about those who brought us here and don't want everyone else to know? But why not? What terrible secret could they be hiding?"

"Why would they hide it?" Kaitja's voice remained flat while asking.

"Because it's terrible? I would think that would be obvious." Robterns seemed convinced of his statement.

"That's a self-fulfilling reason. Until you have a real reason, your argument is meaningless." A branch trail appeared to the left but they avoided it.

"So what would *you* suggest?" Robterns' question wasn't a real question, more of a statement intertwined with an accusation.

"Wait for the council's response. It should be an indication of what is going on with them."

"So your advice is sit and wait?" The tone which Robterns' voice went up indicated his surprise.

"I said nothing about sitting. Continue on your path but watch what goes on around you and prepare for the worst."

"I'm not sure that's a great perspective on life." The words were said almost in a grumble.

"It's practical."

"Which is exactly what I would expect you to say."

At that statement, the conversation ended. The two men were left to ride their horses down the trail in silence. The silence did not extend to the rest of the group, which chatted behind them. Bringing up the rear was Xitano and Tarn, who was leading one of the pack horses, engaged in much less conversation than the main group but sharing many more glances at each other.

Chapter Three

"Stars, I'm glad to get rid of them." Xitano stretched as she watched the group of scientists melt into the mass of people moving in the city street. "Three days crossing the countryside with them is at least two days too many."

"One of the company excepted," Kaitja added.

"Even then, one needs a break every so often." Her face got softer. "Though I could have spent a few more days without complaint." Becoming almost joyful, she added, "At least we're free of that kid."

"I don't know, I think he was starting to grow on me." Straightening, Kaitja let a smile grow on his face as he turned to Xitano. He was met with a scowl.

"Don't even joke about that."

"Who says I'm joking?"

"Well, if you want him for your next apprentice, I'm going to find a new assignment before then." A smile returned to her face. "Maybe somewhere closer to the city."

Both Arms stood for a while watching the activity around them. It didn't take too long for Xitano to turn to Kaitja. "Are we waiting for someone?"

"Nope."

"Then why are we just standing here?"

"We need to report in to headquarters."

"Did they move or are they coming to us?" The question was

asked as if by someone who knows the answer.

"They're not open at the moment so there's no hurry." In a relaxed position, Kaitja made no effort to encourage movement through the throng. The throng didn't complain.

"Well, if we have time, how about we get something to eat?"

"You ate a couple of hours ago."

"I'm talking real food, like a bakery. I could go for some of those sticky roll things." Xitano licked her lips as she looked around.

"You mean the ones covered in honey? The ones you ate like six of last time?"

"Yeah, those. Where's a bakery around here?" Straining her neck, Xitano looked around.

Laughing and shaking his head, Kaitja straightened up and shifted the pack on his shoulders. "This way, oh hungry one."

The smell of the hot bread was found before the bakery was in sight. The horde of people waiting to get in didn't help one see the establishment but was a clear indicator if you knew what to look for. They also did not deter Xitano from waiting her turn.

"They're moving quickly," she kept saying. Kaitja wondered if it was also a suggestion to the crowd.

Amazed that there were any left, Kaitja paid for eight sticky-rolls, as they were called. He ate two of them while Xitano ate six. Just watching her wolf them down was entertaining. He left her alone until she was licking her fingers of residual honey.

"Sure you've had enough?" he asked. "Going to make it to your next meal?"

"I think I will make it, but why take the chance." Xitano's eyelids flashed up and down once. "Especially when there are sticky-rolls."

"Well, if you are done, we have people to see." Standing, Kaitja gathered his things and left, not waiting to see if Xitano was prepared. She made it to the door at the same time, still wiping one hand on her pants as if the last of the honey would not come off.

The streets were more crowded with every minute. Street-panderers announced their wares, some in plain speech and some in elaborate descriptions that stretched the truth. A few used poetry with simple rhyme and plain words. The most popular were the ones selling hot liquid, for which one had to bring their own cup. Because it wasn't raining, cloth and clothing sellers brought their goods just outside their shops or removed the covers from their wagons. Of course fresh vegetables, fruit, and meat from the countryside were there, central features of wide intersections, but also from the backs of women and boys. One man had six dogs, all black with white patches on their chests, sitting in steady form as the people walked by.

"A dog could be a handy thing to have around," Xitano said as they passed the animals.

"No thanks." Kaitja's words had the tone of finality to them.

"Why not?"

"Just another thing I'd have to take care of." Even in the flow of people going the direction he intended, Kaitja had to dodge those passing across the road or pass those moving slower due to loads or age.

"What if I took care of it?"

"His food comes out of your portion."

"You're *so* generous." Turning her head to take in the sounds, Xitano frowned. "Sure are a lot of people selling vegetables here."

"The fall crops are in. You know, potatoes, onions, squash, pumpkins. People are buying to preserve over the winter, especially cabbage." Kaitja dodged a horse-drawn cart.

"Cabbage?" Xitano's turn came to dodge the cart. "How do you preserve cabbage?"

"Pickle it. People take a lot of pride in their pickled cabbage. Some versions have quite a lot of flavour."

"I don't understand why they let these sellers roam the streets. We had regular market days and locations."

"They tried that." Kaitja shoved an over-eager street-seller out of the way. "People complained the markets were too far away. Most of these street-sellers have a regular circuit and even regular houses they stop at every trip. People like the convenience."

"I bet." Xitano turned away a lady holding up fabric. "Anything to make life easier."

"Maybe people get tired of barley and potatoes." Laughing at his own joke, Kaitja tipped his head to an older lady, letting her pass in front of him.

"Maybe they're spoiled." Xitano's voice was a grumbled complaint.

"That too."

The Arm headquarters already had traffic flowing in and out the front door, some uniformed but most not. Bypassing the front counter after entering, Kaitja gave a nod to the man guarding the door to the working area as he opened it. Inside was as much activity as outside the door. Some Arms even carried fighting sticks.

"Seems like something is going on," Xitano commented while standing next to Kaitja just inside the door.

"Sure we'll find out."

Kaitja led them to a desk in the back, stopped, and performed a smart salute to the man standing behind it, shuffling small papers in his hands.

"Good, you're back." Level One Commander Keras glanced up before looking back at the papers. "Things are going to hell in a handbasket here."

"What's going on?" Concern filled Kaitja's face, though it was ignored by Keras.

Keras put the papers down. "Rumours have been flying. People are getting worked up thinking the council is hiding something. Exactly what, no one seems to know, but they are sure they are hiding something about the mass grave outside of town."

"They didn't buy the council's explanation that it was just an old grave created during a disease outbreak? Imagine." Shaking his head, Kaitja added a smirk. "Do you have any more information about the grave?"

"No official information. The scientists have dated the grave to some two-hundred and fifty years ago, roughly. Far older than we have records for, so there is no way to know who they were. And the council isn't releasing anything about those symbols we found in the grave."

"What about the scientists?"

"Three circles inside of each other? Too many ideas and no real answers, just like them."

As Keras paced behind his desk, Kaitja rubbed his chin with his right hand. Xitano sat in one of the chairs and leaned her head against the wall. It drew a disapproving stare from Keras but she ignored it.

"I forgot to ask," Keras said, changing his mood. "How was your survey?"

"We brought back someone." Kaitja's tone was flat.

"I hope you brought back all of them," Keras said with a chuckle.

"I mean an extra person."

Turning on his heel in a swift motion, Keras's brow furrowed. "From the village?"

"From beyond the mountain." The ease with which Kaitja said the words contrasted with Keras's surprise.

"Beyond the mountain? People who broke off years ago?"

"We found a primitive tribe. Human, but far older than our colony and still dependent on stone instead of metal. Hunters mostly. We brought one back with us. Kind of forced to since he wouldn't go home. A boy, I would say late teens. The scientists have him." Kaitja rattled off the facts as if giving a report.

"No! But... Stars, the council will have a fit about this. This will upset things even more than they already are." Resuming his pacing, Keras shook his head with vigour. "This... this... Stars, I don't know what this is going to set off. This place is a pile of powder waiting for a spark and you just might have delivered it."

"The scientists won't let the council have the boy. They mean to teach him our language so they can ask him about the plains beyond the mountain. Oh, we also found metal ores. Iron in the mountain along with traces of some others Robterns can tell you about. But there is one thing you might really need to know." Kaitja took a breath as if to brace himself.

"Old gods, there's more?" Keras seemed to deflate.

"They found silver in the river the tribe lived next to."

"Great! Just what we need. Someone to yell 'treasure' all over town."

"Don't worry, it's not an easy trek and they found nuggets in the river, not hoards of it. Plus it needs to be refined. The scientists want it for solder. I doubt it will be worth someone else making the trip." The reassurance in Kaitja's voice appeared to have no effect.

"You don't know people as well as you think, my friend." Keras waved his finger at Kaitja. "They get a whiff of silver and you'll have young men running off into the mountains looking for it."

"Not to mention the farmers in the hills," Xitano said from her chair, one foot pulled up and hidden below her other knee, arms wrapped around her leg. "They get a hint that there is easy money to be made, they'll be scouring those plains looking for their fortune as a way to leave the hills and live easy in the city. That's what they'll think anyway."

"That's the last thing we need." Keras nodded his head at the girl. "A bunch of idiots seeking their fortune and getting killed in the process."

"Kind of eliminates the problem of the idiots, doesn't it?" A chuckle accompanied Kaitja's words.

"Except their relatives will be hollering for us to do something about it." Keras's arms went up in the air.

"We just tell them everyone takes their own risks, as they are legally allowed to do."

"Doesn't mean people won't scream about it when the natives start killing their relatives," Keras said in a huff.

"It's the sabre-tooth tigers and terror birds they need to be worried about, from our experience." Xitano had a chuckle of her own.

"The what?" Keras's face stretched itself as high as possible.

"The professor called them prehistoric creatures. Large cats with larger than normal teeth and huge, meat-eating birds, not to mention anything we weren't told about." Kaitja's head tilted forward. "It's not a safe place to go treasure hunting."

"Stars," was Keras's response as he turned away, head and hands seeking a place to stop.

"Look." Kaitja took a step toward Keras. "That's in the future. Right now we're about to have an explosion when the council finds out about the boy. That's what we need to worry about right now."

He bounced his finger on the desk. "Unless you're going to tell me to do something else, I'm going down to the Hall of Science to try and keep things civil, or something like it. And I'm taking Xitano with me."

"Hey!" Sitting straight up, Xitano's head did a swift swivel. "Do I get a say in this?"

"You're still under my direction," Kaitja said with a nod toward Keras, "unless he says so."

Keras's hand waved at the other two. "Take her. I have enough guys, for now." The look he gave Kaitja said that things could change at any time.

"Then you will know where to find us." Without signalling to Xitano, Kaitja turned and left the room. Grabbing her things and falling in step behind him, Xitano let him create a path for the trek through the room.

"I don't mind going to the Hall of Science, but I'm not babysitting that kid." Xitano matched her steps to Kaitja's to remain as close as possible.

"I doubt you will need to." After a short pause and in a more cheerful voice, he added, "I'm sure there is someone else you would rather spend your time with anyway."

"Just about anyone," came the grumbled reply, "except maybe Robterns."

"That, I am sure, will also not be a problem, at least until trouble starts. If it hasn't already."

Halfway to the science hall, they noticed whispered conversations in the streets. The conversations grew louder and more involved as they neared the hall. Shaking his head, Kaitja tried to ignore them.

"Not hard to guess what the topic of conversation is," Xitano said as they walked side-by-side.

"No, and not unexpected."

As the hall loomed ahead of them, a crowd was seen in front of the building. Not pressing to get inside, they did peer through the windows often and examine anyone who went into or out of the building. When he reached the doors, Kaitja turned around to the crowd.

"Don't you have anything better to do?" He made his voice loud enough for all to hear. Some returned indignant looks, others dared not to look at him. After a few seconds, most started to wander off in all directions, but not the ones with stubborn looks on their faces. With no further address in word or expression to the crowd, Kaitja turned back to the doors and went inside, Xitano in tow.

Inside the building was even more hectic than at Arm headquarters. Many had not even bothered to put on the white long-coats that were the trademark of the scientists. As the two Arms stood and watched, the scientists didn't appear to be accomplishing much or know what they were doing, confused faces being common. Frequent collisions happened in the hallways.

"This has really thrown them for an end-over, hasn't it?" Kaitja said without looking at Xitano.

"Not sure why. They're supposed to be all about the unknown, right?" she replied.

"You remember how confused Robterns seemed at times. Guess it's the same for everyone else."

"Pitiful."

"You're not wrong. Let's take up station over there, out of the way but near the entrance."

Waiting was not an uncommon activity for an Arm, and their surroundings were more entertaining than many instances. Everyone accepted the presence of security in the building without asking questions, though one lady did ask them if they needed anything in a polite voice.

It took a couple of hours but Xitano started to fidget. When Kaitja gave her a look, she responded, "Are we going to have lunch?"

"Hungry already?"

"Standing around doing nothing makes me hungry," she said in a firm voice.

"I thought doing something made you hungry?"

"That too."

"Did you bring anything?"

"Travel rations?" Her face cringed as if hurt. "When we're in town with all the great food vendors around? You would really make me eat travel rations?"

"Did you bring money?"

"You're the one in charge. That's your department." She huffed at the end of the statement.

Rolling his eyes, Kaitja dug his hand into his pocket and extracted a few small bills. Handing them to Xitano, he instructed, "Get something we don't have to look at to eat, like a sandwich. I don't want to miss something because I have to stare at my food."

"What about me?"

"Same goes."

"Spoil-sport." Her head tilted downward, Xitano exited the building, slipping into a crowd of people going her intended direction. Kaitja laughed at her as she did. She returned after a short while with sandwiches for both of them. Tasting ham as he bit into his, Kaitja smelled something else from Xitano's.

"You got yours hot?" he asked without changing his gaze.

"Why not?"

"But mine is cold." It was almost an accusation.

"You only gave me so much money." An unnoticed shrug went with the comment.

"You couldn't have gotten me something with more flavor?"

"You only gave me so much money." The comment brought a laugh from Kaitja.

Well after the sandwiches had been consumed, a different crowd gathered outside, drawing Kaitja's full attention. The people in the crowd were better dressed than the previous ones and appeared to be waiting for someone or something to happen. Pushing off from the wall, Kaitja walked to the door in a deliberate slow motion, standing just inside at the intersection of the two main doors. As someone pushed their way through the crowd, he exited the building. Head Councilman Noisa made his way to the front of the crowd, flanked by two Arms. Kaitja took a stance in front of the doors.

"Remove yourself," Noisa said with a wave. "We have business here."

"I have been assigned to this building." Kaitja's voice held no emotion. "What business do you have here?"

"We have come for the boy. These men will retrieve him from this building." Noisa made shooing motions with his hands, causing the Arms to step forward.

"And what crime has the boy committed?" Kaitja asked.

The question caused the men to stop, their heads turning toward Noisa. Without blinking, Noisa stood stiff-necked. "That is none of your concern."

"As an Arm of the Law, yes, it is my concern and should be these gentlemen's concern also. No one may be arrested without a formal charge of a crime." Arms crossed, feet shoulder-width apart, Kaitja made no move.

"I never said he was under arrest." Noisa's tone became defiant.

"Then you won't need Arms to retrieve the boy." Kaitja's eyes shifted to the Arms. "You need to think very clearly what this man is asking you to do."

"Get out of the way!" Noisa shouted at Kaitja. "This is none of your business."

"Any illegal action is my business and until I am satisfied that no illegal acts are being committed, I will stand right here." The sound of the door opening was followed by soft steps and the hint of a spicy sandwich residue.

"What is the charge against the boy?" one of the Arms asked Noisa.

"Disturbing the peace," Noisa shot back. "Just look around at the disturbance he has caused."

"I don't see the boy out here," Kaitja interjected. "I don't hear him shouting from a window. How is he disturbing the peace? And where is the warrant?"

"You don't need a warrant if a crime is being committed," Noisa shot back.

Turning his head to scan the scene, Kaitja looked back to the councilman. "The only one I see disturbing the peace here is you."

Head drawn back, Noisa didn't manage a reply, only several huffs from his nose. His feet changed position as he huffed as if not knowing where to go. Looking at each Arm in turn, he pumped his shoulders. "You'll regret this. The council will not be disobeyed!

There will be consequences." His speech done, Noisa turned and made his way back through the crowd, which turned to follow him. The Arms stayed. When the crowd had left, they turned to Kaitja.

"He didn't tell us what he wanted us for," one said.

"Things are becoming heated." Kaitja stared at each in turn. "You may have to choose a side. Choose wisely."

The comment caused the other to laugh. "Choose Noisa? Why?"

"He does lead the council," Kaitja said with ease.

"Not all of it," the man replied. "You've been away. Some on the council are getting nervous. Noisa is losing support, slow but losing it. They're afraid of the people."

"What have you heard?" Kaitja asked.

"Nothing official, of course, but it has to do with the grave they found." The man looked around to see if anyone was listening to them and continued when he was satisfied they weren't. "Rumour is that the people in the grave were part of some old cult but no one seems to know which one. The fact that they were religious is disturbing enough, and the fact that they were part of one we don't know about is even more. People think there was some kind of conflict between two groups, and wonder if it wasn't the cause of the loss of life after the colony was established, instead of the plague we are told about."

"Sounds like pure speculation." Kaitja's voice conveyed his lack of confidence in the information.

"With the council not sharing information, everything is." The man looked around. "I better tell headquarters what is going on here, see if they want to do anything about it."

"Good idea." Turning to the other man, Kaitja asked, "You?"

"Noisa will be back. I better stay."

"Welcome and appreciated." Grasping the man's right shoulder with his right hand, Kaitja received the same gesture from him. "Outside or in?"

"I'll take the outside. Would rather be in the sun." He gave a weak smile.

"We'll be right inside the door if needed."

Nods exchanged, Kaitja moved back inside to their place along the wall. With nothing better to do, Xitano followed. "You know those guys?" she asked once inside.

"Not personally but by reputation," was the reply.

"So you weren't worried about them attacking us?"

"I didn't say that. They've worked for the council for a long time. Who knows for sure."

"How good are they?"

"The best."

Huffing, Xitano shook her head. "So we would have gotten our butts kicked."

"They wouldn't have tried to do any permanent harm." Kaitja's voice did not convey concern.

"Being with you is getting more dangerous all the time."

"At least they aren't sabre-tooth tigers."

"I might prefer the tigers."

In time, people went back to their routines. Just about the time things had settled back to normal, a whistle came from outside. Jerking alert, Kaitja hurried outside to find a small crowd led by Noisa walking toward the building with purposeful steps. He and the other Arm took up positions in front of the two doors. As he drew close, Noisa held up a folded piece of paper, almost shoving it up Kaitja's nose when he got close enough.

"I have a warrant here for custody of the boy," Noisa all but shouted.

With slow motions, Kaitja took the document, opened it, and read it as Noisa waited, shifting from one foot to the other. "There's no seal of the court," Kaitja said, crumpling the paper.

"It's signed by a judge," Noisa said with indignation.

"But without a seal it is a worthless document." Kaitja looked at the man with hard eyes. "Of course, if it had been sealed, it would have become a permanent document in the records, subject to later review. Since it is only signed, it was not entered into the record." He let the statement hang like an accusation.

"The judge says you must give me the boy!" Spit came from Noisa's mouth as he shouted.

"Your paper is worthless. Be on your way."

Altaterra 197

Face turning red, Noisa expelled a loud huff. Body shaking, he turned and stomped back the way he had come. As he did, the crowd that had formed cheered his departure, bringing more shaking to his shoulders. The cheering continued after he was gone from the scene.

"Sloppy of him." The other Arm's words came out without real confidence of their accuracy.

"He doesn't want any record that the boy was ever here, or to be investigated in the event of his disappearance."

"Do you think he would go that far?"

"Yes." The flatness of the statement emphasized its conviction.

"It has to have something to do with the mass grave then."

"It has to do with the accuracy of the story we have been told of why we are here. The existence of more primitive humans that have been here for much longer raises questions of how we got here and why we are here."

"So we are not a colony from the original Earth that has been forgotten for some reason?"

"I don't know. If that is so, how did the others get here? There is no way they developed space travel in their time."

"Maybe they were sent here so they could preserve their way of life."

"Thousands of years ago? Then how did Earth lose touch with us?"

"Maybe our ancestors were exiles? War? Collapse?"

"All possible but not what we have been told. And if Noisa is so keen to keep it quiet, it can't be that simple."

"True."

Hours passed. Nothing happened. As evening wore on, Xitano came out of the building to stand next to Kaitja. "Supper?"

"Try headquarters," was Kaitja's reply.

"You staying here?"

"Yep."

"Want me to bring you something?"

"I'll be fine. I have travel rations."

With a small shiver, Xitano turned to leave. "Have fun."

The buildings made long shadows in the road as Xitano made her casual stroll toward headquarters. The merchants were making their last appeals to passersby and it was too tempting not to at least look at their wares. So many things were not found in her home village and the array of colours were fascinating. Some items she had no idea what their purpose was, but they were bright and cheerful and brought a smile to her face. Some small, globe-shaped pottery caught her eyes. It had a small hole at the top. "Maybe to set flowers in?" she asked herself.

Absorbed in the pots, she did not take notice of the steps behind her. A soft, man's voice said, "Excuse me, miss," right before a sharp point pinched her flesh. Turning quickly, she had time to see the man's face before her eyes started to make the world swim around her.

"You don't look well," the man said. "Maybe I should take you somewhere you can lie down."

Wanting to resist the clamp of his hands brought no response from Xitano's limbs as her head lolled back. The world melted from shadows to darkness.

Chapter Four

It was around midnight when Kaitja was informed that there was someone asking for him at the back entrance of the Arm headquarters. It was rare that visitors at the back entrance brought good news unless they were informants, and he hadn't been back in the city long enough to re-establish any in his mind. Rolling off his bunk and putting on his boots, Kaitja did not hurry to the meeting. The man who was waiting for him occupied one of the shadows, of which there were enough that it made one wonder if the building had been designed that way on purpose. It wasn't until he got close that he recognized Chief Councilman Noisa.

"What could you want?" he asked the councilman.

"I am here to affect a trade." The man's voice was calm, too calm.

"You have nothing I want." He was about to leave when Noisa continued.

"What about your apprentice?"

Before Noisa could blink, Kaitja's hand shot out and grabbed his jacket and pulled the smaller man's face within inches of his. "What have you done?"

"I have done nothing, but seen things." Noisa's voice was still without fear. "I know who has her and I know they will trade her for the boy."

"And you expect me to believe you had nothing to do with this?" Kaitja's face took on the look of an angered mountain cat.

"I only admit to knowing things."

"I could arrest you for assisting in a crime. Where is she?"

"And then she would sit where she is and maybe starve to death. Besides, telling you would be cheating. We can't make this too easy, can we?"

"She must have put up a fight. How bad off is she?"

"She didn't put up any fight at all." Noisa gave the other man a broad smile. Kaitja examined his face for a moment.

"You drugged her. Cowards." Kaitja all but spat.

"This way she is unharmed and secure. Now, about the trade. First thing in the morning?" The smile continued.

Letting the man go, Kaitja shook his head. "I don't even know where the boy is or how secure they are keeping him, or if they will even let me see him. Plus I would have to create an excuse for him to come with me. If I was going to do the trade, that is. Just because you are eager for something to happen doesn't mean it's possible."

"Just take him." Noisa shrugged.

With a single laugh, Kaitja said, "You haven't met him. He's a born hunter with all the energy of youth. And he's not stupid. Give me time to think about it."

"The more time you take, the more time your apprentice sits tied to a chair. But, if that's what you want..." Turning, Noisa waved to Kaitja as he walked away. "Take all the time you want."

Kaitja watched the man leave, not huffing until the man was around the corner. "The time's not for me, you idiot. You think I taught my apprentice nothing?"

Consciousness came like a slap in the face. Eye focus was slower to arrive, requiring more effort on Xitano's part. The first surprise was that she was sitting up. The second was that her hands were tied behind her back.

"What the..." She stopped talking when she heard someone approaching. The footsteps were followed by the sound of a door opening. In the darkness she couldn't see the door or the person who came through it and stopped just outside of the tiny circle of light given by the small lantern. Feeling with her fingers, she could tell that the knot of the rope had been placed where she could not reach it.

"Don't waste your time struggling with the ropes," a man's voice said. "I know how to tie knots."

"You're in a lot of trouble," was Xitano's reply.

"We'll see who's in trouble," the man huffed.

"What do you want?"

"We want nothing from you. You better hope your boss is reasonable or you may rot down here." The laugh from the man sounded as if he found the possibility amusing.

"Fat chance."

"We'll see." Sounds of the man walking away and exiting the room followed.

"Ouch!" came from Xitano in a sharp voice.

"Told you I knew how to do knots," the man said as he closed the door behind him.

At the sound of the door closing, Xitano slipped her hand from the cords. "Damn if that doesn't hurt every time still."

Pushing his way through several people, Kaitja stood in front of Keras's desk, interrupting whatever Keras had been saying without caring.

"What now?" Keras asked.

"Noisa kidnapped Xitano, wants to trade her for the boy." While the words held no emotion, they came out with force.

"We need to find out where he is holding her." Keras raised his hand to snap his fingers.

"Unnecessary," shot out from Kaitja's lips.

Keras's face distorted. "You already know?"

"I taught her well." Kaitja shifted his weight. "I'm not worried about finding her, she'll get out on her own. We need to move on Noisa when she shows up."

"You're sure?"

"Yes and yes. I don't want to give that slug any manoeuvring room before we arrest him."

Keras gave his head a tight shake, trying to keep up with the conversation. "Do you have any proof he's involved?"

"He's the one who told me they have her, which makes him an accomplice if nothing else. Though I would bet the guys doing his dirty work will more than willingly give him up once Xitano is done with them." Kaitja looked around the rooms. "Any volunteers?"

"That's my department," Keras said, pointing. "When do you expect to hear from her?"

"Just about any time now."

"I got a plate of food here for you," came the man's voice from the other side of the door as he opened it, "but I ain't feeding ya so I guess you'll have to stick your face in it if you want to eat."

As the man walked into the room, the end of a wooden pole struck him in the stomach and up into his diaphragm. Bending double and dropping the plate, he received another blow to the back of the head. At least in his unconscious state he didn't notice his nose bleeding from contact with the floor.

"Eat it yourself, idiot," came a soft, female-voiced reply.

Making her way out the door with caution, Xitano noted one other man who was turning toward the room. His head was tilted to one side.

"You drop the plate again?" the man said as he walked toward the room.

With darkness all around, it was easy for Xitano to move clear of the door without being seen. Waiting for the man to approach, she gave him an uppercut to the jaw with the pole, followed by a strike to the back of the knee and one more to the stomach after he had fallen backwards to the ground.

"Guess you guys thought this would be an easy job," she said as she walked over the groaning man toward the stairs. The stairs led to a hallway with a door not a meter away. Opening the door led to the outside. She did not recognize the neighbourhood but it was one of the better business districts in the city. Only a few people were milling around and no one looked at her.

"Hey! Hey!" Even shouting at them, people gave her a quick glance and a glare before moving on. "Assholes," Xitano muttered as she picked up a rock that was part of the flower garden just outside the door. Taking aim, she threw the rock through the large window across the street. That drew people's attention.

"Call the Arms," Xitano commanded them as she went back into the building.

Kaitja had just finished strapping on the last piece of hardened leather to his body when Xitano walked into the room. She didn't look flushed but rubbed her left hand with her right. Grinning, Kaitja nodded his head.

"About time you showed up."

"Thanks for the rescue," she shot back in a sour voice.

"It appears you didn't need one, just like I taught you." Pulling on his vest, Kaitja shifted inside of it for the most comfortable fit.

"And you had every confidence in that. Not sure if that's a compliment or something else." She gave him a sideways glare.

"Compliment, of course. You coming with us to arrest Noisa?"

"Can I tie the ropes on his hands?" The first spark of joy showed in her face.

"Why not. Let's go."

Outside the room a group of eight Arms waited, six men and two women, all hand-picked by Kaitja. From the look in his eyes Keras was dying to come, but it was Kaitja's operation and Keras would have out-ranked him, so he stayed. All were dressed in the anticipation of combat and carried either short spears or fighting sticks, except for Orlan, who had repeatedly voiced that using weapons was unnecessary. For him, they were.

"Do I gear up?" Xitano asked, surveying the group.

"No time." With a small nod to the group, Kaitja led the way out the rear of the building. "You should have been here sooner."

"Thanks a lot," Xitano grumbled. "I had to wait for someone to take the prisoners. Not like I wanted them disappearing on us."

Taking alleys and back streets, Kaitja made his way to the town hall. The Arms spread out so that no one saw all of them at the same time when they crossed a street or alley. All eyes looked for anyone following or taking too much interest. None were found but they stayed vigilant.

Upon reaching city hall, the group gathered together and entered as a compact group, Kaitja in the front. A man at a desk four meters into the building took notice of them with alarm, stood up, and held up his hand. "You can't come in here."

"We are exercising the law, we can go anywhere we need." Ignoring the man, Kaitja led the group up a curved stairway to a hall decorated with pillars and scrollwork at the corners of the ceiling, and pictures of past legislators of note. Long, quick strides took Kaitja to the office at the end of the hall. Pushing open the double door, he varied his path to bypass the desk inside the door as he made his way to the large wooden door on the other side of the room.

"He's in a meeting..." the lady behind the desk started in a panic, but none listened.

Pushing the door open resulted in a crash from hitting the wall. Kaitja found Noisa behind his desk. No one else was in the room. Papers and a redwood pen were scattered on the desk, just dropped from Noisa's hands. Noisa looked surprised.

"You can't come in here like that," he said, trying to gather confidence by the tone of his voice.

"I am an Arm of the Law and I go where my duty takes me. City Councilman Noisa, you are under arrest for kidnapping." Standing as tall as possible with his chin elevated a centimetre, Kaitja's eyes gleamed at the councilman.

"You can't arrest me!" Noisa protested.

"I can arrest anyone who breaks the law, no matter who they are. All are equal under the law."

"You have no proof!" Confidence returning, Noisa also stood up as tall as possible with his chin elevated higher.

"Am I proof enough for you?" Xitano asked as she made her way through the group, rope in hand. "Not to mention those stooges who you left to hold me that are talking like little girls now."

Eyes wide open, Noisa huffed at Xitano several times before

looking past the group. "Defend me!"

The group of Arms turned to find guards flowing into the room. They carried short, small-headed maces made of a soft wood that could injure or knock out a person. They were the council guards, loyal only to the council. As they entered the room, they were met by the staffs and sticks of the Arms. All except Xitano, who jumped the desk in pursuit of the fleeing Noisa.

The guards entered the room one at a time but paused, maybe to gather strength or maybe to take note of the situation. The Arms demanded that they drop their weapons as soon as they were in the room. This didn't happen, even when faced with six Arms with weapons. Once a small group had been established in the room, they attacked. The sound of wood hitting wood in irregular beats filled the room. Because of their shorter weapons, the guards tried to get as close to the Arms as possible, but this meant they had to come within range of the Arms' weapons for at least a few seconds, seconds the Arms did not waste. The Arms did not waste their efforts on swings but poked at the oncoming guards in the face and the gut. The guards tried to knock the Arms' weapons aside, weapons that may not be in the same location when their maces swatted at them. The unified front presented by the Arms made progress difficult.

Because of the confines of space and the number of people, the office accessories took as much of a beating as any person. The Arms formed a crescent across the room, defending each other's flanks and using furniture as defensive obstacles. When the guards tried to charge the centre and divide the group, the sides of the crescent collapsed so that the guards became surrounded. In the centre and the most free for action was Orlan, whose fists and feet hit their targets with such speed that a guard had little time to defend himself. It only took a few minutes for the guards to think better of the encounter but had little space for any to extract themselves from the room. Only a few managed to leave while eight others lay on the floor, moaning from their injuries. Two Arms sustained injuries from the short maces but still stood. Orlan wore a broad smile and look of joy.

"That was exhilarating," Orlan commented.

* * *

Though a short, squat man, Noisa had moved fast. Exiting a door at the back wall while the fighting was still ongoing, Xitano ran down a hallway in the back of the room that made a left turn into an intersection of three other hallways. She lost a few seconds finding which direction the man had gone. Noisa had time to exit through a door on the right before she caught up. The door led to stairs going down and another door. As she made the bottom of the stairs, Noisa opened the door, letting in sunlight. He tried to close the door behind him but Xitano kicked the door with the flat of her foot, spinning Noisa around. When he started to flee again, she kicked his feet from under him, sending him to the ground. Before he could get back up, she placed a knee in the middle of his back and grabbed a wrist.

"Help! Help!" Noisa screamed. "I'm being assaulted!"

"In the name of the Law," Xitano said in a equally loud voice, "I place you under arrest for kidnapping." After looping the rope around the first wrist, she grabbed the second, fighting the bucking Noisa the whole time. With both wrists secured together, she pulled the man up by his shoulders.

"Help! Help!" Noisa continued to scream.

"Scream all you want," Xitano said with a shake. "You're still going to jail." Holding the man by his collar and bound wrists, Xitano pushed him around the building to the front. Noisa talked the whole way. By the time she made it back to the front doors, several Arms, including Kaitja, had made their way out of the building.

"I think he intends to escape by talking us to death," she told Kaitja.

"He'll wear out eventually," he replied with a sigh. "You fine?"

"Yeah, no problem." She shook her hand after giving Noisa to another Arm. "Thumb still hurts though."

"Give it a couple of days." Kaitja looked around at the gathering crowd. None looked like they intended to interfere.

"Some ice would be nice."

"Where you going to get that?"

"Just saying. No cold mountain streams around here either."

"They probably have some ointment at headquarters to dull the pain."

"How bad does it smell?" Xitano's face twisted in anticipated dread.

"It's not used often," Kaitja conceded.

"I'll take the pain."

Chapter Five

Looking out from the second storey window of the headquarters building could be an impressive or scary sight. People gathered outside, formed talking groups, left, and were replaced by others in a continuous flow like water being trapped, then released in small whirlpools. A few entered the building to leave a few minutes later and feed the talking groups with their vital nutrient.

"You made quite the stir," Keras said as he stepped up next to Kaitja, watching through the window.

"Inevitable," came the neutral reply.

"Worried?"

"No." Kaitja shifted his weight and waved his hand at the crowd. "Noisa doesn't have that many friends and I would bet that most of the people down there only want to know what he knows."

"Probably true. I hear there's a crowd over at the science building also. Everyone wants to get a look at the 'primitive', as they are calling him." Keras chuckled.

"That needs to be stopped." Concern showed in Kaitja's voice. "He's not a primitive, they just have a different culture based on where they live. His leader didn't strike me as primitive at all."

"You know how people are." Keras's head wagged. "Have to think that they are superior for some reason. Damn fragile egos."

"Talking about egos," Kaitja said, turning from the window to face his friend, "Noisa ready to talk yet?"

"One way to find out." With a quick grin, Keras turned from the window and walked into the interior of the building. He led Kaitja to a room that had one door and no windows. Inside, Noisa sat on a chair with his head on the table but raised it as soon as they walked in.

"Have a nice nap?" Keras asked as he walked to the other side of the table.

"This is cruel and unusual punishment," Noisa muttered in a half-awake voice.

"Unusual, no. Cruel we leave to personal opinion." Sitting down, Keras stared at the man. "You might as well tell us everything. Your stooges already told us their story, blaming you for everything of course..."

"They lie!"

"How did I know you'd say that?" Kaitja interjected.

"Then how about you tell us your story?" Crossing his arms, Keras leaned back in his chair.

"I'm not saying anything without my lawyer." Clamping his mouth shut, Noisa stared back.

"You just did," Kaitja said with a suppressed chuckle. It earned a glare from Noisa.

"That's your right, of course, but the more cooperation you give us, the easier we go on you."

"Right. I'm sure your man there will be so generous." Noisa nodded his head at Kaitja.

Tilting his head, Keras raised an eyebrow and then let it fall. "No? Okay, have it your way. Rot in this room for what anyone here cares."

With that statement, Keras stood from the chair. Before he could leave, the door was opened by another man who poked his head into the room. "Commander? I think we found something you'll want to see."

"You can't look at my papers!" Noisa shouted. It caused Keras to turn back to the man and smile.

"Yes we can, we have a signed and stamped warrant. And are you saying that the papers they found are yours?" Keras asked.

With a sheepish look filling his face, Noisa avoided his gaze. "No,

I'm not saying anything."

"Then you won't object if we look at them." As he left, Keras added, "And if you did object, it won't matter. It's called evidence."

Both men exited the room, stopping outside after the door was shut. Kaitja noted a well-dressed man making his way across the floor but gave him no further thought. Instead he listened to Keras and the interrupter.

"So, what you got, Rade?" Keras asked.

The man handed him a stack of papers. "We found these in a hidden compartment in the wall. There's more, older, but these were on top and appear newer. And the subject is most interesting."

Keras took the papers. The folder that contained them was blank but opening it revealed a paper on top with the title "Report on Remains from the Mass Grave." Eager eyes started reading.

"We were never sent this," Keras said as he read.

"What does it say?" Kaitja asked.

"It talks about the articles in the grave: clothes, amulets, other trinkets. Some we knew and some we didn't. And it keeps saying that they verify the situation in Report 117."

"We haven't found that yet," Rade interjected, "but we're still looking through his papers."

"I doubt it's in the official archives," Kaitja scoffed, "unless there's a section we don't know about."

"Don't discount that." Keras turned a page. "It says that the people in the grave appear to have been executed."

"Executed?" Kaitja's head went back.

"Shot through the front of the head, though no bullets found. Sounds like an execution to me." Keras flipped another page.

"Old weapon then."

"Yes. We could ask the scientists what kind but I doubt it matters. Ah, it states that they are sure the people in the grave were worshippers of the Three, whatever that is, and that the grave is from the time of 'the cleansing'." His head shaking, Keras kept reading.

"That sounds ominous," Rade put in.

"Cleansing what? Disease?" Kaitja's face showed no more understanding than anyone else's.

"That would be answered by Report 117, I assume. We find that, we find answers." Closing the first folder, Keras put it on the bottom of the stack and opened the second.

"I think I need to visit the science centre and ask a few questions." Kaitja waited for Keras to reply.

"Sure. Go ahead." Hand waving in an absent-minded manner, Keras continued to read. "You taking your apprentice with you?"

"I gave her the day off. Dislocated thumb pain, you know."

"Oh, yeah. Never doesn't hurt, does it?" Continuing to read, Keras did not watch Kaitja leave but slowly made his way to his desk. "Bastards," was said at one point.

The trip through the city did not take long. At least there was no gathering of gawkers at the Hall of Science. At the front desk he asked to see Robterns and was not asked why or put off. After a couple of minutes a young woman appeared and asked him to follow her. Led up to the top floor, Kaitja was shown into a large office full of books and papers on all available surfaces except a couple of chairs near the desk. Inside was Robterns, pacing while reading papers. His head came up as Kaitja neared.

"Wondered when you or another Arm would show up." Robterns put the papers on his desk with no apparent effort at organization.

"I'm half surprised you've heard the news, as busy as you are."

"Others are busy. I have to run this place, which includes knowing what is going on outside of these walls." Robterns' finger rose in the air. "Not that I wouldn't rather ignore it, but at least one person in this hall has to know." His mood suddenly changing, Robterns clasped his hands together and his face got more eager. "Please tell me you found something in Noisa's office."

"We found some papers." Robterns' face got brighter as Kaitja talked. "They don't tell us much and reference a Report 117. You ever hear of it?"

"117!" Robterns looked shocked at being asked. "117! Of course I've heard of it." His arms started to flail about as he went back to pacing. "In rumours only, of course. Never seen a copy myself but I've heard things. Haven't you?"

Kaitja shook his head.

"Stars! I thought everyone had heard of Report 117. Guess I was wrong." Robterns continued to move about the office. "Anyway, Report 117 is supposed to contain the only written record of what happened right after humans came to this planet. The only record of what happened during the formative years of the colony, including the record of the great plague, or whatever it was. Of course that's probably asking too much for one report. I mean, it would have to be massive, wouldn't it?" He turned back to Kaitja with a questioning look on his face.

"Not necessarily," Kaitja replied. "It could be concise. All the much better to keep it hidden."

"But it should contain the data." The back of Robterns' right hand slapped flat on his left as he faced Kaitja.

"If written by a scientist. If written by a politician, who knows." Kaitja shrugged.

"That's too depressing to think about." Turning away, Robterns went back to pacing.

"So you don't know any more about this Report 117?"

"Facts, no, only rumours and those can't be trusted. But, if you get a copy, I would love to read it." Flaring his eyebrows, Robterns looked encouragingly at the man.

"That will depend on what's in it. By the way, how's the boy doing?"

"Great. He's taking to our language well, learning every day, and is fascinated by everything else." Leaving his pacing, Robterns turned toward Kaitja and seemed to be absorbed by the subject. "We've even dressed him in real clothes and taken him out and around the city. No one seems to notice, they think he is mute. He loves all the shops and goods. It's quite fun to watch, though I don't think he has the concept of commerce and money down yet."

"Not surprising. Anyway, so you are saying that you know nothing about what's in Report 117?"

"Correct."

"What do you know about the great plague?"

"Only what everyone has been told. There are no records. I can tell you, though, that the bodies we were able to examine did not die of disease, unless it had something to do with the head because they would not send us one of those." Robterns flipped his hand in disgust.

"That's because they were all shot in the head." The calmness with which Kaitja delivered the information caused Robterns to pause before realizing the significance.

"What? Are you sure? Have you seen one?"

"No, just read about it. No bullets, though, just holes."

"Really? Of course, that would be when they had a working model of the old weapons. Did they report burn marks or anything like that?" Robterns' eyes filled with expectation.

"No details, just the one comment." Kaitja shook his head while talking.

"We *have* to get one of those skulls. It could tell us so much." Random steps and emphatic flailing resumed as if Robterns was a toy that wandered around the floor. "We have some old weapons left, but of course they don't work and we have no idea how they are supposed to work. Why, I don't know. It's as if someone was afraid of what we would do with them. What did they expect, we would shoot each other?"

"I think that's exactly what they were afraid of." Kaitja's voice was emphatic. It caused Robterns to pivot toward him.

"Why would we do that?"

"You don't think that if Noisa had some of those weapons he wouldn't have used them to take that boy?"

The words caused Robterns' whole body to pause, as if thought was the only thing left functioning. He stood mouth open and eyes unfocused for a few seconds, then spoke. "Oh, I see what you mean. Yes, I am sure he would have."

Shifting his weight, Kaitja continued. "I am also of the opinion that the great plague wasn't a plague. So, what else would cause a large number of people to die suddenly?" He paused to let Robterns answer.

"Famine?" the man said in a weak voice.

"How about a revolt, or all-out war between factions?"

"But, but, so soon after settling this planet?" It was clear from

Robterns' face that he could not conceive of such an event.

"Yes. Once you've established the settlement you need a government, and that's the prime time for armed conflict. I am actually surprised that they had any weapons. Of course they could have excused having them for hunting or defence against unknown animals, but we know who the most dangerous animal is, don't we?" The grin on Kaitja's face said the question was rhetorical.

"But we have very little violence anymore. The last few days have been the most violent in years in the city. And before that it was mostly the Infected."

"Violence is about desires and frustrations." Kaitja let his arms uncross. "There isn't much people can want besides what we can provide. Food, clothing, a few luxury goods is about all our society can make. Of course, if we start producing metals, that might change. Just think of the change that could happen if we could get the robots working again."

"Oooh, that would really change things. Walking, automated machines performing work functions. What would we use them for first?"

"Exactly. Point taken. But that's for the future. Right now we have other things to worry about. If you learn anything about Report 117, you contact us immediately. And I mean *immediately.* Got it?"

"Of course, of course." The distracted way in which Robterns said the words did not convey assurance. Kaitja stood for a moment, then turned as if deciding it was the best he was going to get.

"Don't make me hear about it somewhere else and come calling."

"Of course, you can count on us." The trailing nature of the words spoke to the fact that Robterns had transitioned to the next subject.

The same young woman waited outside the office when Kaitja exited. "You been here the whole time?" he asked.

"Yes," came a crisp reply.

"What, you his gofer or something?"

"Granddaughter."

"You a scientist too?"

"Yes, sir." She said the words with some enthusiasm. "Chemistry."

"Have you seen the boy we brought in?"

"Idula? Yes, sir." The girl hadn't turned to lead him out of the building.

"What do you think of him?"

"Different." She paused only a second. "Young. Overall healthy. Abundant curiosity. And polite, or maybe just cautious."

"Sounds about right. Any problems?"

"Other than those experienced from a normal, say, ten-year-old? Nope." She grinned as she said it.

"Sounds just about what I would say. Okay, let's go."

Back at headquarters, Kaitja relayed the nothing that Robterns had told him.

"Do you think he's being honest with us?" Keras asked.

"Yes," Kaitja replied with a little huff. "He's way too enthusiastic to be hiding something. Have we found Report 117 yet?"

"Nope. Just have to wait for people to look through everything, I guess."

Taking a seat, Kaitja waited in Keras's office while the man went about his normal duties, many of which were comprised of paper and signatures. After an hour, Kaitja dozed off sitting upright, head resting on the wall behind him. He woke up two hours later, just before Rade came into the office.

"We found it!" Rade announced in a voice louder than needed, waving a folder in his hand.

"Let's see it." Extending his hand, Keras took the folder, cleared a section of his desk, and placed it on the surface before opening it.

"Where was it?" Kaitja asked.

"In a safe in the council chamber hidden behind a painting." Rade huffed for breath.

"Behind a painting? How cliché." Kaitja laughed with the statement.

"No one ever said bad guys had imaginations," Keras added while opening the folder.

While Keras read, the other two men stood back, knowing better than to intrude. While they waited, light steps entered the room from behind. When Kaitja turned, he saw Xitano taking up a station behind them.

"I thought you were taking the day off?" Kaitja asked.

"Which means I get to do what I want, right?" She looked at him for a moment, then looked away. "So if I want to spend my day sitting at an outdoor table of a cafe watching Town Hall for something that looks interesting to happen, I can do that. Right?"

"I suppose so. I told you to rest."

"I was resting. I was just sitting and watching. More rest than I've had in weeks. Of course you didn't say where to rest either." A small smirk grew on her face.

"Next time I will be more specific." Kaitja shook his head as he talked.

"Hey, my time is my time. No intrusions."

"I expected you to go see Tarn." There was a lilt in his voice as Kaitja turned back toward Keras.

"He's busy in the chemistry lab calibrating some scales or something. Plus there was some girl there I didn't much care for, so I decided to leave before I poked her eyes out." A small huff followed the words.

"What was wrong with her eyes?"

"It was where they were focused."

"I suppose Tarn has become somewhat of a celebrity over there after their trip." A suppressed chuckle rippled through Kaitja.

"If she wasn't interested before, there's no reason for her to be interested now." The statement was made with a little animosity.

"You feeling insecure in your relationship?"

"No. Doesn't mean I'm not going to protest my territory."

Turning his attention back to Keras before he broke out laughing, Kaitja asked, "Well?"

"Interesting stuff. Stars, this must be old, like over a hundred years old. The information is presented in a way that makes it sound like the person was there when it happened." Keras shook his head.

"The paper would have degraded by then," Kaitja pointed out.

"Oh, this isn't normal paper. It feels different. Lighter, stronger. Haven't felt anything like it before. Smoother too." Keras rubbed his thumb on the paper as he read.

"You going to share?" Kaitja asked.

"Once I get the whole picture." Looking up, Keras glanced between those in front of him. "I think everyone needs to hear this at the same time so everyone hears the same story. Call a gathering in half an hour. Main hall."

As Rade left, Kaitja turned to Xitano. "Go tell Robterns he wants to be here in half an hour. But don't tell him why."

"Why me? I'm off today, remember?"

"And yet you are here." It was said almost in a exasperated tone.

"Fine." Xitano started to turn, stopped, opened her mouth, closed it, then left. Keras furrowed his eyebrows and looked at Kaitja.

"Was she going to ask you something?"

"Yes," Kaitja answered as he turned back to Keras in a calm manner.

"Then why didn't she?"

"She didn't want me to say no."

Eyebrows going up, Keras added, "Smart girl. You know what she was going to ask?"

"I can guess."

"And yet you said nothing?"

"She didn't ask."

The hall filled fast. Some, like Xitano and Tarn, sat on chairs near the front. Most stood. All talked in quiet whispers. Some milled about from one person to another as if taking a survey. But when Keras walked in, all hushed and looked toward him. He stood behind the column of a podium at one end and banged the top with a wooden fist. Any traces of conversation disappeared with the official call to order.

"As you have heard, I am sure," Keras started, "we have found a copy of Report 117. I have read the whole document. I will not read the whole thing here. We will be sending a copy of the document to all periodicals and the original to the Hall of Science."

A small moan of disappointment was heard from some areas in the room. Keras held up his hand. "Don't worry, I have called you together to give you a summary of the document. I am doing this because I am sure it will cause a disturbance in the city. As distasteful as it might be to some, we must protect City Hall and those who work there. I am sure only a few knew of this document and less knew what it said. Remember that. Remember that most of the people at City Hall are innocent of any crime connected with recent events." The comment drew a chuckle from the crowd. "And we need to treat them as such."

Straightening himself and clearing his throat, Keras paused for a moment, then continued. "Now, to what you all want to know. I will just say that there is no way we know to verify these facts, but there is also no reason to doubt them.

"Our colony was settled approximately three hundred years ago by people from Earth, but it was not Earth that brought them here." The statement caused gasps. "An alien race for whom very little information is given brought the settlers here. No reason is given. What is said is that many of the humans that were brought worshipped them as God, or gods, though we have no idea how this worship was conducted." Confused looks and single syllable words could be seen and heard. "The aliens stayed for about a year, enough to establish the colony and ensure crop production. Then they left and have not returned since. No reason is given for their absence. The colonists slowly formed into two groups, those who worshipped the aliens and those who did not.

"In year fifty-one of the settlement, this came to a head. The religionists tried to assume power over both groups and a civil war started. The religionists lost. The mass grave we found were the leaders of the religionists movement, all executed for their 'crimes' against the people. After that, the religion was abolished and enforced with severe consequences. All mention of the aliens was erased. The cause of the deaths from the revolt was listed as a plague. Basically they covered up the revolt and their past history. For whatever reason, Report 117 was the only record left of events."

Keras shifted his weight and paused a couple of seconds before speaking again. "I know that people are going to be mad that they were lied to and they are going to want more information. The truth is everyone was lied to and this is all the information we have, and it only states the bare facts. Plus I know the idea of worshipping anything will seem strange. Do not try to give them answers. That is not our job. Our job is to keep the peace, which will be enough I am sure. We have arrested all of the city council and are determining who knew and who didn't. As you can imagine, it can be hard to tell which members of the council are telling the truth."

Laughter spread through the group for ten to fifteen seconds. Some of the tension in the air disappeared. One, "Typical" was heard, which induced more laughter.

"Please assure everyone," Keras continued, "that we are on top of this and will not stop until all included in the crimes and cover-up are found and brought to justice, though I am not sure there is any punishment for just keeping a secret not related to a recent crime. I am sure that there will be more repercussions than just legal, though. I don't want the repercussions to be the violent type. Dismissed."

Some Arms left as if the meeting was an interruption of required business. Others stayed and talked. Xitano lounged as if waiting for the crowd to leave, eyes closed and head back. Tarn sat wide eyed, staring at nothing in particular. After a while he said, "Wow."

"Wow what?" Xitano asked, only peeking out to see if most of the crowd had left, which it hadn't.

"That's… that's… a significant change to history." Tarn stuttered.

"So what? It's ancient history. Who cares?" Xitano leaned her head back again.

"It matters. It matters how we got here and what happened."

"Why? Doesn't change anything. We're still the same before and after knowing. It happened hundreds of years ago. It's done, gone."

"But it changes *why* we are here." Tarn's voice became emphatic.

"So?"

"We always assumed that we were a colony sent from Earth. Now we know we're not. Does Earth even know we are here? Do they even have the technology to come here if they want to? What did the aliens want from us? Was Earth dying and they were saving the last of humanity?" Tarn's hands and head jerked from side to side with each idea.

"Until we can find out, what does it change?" Xitano sat up in her chair. "I mean, if we have no way to find the answers, why worry about them?"

"What if we're the last humans left?" Tarn looked at her with wide, desperate eyes.

"You mean besides that tribe we found and, who knows, others that the aliens placed around the planet maybe? We don't even know how many tribes there are across the mountain." Eyes rolling, Xitano flipped her hands in dismissal.

"Eleven." Robterns walked in front of their chairs, grinning. "We have learned a few things from our friend. From his descriptions, I would say an average tribe has around one hundred and fifty people, women and children included, making a total of about seventeen hundred people on the plains. Assuming we understand him correctly."

"Seventeen hundred? Is that all?" Xitano asked.

"Given their primitive lives, it doesn't surprise me," Robterns said dismissively. "And don't forget the low birth rate. From what we think we know, the birth rate barely exceeds the death rate, most of the time."

"Just doesn't seem like many." Standing up slowly, Xitano stretched as she did so. "Anything else we've learned from our friend?"

"Not much. Still working on language skills. He appears to be learning more about us than we about him." Robterns gave a small huff. "One thing is for sure, he knows almost nothing about metal."

"Stone age," Tarn piped in as he stood.

"But with sophistication." Wagging a finger as he spoke, Robterns appeared to muse about something. "Making the best of what they have, it would seem. Now if you will excuse me."

"I really should be going back to the lab," Tarn said, head down and foot shuffling.

"Haven't you ever just *not* gone back to the lab?" Xitano gave him a mischievous smile.

"Only when I was sick." Looking up into her eyes, Tarn smiled back. "Of course I never really had a reason before."

Chapter Six

"I didn't really expect this level of response." Kaitja looked out from a second-storey window of City Hall at the people outside.

"You thought that once the people knew the truth, things would quiet down?" Xitano raised an eyebrow at him.

"Well, yes, I did." The statement was made with a small dab of nervousness.

"Don't know people well, do you?" A chuckle followed Xitano's question.

"I thought I did. Why are they so upset now?"

"Because now they know more." Xitano made the comment as if it was obvious.

"I thought the idea was to know more." Kaitja watched the crowd, who walked in a circle, stretch across the front of the building. "And why are they walking in a circle?"

"Work off energy, I hope."

"Or work up to something." Kaitja's voice was either nervous or suspicious.

"That's what I'm not hoping. The more they know, the more they have to be upset about."

"So," Kaitja sighed as he shifted his weight to the other foot, "what do they think they are going to do about it? The council is in jail, being investigated for 'lying to the public.' As if *that* never happened before." His eyes drifted upwards.

"This time it was important and it can be proved."

"Sure, but what then?"

Xitano pointed down at the crowd. "I think that is your answer."

A lone figure stood on something, head and shoulders above the rest of the crowd. A woman in a green blouse and blue-green pants raised her hand, hammering it forward and backwards as she shouted. "*We need new elections now!* We need a new city council, one that will address the concerns of the people and one that will address what this new information means and what we should do about it! We are not some alien's farm animals. We are human beings with our own destinies and own decision-making power. And we need to elect people who know this and exercise the will of the people with independent thought, not driven by instructions from some aliens."

The crowds cheered. Xitano furrowed her brow. "I thought the knowledge about the aliens was being suppressed, not followed."

"Don't confuse them with the facts." It was Kaitja's turn to chuckle. "Besides, it makes good political speeches."

"Makes me wonder if people even bothered to read the report."

"Most, probably not. They read the summary in the paper."

Huffing, Xitano commented, "As if that can be trusted. They only throw in the most dramatic parts."

The woman continued to shout. "We need to find out why Earth has abandoned us. Why haven't they contacted us?"

"Maybe no one is left there," a man shouted.

"Billions of people just disappeared? No way," the woman shouted back.

"Maybe an asteroid hit the planet or…"

"Then why is there no record of it? Tell me that. No, we were abandoned here and I want to know why." The crowd responded with a cheer.

"And exactly who are you going to ask?" came a snide comment from within the crowd.

"Guess who's going to be running for office," Xitano said through the corner of her mouth.

"You think?" Kaitja asked with a laugh.

"Call it a wild hunch." Xitano tilted her head and shrugged.

"How do you think the people in the countryside will take the news?"

Chuckling, Xitano barely shook her head from side to side. "If it doesn't put more food on their table, they won't care. Those people down there obviously don't work hard enough for a living if they can spend their time shouting at each other in the street."

"At least we won't have to worry about riots in the countryside then."

"Riots? If the countryside rioted, I'd suggest staying away from it. By the time they get worked up to it, there's no stopping them. Besides," Xitano shifted her weight, "if they rioted they'd be coming here."

"Good to know. Shit!"

As Kaitja turned and ran toward the stairs, Xitano noticed that the woman outside was pointing at the building as she shouted. "That's our City Hall. We paid for it and have paid to keep it there. We own it. We should make it ours!"

"Lock the doors!" Kaitja shouted as he bounded down the stairs four and five at a time. "Secure the premises."

To the sound of bolts being thrown, Xitano ran to the back of the building where several single doors led outside. As she threw the bolts for the back doors, the first wave of people hitting the front resounded like a mallet hitting a drum. "At least they're not glass," she reassured herself and she found the other doors and locked them. The last was Noisa's secret door. As she ran back to Kaitja, he looked at her.

"You get them all?"

"Unless there's one we don't know about, yeah."

"Let's hope there isn't." The boom from the front door sounded again.

"You know you're only making them more angry?" she asked.

"I'm not letting them in here to destroy the place," Kaitja said in a firm voice.

"You also know we're now trapped in here," Xitano pointed out.

"That's a very negative way of looking at it." Kaitja's voice had more confidence than Xitano felt.

The crash at the doors continued with no sign of stopping for fifteen minutes before other sounds, such as whistles being blown, could be heard. Shouts and commotion followed, which subsided in a slow manner until the sound from the other side of the door returned to normal. The silence was followed by four knocks on the door. Kaitja unbolted one door and opened it.

"Just can't leave you alone, can I?" Keras said with a snide smile.

"It's my popularity. It's irresistible." Looking out showed a dozen Arms forming a semi-circle in front of the building, encouraging people to move on.

"I think we need to close this building for a while, until things settle down."

"With a couple of men inside in case the protesters find some rocks to break windows?"

"Of course. Not that I will envy the boring duty they'll have." Keras turned his head to the side. "You volunteering?"

"Not hardly." Kaitja huffed. "There has to be something better to do."

"Like secure the science centre?" Keras gave him a look. "That would be my guess where they will go next."

"On it." Waving at a couple of Arms who had been in the building with him, Kaitja left through the door. The science centre was only a couple of blocks away and the number of people grew as he neared the building. The crowd of people at the front door was small but insistent. Inside the door, Robterns was equally insistent that they were not welcome. In formation, the Arms inserted themselves between the people outside and inside the building and took up a cross-armed stance that announced their intent.

"Thank the stars you're here," Robterns said from inside the door with a heavy sigh. "I don't know how much longer I could have held them off."

"Any get inside?" Kaitja asked.

"I'm not sure. I haven't been able to look."

"Go. We got the door."

Without further comment, Robterns closed the door. The click of a lock was heard after the door was shut. Turning, Kaitja took a deep breath before starting his next actions. Walking to the crowd in a stiff, upright manner, he let his voice boom.

"All right, everyone. I don't know what you think you are doing standing around here but there will be nothing of interest going on. Get back to your lives. The scientists inside had nothing to do with town hall."

"They're supposed to know things," someone in the crowd called out.

"Only if they have data and we asked them before and they had none," Kaitja answered to the whole crowd, spreading his voice in an arc.

"That's what *they* say," came the voice again.

"We're not starting that!" Kaitja stared as he spoke. "You want to say everyone lies, then start with yourself. Stupid conspiracy theories to make yourself feel better help no one. Go back to your jobs and do something useful today."

Most of the crowd started to shuffle their feet in the early stages of leaving. A few still looked defiant. "You can't make us leave."

"I can haul you off to jail for blocking traffic, and while you will eventually be released, I can guarantee it won't be a pleasant experience." Able to identify the speaker this time, Kaitja stared straight at him until the man flinched and looked away. As the crowd dispersed, he shook his head. "People," he muttered.

A week later, the town square was again filled with people. This time, instead of milling around they gathered in groups around individuals who stood on anything that raised them above the rest of the crowd. A few huddled in smaller groups with their heads together in order to hear over the sound of the speakers and those answering them. Kaitja and Xitano watched from the top of the town hall front steps together.

Xitano bent toward Kaitja. "What did they call this again?"

"A convention," Kaitja replied without removing his eyes from the scene in front of them.

"And this is how they are going to elect the new town council?"

"No." Kaitja barely shook his head. "They are just picking the people to be voted on."

"I thought people just voted for who they wanted to."

"First off," Kaitja's head tilted to one side, "there are too many people who would run. Second," his head tilted to the other side, "people really want to win because they care so much about what they call the 'issues,' whatever their issues are. Third, in order to win they have started to form what they call 'parties.'"

"So they are having a party in order to get people to vote for them?"

"No, the groups are called parties."

"There's going to be parties?" Xitano's eyes brightened.

"Not that kind of party."

"So they sound fun?" Xitano turned her head as her eyebrow tried to cover her right eye.

"It's a historic name, I am told."

"Hmph." She turned back to watch the crowd. "They should call it something more descriptive, like a clique or gang."

"That would sound negative." Kaitja gave a small laugh.

"People who gang up to get a person elected? Sounds negative to me." A head shake by Xitano was included.

"Supposed to cut down on the chaos." Keeping his voice even, Kaitja showed no emotion about the subject.

"Yeah, but at what cost? We get to chose from those others have picked? Who made them so smart?"

"If you want to help make the choices, join one of the parties. Or start your own." Kaitja casually cast out the statement.

"Right, just what I want to do. Join a bunch of screaming idiots."

"If you don't, you leave it to the idiots."

Huffing again, Xitano shifted her weight. "We should just make them illegal."

"Then they would just meet in secret and we would have to do even more work to monitor them. This is the best option." The comment was said as if it closed the subject with some self-satisfaction coming from Kaitja.

They stared at the gathering, the speakers getting louder every minute. "Are they competing for attention?" Xitano asked. "Or are their egos so fragile that they can't think of someone else getting more attention?"

"Who knows." Kaitja shrugged. "They only have two more days until the election so they might be feeling desperate."

"There *are* twelve seats on the council now."

"But if they don't get enough seats, they won't win enough council votes to get their agendas through."

"Poor babies." Xitano said the words with no sympathy.

"Those are your future leaders you're talking about." A grin spread on Kaitja's face as he said it.

"Don't remind me." The comment was almost a groan.

"You are going to vote, right?" People continued to mill about and speakers continued to raise their voices. Most looked like they ignored them.

"Might as well." She huffed again. "Maybe we can keep the worst of them out."

"And those would be...?"

"At this moment, all of them." Xitano's hand swept across the square in front of them.

There was a pause before Kaitja spoke again. "Maybe you should run for the council."

"*Me?*" The volume of her response shocked him as Xitano's body reacted as if it had been struck. "Sit in a room and argue with people all day? Forget that." She managed to recover her poise.

"Then you have to trust others to do the job for you."

Xitano's head went back as her eyes went to the sky. "Are there no good options?"

"Define good." Voice flat, Kaitja showed no reaction to Xitano's theatrics.

"You're no help." Disgust dripped from her voice as she looked away from Kaitja.

Happy to stand and just watch for a while, Xitano was the first to speak again. "So how are people supposed to choose, besides if they like the person?"

"What they stand for. Or at least what they claim to stand for."

"Which would be, what, who gets to sit in a council chair?"

Kaitja huffed. "If you listened, you would know. That woman to the right," he said as he pointed, "is for, in her words, 'more equitable distribution of resources.'"

"So taking from people who have and giving to those who have less?" Xitano cocked her head while she asked.

"I would assume."

"And who decides who gives and who gets?"

"She does, I assume." Gesturing toward the middle, Kaitja continued. "Our boisterous man in the middle is for exploring the planet to find out who else has been stranded here and how we might help each other."

"And we're going to walk across the planet?" A snicker travelled with the words from Xitano.

"Build ships, sailing ships."

"Sounds real safe." Xitano stopped and then spoke again. "And if the wind only blows one way?"

"Details, details," Kaitja said in playful dismissal. "And the man to our right wants to develop our technology first, exploiting the mineral deposits we found."

"Wait, doesn't he work for the science centre?" Xitano's eyes squinted to examine the man from afar.

"Details, details," Kaitja said with another laugh.

"Like I said," Xitano said with sagging shoulders as her eyes went back to normal, "no good choices, only motivated self-interest."

Turning toward her, Kaitja asked, "You expected different?"

"Exactly as I expected," Xitano said with disgust as she watched the voting line entering and exiting city hall two days later. "Chaos."

"Controlled chaos," Keras said, walking up behind her. "I think it's called democracy."

"Do we trust these people to make the right choices?" Uncertainty filled Xitano's voice.

Altaterra 229

"It's not about trusting the individual." Settling in beside the young woman, Keras rocked back and forth a little. "It's about trusting that the collective decision is as good as it can be."

A huff came in response. "Sounds unlikely to me."

"You want to go back to a council that basically picks its successors?" Keras raised an eyebrow at her.

"Not really. Just seems like there should be a better way. Maybe we can find the people that would actually be good at the job and force them to be in charge."

"And who picks them?"

Silent for a few moments, Xitano said, "I have no idea."

"And thus…" Keras said with a wave of his arms.

"Great." Her words were filled with shoulders slumping. "Any idea who's winning?"

"They won't count until all the ballots have been cast."

Xitano huffed. "Way to drag it out."

"It's only fair." The line moved forward in spurts like a giant insect, a section at a time with frequent stops and short movements forward.

"Because people would change their vote to whoever is winning? I'll never understand that." A head shake went with the words.

"Maybe," Keras said as he shifted his weight and widened his stance, "they just don't want to be on the losing side."

"If your mind is that easily changed, don't vote at all." A disgusted scoff from Xitano followed.

"And thus why we don't tell anyone before it's over."

Xitano replied with one word. "People."

The two watched as serious-faced, dour, or excited people entered the building, while relieved, talkative people left. Most kept their voices low to others in groups of two or three, or didn't talk. The few that appeared to want to speak louder needed only one look from the Arms present to hold their tongues, though they did not look happy with the situation. Louder voices could be heard two blocks down the street, the agreed upon distance for any discussions from city hall. After a while Keras left, but after ten minutes he was replaced by Kaitja.

"Don't trust me to hold the line alone?" Xitano asked the man.

"How you got the best place to stand I will never know," he replied in a false-grumpy voice.

"You got to know people," Xitano said, emphasizing every other word.

"You know someone I don't?"

"I'm sure I do but I doubt they're in town." The reply brought a single huff from Kaitja. "So, how are the other entrances doing?"

"About the same as here. Should be done in another couple of hours." Kaitja scanned the area.

"It would go faster if they had more than one location."

"Then we would need more Arms to watch them."

"And that would be a bad thing?" The question came from Xitano's face as well as her voice.

"Didn't say that." Kaitja's voice got lighter. "Maybe you can convince the new council to train and employ more Arms."

"What are the chances of that?" Doubt flowed with the question.

"About the same as Keras buying us all dinner after we're done."

Sighing, Xitano's shoulders fell. "Zero then." Her voice took a mildly playful tone. "Wait. You're saying if we convince him to buy us dinner, then the council will hire more Arms."

"Didn't say that either," Kaitja replied without looking at her.

"But you implied it."

"All implications are produced by your imagination." Lifting his chin, Kaitja stared straight ahead.

It was Xitano's head's turn to swivel. "Darn, no witnesses." She took in a deep breath and let it out. "So when will they announce the winners?"

"Tomorrow morning."

A series of laughs came from Xitano. "Make them sweat the night out."

"Last bit of revenge maybe."

Chapter Seven

"You sure this is the easy way?" Chief Engineer Mical Strove bent back to gaze up the mountain.

"Yes," Kaitja replied without following the man's eyes.

"I just thought it would be... straighter. You know, like right up the mountain." Mical's hand made an upward swooping motion.

"We could do that, but it would be a lot steeper and head toward a peak instead of between them."

"That wouldn't be good." Mical took a few breaths before speaking again. "I guess nothing to do for it but get back to it. Guess we got spoiled building roads on the nice flat plain."

"The place with water everywhere?" Kaitja gestured over his shoulder. Mical laughed.

"We've been dealing with water for three hundred years, we're used to it. First time I've known someone tried to build a road up a mountain, at least here."

"You'll be famous." Kaitja gave him a cheesy smile.

"One way or another, I'm sure I will be." Shaking his head, Mical turned to head downhill.

"By the way, what are they going to name the road?" Kaitja asked.

"I heard several suggestions: Fortune Highway, Mountain Ascent, and my favourite, Mical's Folly." A huff joined the end of the statement.

"Then you'd really be famous." A laugh joined the comment.

"Like this was all my decision. Blame the poor engineer just doing his job." Mical's body and head swayed as he walked.

"You should try being an Arm sometime," Kaitja called to the descending figure. Turning back to look up the mountain, he said to himself, "They're going to ruin my running path."

Fulfilling his lifelong dream of becoming a famous author just before he retires, Dale McClenning is transitioning from a job as a mechanical engineer in controls and project work into the exciting and glamorous field of being a world-famous author (still waiting for the last part to take effect). With his wife of 37 years at his side and encouraged by his 10-year-old granddaughter, who is still waiting for the book inspired by her to be published, Dale plods on putting out hard science fiction works in that little appreciated field (everyone wants fantasy these days it seems). But never fear, Dale shall continue to write in the literary desert of Indianapolis until he is sure that genre specialty again is fully appreciated.